SPLINTER

Facts of Life Series: Book 1

JR Sheridan

Straits Line Publishing
Gwynedd, Wales, UK

Compiled by Straits Line Publishing, Gwyneedd,, UK

Publisher's Note: This is a work of fiction. Names, characters, places, and incidents are a product of the author's imagination. Locales and public names are sometimes used for atmospheric purposes. Any resemblance to actual people, living or dead, or to businesses, companies, events, institutions, or locales is completely coincidental.

Book Layout & Design ©2013 - BookDesignTemplates.com

Printed by Create Space
Imprint 1
Facts of life series Splinter/ J R Sheridan. -- 1st edition
ISBN:978-14910420

www.jrsheridan.com

Acknowledgements

To Karen for everything (in capitals)

Rebecca for her young wisdom and
Gavin Ingham for the brainstorming.

Gary Smailes for editing (www.bubblecow.com),
Jane Dixon-Smith for the cover
(www.jdsmith-design.co.uk)
Joanna Penn (www.thecreativepenn.com) for being
an invaluable resource to an aspiring author.

Julie Youdes and Ian Drummond for their encouragement that I was on the right track

Rob & Andy Kemp for giving me the only job that I didn't mind getting up at 4am, to catch the tide.

Also to my Welsh Friends who were so helpful on my Facebook requests for spelling of the Welsh Words that I hear every day and have used to provide flavour to the characters and location for Splinter. Especially to Dafs Pritch for telling me that 'Cymru Am Byth' means 'Have a look at my book'. Fortunately I now know that what sounds like 'mallycachy' is actually spelled 'malu cachu'.

Diolch yn fawr,

JR Sheridan Gorffennaff/July 2013

www.jrsheridan.com

1.

The red-hulled fishing boat nosed its way out into the channel. The dawning sun was low and vague in the sky. Its pale light reflected across the muddy sandbanks that were now being met by the flooding tide. The greys and yellows of the early morning merged into the silver of the water as the boat headed along the low headland and navigated the red and green channel buoys of the river estuary towards the Irish sea.

Inside the wheelhouse Dan Richards moved the throttle forward, turned the wheel and the boat responded. When they were clear of the headland he pointed towards the fishing ground where they had laid their pots the day before.

The boat's diesel engine was strong and steady

against the incoming current. The breeze was gentle today though Gwilym and Dan were wrapped up against the late autumn chill. Dan was in his late 30s. He wore thermal long johns underneath his old combat trousers. Above them the thick yellow oilskin dungarees helped to keep the wind out, but the cold still cut through to the scar tissue on his thigh.

Gwilym the owner of the boat was in his mid 50s. They were hoping for an easy profitable haul.

Dan always relished passing out of the lee of the land and into the open water. Through the open window of the wheelhouse the salt air was fresh against his face, waking him up and switching him on to the job in hand. He did not sleep much these days anyway so the early start was no hardship.

Dan had been going out to the pots with Gwilym for three years. So three years since he had seen his first whelk. Horrible slimy creatures, the hermaphrodite sea snails, which they caught in roped lines of pots lain along the seabed. Now they were keeping the wolf from Dan's door but more importantly the monotony of shaking the pots had brought him back from the edge of insanity.

Dan did not think they were much of a delicacy but he had eaten them and eaten worse. He knew that they lived off sucking the silt and everything else that fell to the seabed. He saw what came up with the whelks in the pots and it was unappetising to say the least. Saying that, stir-fried in a wok with rice, vegetables and plenty of soy sauce and chilli, washed down with beer meant that Dan did not starve. For a long while after his discharge from hospital he had avoided shops.

Gwilym, oil stained sailor's cap planted on his head, wiry hair escaping from underneath, squeezed his belly through the narrow wheelhouse door. He accepted the flask top mug of coffee and took the cold bacon sandwich out of its foil. The congealed grease mixed with ketchup, catching in his bushy greying beard.

"Iawn boi?"

"Iawn diolch, Gwil."

Dan had learnt some Welsh but not much. Gwilym in the early morning was not much of a conversationalist anyway. The lack of chatter suited both of them well enough as they chugged on in companionable silence. The marine radio was switched on, its tall antenna on the roof reaching high into the sky. This late in the year there was only the intermittent chatter from a coastguard navigation warning to keep them company.

The headland was fading into the background, the sand dunes becoming an indistinct yellow and green merging with the grass of farmers' fields and the dark of the pine forest plantation along the coast. The mountains of Snowdonia and the Lleyn Peninsula lay off to their south, dark and brooding in the morning light. Within a month their tops would be covered in snow.

Yesterday they had laid down five lines of 40 pots, each line stretching about 200 feet across the seabed. There had been plenty of time for the whelks to sniff out the bloody dogfish morsel left as bait in the plastic pots. Then the whelks would climb in and be trapped by the netting around the opening. The pots were made from 5-gallon drums, white or yellowing depending on their age. A big hole was cut for the opening and smaller holes drilled in the sides to allow them to sink, helped by the inch or two of concrete set at the bottom.

Pots wore out or were lost and they kept a small number on board to swap over on the lines when needed. They were both proficient with knots and both wore sharp knives in a blue plastic sheath on a belt outside their oilskins, the knife was to cut off the pots when needed, or heaven forbid, themselves if they got tangled up in the ropes and were pulled over. The knife was long bladed with a sharp blade leading to a sharp point. Commercial fishing was a dangerous occupation.

Being dragged under by the tackle had been known to happen and they were careful where they put their feet.

Taking a marker from the surrounding land-marks, the cliff top, the radio mast and the light-house they headed towards the fishing ground. The setting up chores completed they settled into the thirty minute voyage. The low thump of the Per-kins diesel engine vibrated through the decking and up through the soles of their wellington boots. The sun was becoming stronger in the sky and the blue reflected on the green of the sea.

"Not a bad view from the office window," was Gwilym's standard opening line. "Those sons of mine with their high-powered jobs don't know what they are missing."

"What? You moaning about your stiff old bones." Dan replied used to his friend's train of thought. .

"I wish they would come up more, Annie misses seeing the kids. Gethin rang last night to say that they definitely are not coming up for Christmas. Again."

"You could go down to see them. Take Annie away for the weekend."

"Annie doesn't want to leave her chickens."

"I will look after the bloody chickens. You don't want to be away from the pub gossip more like."

"She doesn't enjoy visiting them. The sons' wives make her feel out of place."

"But seeing the kids makes up for that. Annie bites the bullet when she goes down. We will be finishing for the winter soon so take her down before Christmas. A couple of days in Cardiff, then across to London. See them both and get it out of the way. Or do it over two weekends, take Annie to see a show, take the grandkids to see a pantomime with their Nain and Taid."

"Hark at you Danny Bach. When was the last time you left the village?"

"I haven't got two sons who have given you five lovely grandkids."

"And sour-faced English mothers, who want to climb social ladders and look down on my Annie," said Gwilym. "They are pretty enough but cold, not warm like a good Welsh girl. Like my Rhiannon. When are you going to trap a good Welsh girl then Dan?"

This was a well-trodden path of banter between

them both. Gwilym wanted Dan to be happy, find a girl and settle down.

"I will find one when the time is right. You just want to hear about my sex life and you are the last one I'd tell my most intimate details to, with your voice like a foghorn in the pub. Bloody hell this boat is slow today."

"You say that every day. I know it not like the fast pursuit boats you used to drive into danger with that green hat of yours. If you want to change the subject on me then what about the remembrance parade in the town. Are you going?"

"Not this year."

"Your Taid went and marched with pride, Green Beret on his head and medals on his chest. Went with my dad and they marched together."

"Then they all went to the pub and everybody bought them a whisky, that's why they went. That was a World War, Gwil. Not a forgotten skirmish against freedom fighters."

"Its not forgotten boi, It's on the news every night."

"Yes another squaddie gone and nobody understands why?

"You know why. You fight for your mates my dad said and stuff the politicians."

"I won't go this year, maybe next."

"You have a medal to be proud of boi, wear it."

"We are nearly there, start looking for the flags."

They searched around for the danbuoys, the floating poles with a flag on top that marked each end of the line. New technology was available with transponders on the flags to guide them in but Gwilym insisted he had fished this patch of sea for 40 years and had a mariner's sixth sense of their location. He mocked the younger lads down the coast who used the modern technology, neither admitting that it could be useful nor that he was too tight to pay for it.

Gwilym pointed and as Dan looked at the empty water the first flag, then the second and third popped into view. They motored to the outermost flag of the field and Gwilym, leaning over the side of the boat, pulled the pole with its bedraggled flag and barnacled polystyrene jacket that kept the pole floating upright, onto the deck.

Dan switched the engine into neutral and

transferred the power to the winch on the stern gantry. The weight of the line and the pots anchored the fishing boat, which bobbed gently. Gwilym was frowning as he looked around his bare field of flags.

"The ends are too close together boi. I think we have been trawled again. Bastards!"

Dan shrugged back, pulling on his heavy-duty rubber gauntlets. "Let's get these up and see what we find?"

The hauler wheel was constantly turning and as Gwilym put the line over the pulley, the rope started rapidly pulling out of the water, pieces of caught seaweed dropping off back into the sea. Both men worked to pull the line up. As the first pot came out of the water and up to the hauler Gwilym placed each pot on to the waist level shelf. He then slid it along towards Dan, taking care for the rope not to be tangled. With the seawater gushing down his oilskins and over the feet of his wellington boots, Dan picked out any seaweed and starfish that had come up with the pot. He threw them unwanted back into the sea where they sank. He turned the pot upside down shaking out the whelks into a big round red plastic basket. The remaining water flushed out of the basket and over the deck leaving behind the seafloor loot of writhing sea snails.

Dan stacked the first pot and pushed the bloody dogfish bait onto the four-inch nail set in the concrete base. He set the pot in place against the wheelhouse. With the next five pots, he did the same, each one stacked and laid with its ropes free. He emptied the bucket of whelks into a grey nylon sack and put the first bag of the day's catch against the sidewall of the deck. The whelks were a good size and the Koreans would feast well.

Twenty sacks made roughly a tonne and each tonne would make £600 when delivered to the quayside processing plant in the harbour town down the coast. Two tonnes landed in the day if they were lucky was good money. After costs of fuel and insurance and paying for the regulatory necessities Gwilym would have earned enough to pay Dan for a few pints. A good catch late in the season made up for the plenty of days when they could not fish. The summer had been wet and windy. Strong winds and big waves made the pots harder to haul. Wait too long before picking up the pots and the bait would have washed out and the catch would have escaped. It was not a reliable way to make a living but like fishermen over the ages it kept them in clothes, food and beer.

One of the pots brought up an edible brown crab with its claws snapping in defiance. Dan picked it up by the back of its shell and dropped it into a bucket under the loading shelf. He found a weaver fish in another pot its thin body and poisonous spines burying itself in the mud as the water escaped through the drilled holes in the plastic. The spines could easily pierce his rubber gloves, very painful if not deadly. Dan picked it up by the tail and flung it overboard.

With the 40 pots of the first line emptied, stacked and baited, Gwilym went into the wheelhouse and aimed the boat to a fresh patch of empty sea. Dan pulled off his khaki scrim neck scarf and wiped his forehead. The weather was cold and this far out from land even the mild breeze was biting. Still his exertions with concrete in the pots, the catch of whelks and the seaweed kept him warm.

He was dressed in many layers to keep out the cold. Above an old T-shirt, he wore an olive drab Norgie sweatshirt with a zipped high neck and over that, a thick blue quilted check shirt. All were tucked into the oilskin dungarees. If it rained, he had a yellow oilskin jacket.

The muscles of his back had widened with all the pot shaking he had done over the past 3 years and his shoulders were square and his waist trim. His days of running and rugby were over, thanks to the Afghan bomb blast, but at least he was fit and healthy in most of his body. His mind was still messed up and despite the fresh air and hard graft sleep was often elusive. His black hair, growing out of a barber's crop chop was becoming flecked with grey and coming to the end of this fishing season his face was tanned and weather-beaten around his blue eyes. If he had seen himself as some of the women in the village did, then he was still a handsome man.

"Iawn boi!" Gwilym shouted and he pushed the throttle forward. The boat speeded up. Standing amidships Dan threw the flagged danbuoy pole, the attached coils of rope and the first pot through the midships gangway opening. He heaved it as far away from the boat's side as he could, so as not to tangle the rope in the boat's propeller. The line shot out. The momentum of the boat and the weight of the pots pulled the rest of the line down from the stack and each one bounced off the deck and into the sea leaving a line of rapidly sinking pots. Ready for the last pot to go through he picked up the pole and heaved it away from the boat's side.

Gwilym turned his wheel back to the next flag along and they repeated the process for the second line of pots and then the third. As they moved to the fourth line they picked up the end pole. Dan sensed trouble. The far end flag was too close and the next flag across closer still. The fourth remaining flag was nowhere to be seen. They hauled up the first 25 pots before the hauler started to groan.

As the rope slipped on the pulley wheel the stern of the boat dipped. Gwilym switched off the power to the winch. He stared into the green depths and followed the line down; he could see the outline of a pot twenty foot beneath the surface. The line was taut and hauling any further could damage the winch. Cursing aloud he pulled his knife out of its sheaf. Looking over his shoulder he called to Dan who stepped back well clear of any backlash. Gwilym cut the rope. The line and the pot disappeared back down to the bottom of the sea. The boat, released from its temporary mooring, bobbed back up and started to drift.

Dan went back into the wheelhouse, put the engine into gear, and aimed at the next flag. They managed to get ten more pots up before the winch groaned a second time. At least they had saved one bit of the line. The fifth and final line was worse. With only one visible flagpole, they pulled up the end and managed five empty pots before having to cut it free. It was obvious that a fishing trawler had gone over the two lines in the night and its propeller had chopped the rope to the flagged danbuoy, which would wash up on a local beach with the next high tide. They kept spare poles tied to the gantry frame in case one was lost but that wasn't the point. They stacked the surviving pots and would make another line of it over the winter. More expense to buy new ones and a waste of time, energy and money.

"I'm betting that was that god forsaken lazy skipper on the Mary Jane. Happy to foul our pots to save a few quid on fuel. I've reported him once and I'll do it again," spat Gwilym.

Dan shrugged. "You know it can't be proven."

"I know it's him. He's a Williams, they are all bastards."

Frustrated and angry Gwilym took the wheel and headed back to their mooring in the river estuary. This time they fought against the ebbing tide, which made their passage lumpy and added to the dark mood. Dan checked their catch of 30 bags and tied up the necks of the sacks with sisal twine. Probably another 10 bags had been lost to the trawler's dredge, half a ton. That was about £300 plus another £200 costs for the rope and raw materials to make up new pots.

He busied himself with swabbing the decks and himself free of the slime, silt and the dogfish guts. It was easy enough to put a bucket on a line into the water and sluice it over the deck and loading shelf with a wooden handled brush. He finished by pouring half a bucket over his oilskins washing the worst away.

They motored up towards the mooring.

Gwilym knew the channel well but with the tide dropping fast kept close to the marker buoys. Messing around with the tangled lines had taken them longer than they would have normally needed. They had a few minutes to get close to the shoreline before mooring up. They needed to off-load their catch.

Gwilym steered to a spot below the concrete slipway. Just as the boat touched on the firm sand he put the engine into reverse and slowly moved back. Ready for the manoeuvre Dan dropped the sacks two-by-two off the boat. They did not have far to sink leaving a line of sacks for the falling water to leave marooned on the sand. Gwilym headed back out to his mooring in the channel.

Dan stood ready with the heavy wooden boat-hook and leaned over to pick up the small orange buoy attached by a short thick rope to the floating white drum, which was itself attached to the thick chain anchored to the seabed. Their white dinghy was tied to the drum and floated lightly on the water. Dan prodded it away with the boathook before hooking at the rope and pulling the buoy on board.

Dan made the fishing boat fast by tying the mooring rope to the heavy bow cleat. Safely tied up to the mooring he placed the old boat hook onto the loading shelf. The length of aged wood had a satisfying smooth feel to it. The boat hook had been used for many years, the wood seasoned with age and salt water fused into the brass of the hook. Not like the aluminium and plastic hooks that the yachties used, which snapped when they judged it wrong. A proper robust piece of kit, like a World War II Lee Enfield versus the modern plastic SA80 assault rifle, both fired bullets and one bullet was enough to kill a man. Dan knew which he preferred to use.

He gave thumbs up to Gwilym who switched the engine off. After the last five hours of the motor chugging, the quiet was sudden and pleasant. It seemed that the estuary was silent. The river channel flowed out, sunken in its confinement of the sandbanks and beach. Nature's noises came back, the gulls called out, the water gurgled against the hull of the boat and a fish broke the surface heading back out to the sea.

Dan stood up and stretched his aching back, the muscles tingling with the efforts of his day's work. He sat back on the shelf and rested looking out over the estuary. The sand dunes and the pine forest stretching away to the south, to the north where the raised headland was scattered with houses and grid lined with the hedgerows of the farmers' fields. He had travelled the wide world over and this certainly was a beautiful place.

They finished off the little jobs that needed to

be done and pulled in their dinghy. It was fibre-glass and utilitarian, the oars laid bow to stern across the two bench seats. Dan stepped in first and Gwilym passed down their gear. The short boat hook, a yellow waterproof ready bag, with their emergency flares and hand held marine radio and the 5-gallon drum of spare red diesel. Gwilym stepped into the dinghy and they cast off.

The dinghy was much lower in the water now. Dan put the oars in their rowlocks and pulled away. It was only about 40 yards to the beach and with the occasional scull to keep his bow aiming straight Dan let the outgoing tidal current take him down towards the line of bags. They beached fast on the sand and the two men clambered on to dry land, their wellington boots splashing up to the waters edge. Together they heaved at the bow of the dinghy and pulled it up away from the tide's drag.

Dan walked up to the car park to pick up the Landrover and trailer. There was only one other car parked, probably a dog walker taking advantage of the dune path and the empty beach. The old Landrover was a long wheel base with a cab and a canvas hood on the back. It was ex-service green, no heated leather seats or air conditioning and smelled of fish, but it started every time. He checked that the trailer was hooked on before driving across the puddle pitted crushed shale car park and down the concrete slipway. The empty trailer bounced behind him as he drove down the beach. He did a tight u-turn leaving a gyroscopic pattern of tyre marks on the hard packed sand. He came to a halt next to the line of, by now, stranded bags.

The trailer was a basic double axel flat back with low side panels that they unclipped and swung down on one side. Gwilym eased himself aboard and Dan started lifting the sacks on to the wooden base. Gwilym then pulled them into place to balance the trailer. They put the oars and the boathook alongside. They finished by tipping over, then lifting the dinghy on to the back, pulling up the sides and throwing a rope over to hold it in place.

They drove back up to the top of the beach above the high water mark of dried seaweed and discarded flotsam. They stopped to take the dinghy off again and drop it on the dry sand and shingle next to the low defending wall and the slipway that led up to the car park. There was a sorry collection of half a dozen upside down tenders tied to a rusty length of chain, which was itself attached to rings in the wall. The unwanted dinghies had paint peeling and their colours had faded in the sometime sun and often rain of the Welsh weather.

One of the tenders was slouched upright and had sunk into the sand and pebble mix of the beach. It was half filled with a green soup of seaweed, water and rubbish. Pebbles had been thrown inside by high water storms, or possibly by mischievous children holidaying on the beach with nothing better to do. Its wooden bench was broken and the exposed plywood boards of the cheaply made hull had warped to snap out of shape. They left jagged edges that would leave a splinter to the touch. Dan felt some sympathy for the lost usefulness of the dilapidated dinghy.

After dropping their dinghy off and tying it to the chain, Dan did another u-turn. Lining up the slipway he gunned the engine on the Landrover and hit the concrete ramp at some speed. The momentum carried the Landy and trailer up and on to the flat car park. He stopped a few yards along, attached the trailer lights, and hooked them in to the tow bar socket. He checked the cargo would not bounce out and they set off the ten miles to the fish processors.

2.

They drove the Landrover along the coast road, through a couple of small villages looking down on to the sea below. Dan then turned on to the main road into the town and headed towards the harbour. As they drove along there was a for sale sign above a pub doorway and from the raised cab of the Landy they could see through the windows into a dark and lifeless interior.

"Tsk," Gwilym clicked his tongue, "bollocks, another one gone. That was a good pub that, in its day."

The harbour town itself had seen better days. Built for a more prosperous time the quay and breakwater stretched into the Irish Sea. On the quayside opposite the commercial dock was a line of terraced town houses, shops and a couple of pubs. On closer inspection, half the shops were closed and only one of the pubs was still open. There were other shopping streets leading away from the sea but the shops here were also half occupied. A big supermarket on the outskirts had leached the lifeblood of the town away from the quayside.

What had been the town's main hotel stood on a promontory at the end of the quayside terrace. The Bay View Hotel looked grand enough and had great views looking out towards the sea. But its white paint had peeled and the sash windows of the bedrooms were loose and rattled in the winter gales. For years there had been a nightclub underneath the hotel, which had been a local institution. The club had been closed down by the police due to violence, drugs and underage drinking and was yet to reopen and the hotel struggled on above.

Gwilym nodded up at the hotel as they drove past. "They say that the Bay is going to be knocked down for flats."

"They've said that for years, they also say that it wouldn't pass planning"

"It depends which councillor is chairing the

meeting" huffed Gwilym.

"God Gwil, you are in a foul mood today."

"We all know whose pockets they are in."

"They are duly elected by the local population," teased Dan. "They can't all be bent."

"Chwarae teg, some aren't to be fair. But the stories I could tell you."

"And you already have told me most of them. Will you not go down and see your sons and come back with some new ones."

There were half a dozen fishing boats alongside the harbour wall. A few years before there would have been nearly a hundred trawlers. Dan noted that the big blue-hulled Mary Ann was there too. There were lights and activity on deck.

Gwilym saw it too and muttered under his breath, "Bastards!"

The Harbour Seafood company's factory and warehouse were set back from the quayside and the corrugated sheds backed into the grey cliff from which the stone for the quay had been quarried. Tall sharp pointed metal fencing surrounded the yard in front, the twisted spikes deterring any unwanted visitors. The big gates were wide open. Dan turned in and drove the Landrover and trailer across the big yard and down towards the end building. He switched the engine off and the bone shaking vibrations stopped. It was mid-afternoon and the light was fading for the day. The yellow sodium lights that illuminated the yard were already switched on.

Still in their yellow oilskin dungarees and wellington boots, Gwilym and Dan got out of the Landrover. Dan pressed the button of the big red bell and waited. After their own race to beat the tide there was never any rush here. It took a few minutes for the chain on the other side of the roller shutter to be pulled and the wide door clattered upwards.

The goods inwards controller, Arwel Price, was on the other side of the shutter in his white coat and white wellington boots. His grey hair sticking out of a black bobble hat, he was spry and sharp, he even wore a tie.

"Sut ydych chi Arwel."

"Da iawn diolch. A tithau? Gwilym, Dan."

"30 bags today. Would have been more but some bastard has trawled us again and we lost a couple of lines. Makes it even harder to make a living in these tough times."

"Well it's a good job for these Koreans wanting your whelks then isn't it?"

"Not at the price you buy them for Arwel."

"Ah now Gwilym, you know you are well paid for these horrible snails."

"I hear that there is a place over in Wallasey that will pay me more."

"Ah but they won't always pay you for them, I heard that too. Not like us now boi."

"Well as long as we are here now you must give us a good price for these beauties, top dollar now Arwel. Fresh out of the sea today."

Arwel clambered on to the trailer, cutting open the sisal ties with a penknife and inspected a couple of bags.

"A bit too much seaweed in here for my liking, Gwilym."

"There was that storm last week, throws the seaweed up, you know that. Will tell my lad here to be a bit more careful next time. Hey Dan, you hear that?"

Dan smiled back at their jousting.

"£550 per tonne today."

"That's rubbish, what happened to the £610 last month, Good big whelks these are boi."

"Just for you and that lovely wife of yours who you treat so badly I will give you £570."

"My wife is very happy thank you now Arwel, will have a nice big meal waiting for my tea before the pub," Gwilym patted his belly. "But she won't be happy if I go below £590 per tonne. You know she keeps a tight rein on me."

"And shouldn't she just. For the sake of Annie and the labour she has to bear with you I will do £580 and that's my limit."

"She won't be happy with me. But you know she has a soft spot for you Arwel bach so we will have to shake on it."

The two men shook hands and Arwel called back into the warehouse. "Three pallets Tommy."

A young lad, his oversized white rubber boots flapping against his thin legs, came out of the depths of the warehouse pulling a pallet truck with three blue pallets stacked on each other. The truck trundled across the tarmac and he laid the pallets next to each other. Dan let down one side of the trailer's walls and helped the lad unload the sacks from the trailer onto the blue wooden squares, ten on each. Tommy wheeled the first pallet back into the warehouse, pressed the handle of the truck, and pulled it away leaving the pallet and the whelks on the big metal weighing bridge built into the floor. The red digits gave the weight of the pallet and the whelks and the known weight of the standard pallet was deducted. This was repeated twice more and Arwel wrote down the numbers.

Arwel signed the billet form and offered Gwilym and Dan a panad, a cup of tea, but they declined wanting to get back and out of their fishing gear. Taking the form Gwilym walked over to the office block to pick up the payment, while Dan readied the trailer for their journey home, putting up the sidewall again and checking the light connection. The oars and the boathook lay across the bed of the trailer and he pulled them to one side in an effort to keep them neat.

He drove a little way over the yard to wait for Gwilym. He sat in the Landrover's cab and yawned. Too many sleepless nights, he had worked out that if he had one bad night's sleep troubled by nightmares the next night was usually better.

As he waited, he saw a group of five fishermen coming through the gate and towards the office block. It was getting darker now but Dan recognised them as the crew of the Mary Anne. The group were loud and two of the younger boys were drinking from big plastic bottles of cider. After cleaning down they were probably picking up the money from their own catch and would be on the way to the pub. It did not help that John Williams, who captained the Mary Ann had gone into the office and would be seeing Gwilym in there.

Hidden in the shadow of the Landrover's cab the young men paid no attention to Dan who sat only a few feet away from them. The lads in their teens and early twenties talked of playing out their fantasies.

"I'm going to break that Hayley Jones tonight, she's been promising it for ages," said the leader. The others laughed.

"She's got these great big tits and a tight arse."

"How far have you got Steve?"

"I've had a good feel inside her knickers but not had her naked yet."

"Her tits look great. Steve, bet they feel firm and pert"

"Pert, what have you been reading you little gobshite. They felt good in my hands and the nipples went ping. Ping!" He was pleased with himself and repeated the word "Ping"

"She's going to suck me off tonight, then I'm going to come on her "pert" tits."

"Has she said so?"

"Why virgin? Do you want to watch? See how it's done by a proper man. Not yet but I will give her a bit of white and she will do what I tell her."

Steve, the one who was going to be doing the "breaking" grabbed his crotch and squeezed, then thrust his hips forward. The other three boys who were probably cousins laughed. Dan noted that the youngest one looked down in embarrassment. The leader flicked his dark hair into place.

Gwilym came out. He was followed by John Williams. John was around the same age as Dan but the years had not been as kind, with wispy hair on the top of his head and a belly to rival Gwilym's.

"You can't prove it was me that went through your pots, you stupid old man."

"We both know it was you, John Williams. The

whole big wide sea and you went through my lines."

"I will head for them next time then Gwilym Jones and make sure I get the lot."

Gwilym was bigger than John Williams and he looked down at him. In his time, he had been a hard man but he was getting old and his temper had not improved to keep up. Under the sodium lights, he looked his age and his ragged hair and beard was grey. The Mary Ann's crew had taken notice and they went to surround Gwilym.

"Go on Dad, fucking have him."

Gwilym squared his shoulders and faced down the smaller man. One of the boys behind pushed him and he turned, while another pushed him again, a pack of dogs baiting a fairground bear.

Dan disembarked out of the Landy. Bullies never noticed their surroundings in a fight; it was the difference between a trained man and a thug. They did not notice as Dan moved back round and leaned in to the trailer where his hand felt the heavy wooden pole of the boathook. He picked it up, held it straight down by his side and slightly behind him, and stepped into the light.

"Right lads what's going on here?"

"Fuck off now."

Dan said, "Boys I am telling you to back away from this man."

"Fuck off, who are you?"

"Come on boys, we don't want trouble," said John Williams.

The loudest biggest boy blatantly ignored his father. "What are you going to do about it hey?"

"Stephen, stop it. Stop it now," said John.

The young buck ignored his father and tried to eyeball Dan. "You are an old man too aren't you? Go on fuck off."

This was the one who fancied himself with the ladies. Good looking and vain, dark hair, tanned face and broad shoulders, he swaggered in his walk. Dan had already marked him out as a fool. The fool then did a stupid thing and pulled out a fishing knife and flashed it at Dan. Dan was not wearing his own knife having taken it off as soon as he got off the boat. He did have the boat hook by his side and the stupid boy hadn't noticed that.

Dan smiled. "Put the knife down."

"Fuck off."

Steve waved the knife in Dan's face. Dan reacted in one fluid motion, bringing up the boat
hook and cracking it down. Hard. The wooden pole
hit Stephen's hand with a heavy smash. In a second
movement Dan twisted the pole in the air, redirect-
ing its path to between the boy's legs. The boy let
out a small whelp and dropped to his knees, his
hands clutching his crotch.

Steve's posse of cousins backed off. Dan turned
to John. The wooden pole held at an angle across
his chest. The brass hook, evil, sharp and menacing
pointed towards the group of fishermen.

"Take him away and tell him never to use a
knife like that again, or next time I will use the
hook on him."

John Williams nodded.

"Gwilym, You ok? Get in the car."

3.

Gwilym and Dan met later in the village pub, the Ty Coch. It was set on a small square with grey houses around an ancient cross. Ten years previously all the local villages would have had the basic life necessities of the pub, a chapel and a post office. Now in many of them the post office had closed, the chapel and the pub sold off to become holiday homes 'with character' or, more lately, just left boarded up.

Carol Pritchard from the Ty Coch had been lucky and had cut her cloth to fit the straitened times. A few sandwiches wrapped in cling-film meant that the kitchen and small restaurant could be closed off most of the time and reopened only in the summer, saving the cost of a chef and the waste of unsold food.

When Dan and Gwilym came in, she poured them their pints, a hand pulled keg bitter, strong and frothy. It was 8 o'clock and they went to sit by the log fire. With the pine forest close by there was plenty of wood and it was cheaper than putting the oil fired heating on.

"I should have clattered him, the little shit," Gwilym said after placing his pint on the small hammered brass tabletop.

"What would that have achieved? You couldn't have taken all of them on," said Dan.

"You would have backed me up."

"What if I hadn't been there, nipped for a slash or something?"

"You clattered him and taught him a lesson."

"Yes but he was only a stupid kid and I didn't have much choice."

"You are a cool one you are Dan. When he pulled the knife, you smiled at him."

"Did I? He was waving it around, it was clear he did not know how to use it. Just wanted to be big and tough."

"Yes by trying to frighten an old man, a typical Williams that one," Gwilym said with certainty

"You are not as young as you used to be. I've heard those stories you tell about the scraps you got into in ports when you were in the merchant navy. I would have thought you would have learnt some lessons by this time of your life."

"Yes, Annie said that too."

"Well listen to your wife then."

"She said to say thanks for looking after me." Gwilym looked at Dan and leaned over and patted his knee. "Diolch yn fawr a ti boi."

"Who else would I get to buy me a pint then Granddad? Go on it's your round."

Gwilym grumbled but went to the bar. He called for their drinks. "Two pints please Carol cariad and when are you going to let my fine friend over there take you out for that dinner?"

"Anytime he asks nicely I will be happy to go with him, Gwilym."

"I'm sure you would cariad. You might have to be gentle with him though, he is a weak man, no strength in him at all. Not like me," he puffed his chest out.

"Don't you worry Gwilym; I would take good care of him."

"I'm sure you would cariad, I'm sure you would. And if he needs me to show him how then I'm your man."

"I can show him myself, now thank you very much."

"Pity he never asks," she said under her breath. Then out loud, "That will be £5.20 please?"

"£5.20 for 2 beers. It's like living in London here these days."

"And when did you last go to London, Gwilym Jones. It would be £10 for 2 pints there."

"That's true," he replied. "The beer might be better there too!" He quaffed the top half of his pint, the spume catching in the whiskers round his mouth.

"To be fair, it's not that bad. But not as good as that Guinness in Dublin, when I took my Annie last year."

Gwilym took the pints back to the table and pressed his head close to Dan so they would not be overheard.

"Dan, the Williams family have been a bad family for a long time. They have their fingers in so many pies, they are dangerous."

"Gwil, they are chocolate gangsters, big names around here but not as tough as they think they are."

"They are supposed to have contacts all over the place."

"That may be so but what have they got against you. They didn't trawl over your lines on purpose, it was a mistake and that Stephen is just a young fool, trying to play the big hard man."

"A few years ago one of the Williams brothers, Cliff was the worst of the lot. He would be an uncle to that Stephen. My eldest boy would be coming into his teens. Cliff started seeing a young girl in the village and caused a lot of trouble. There were a few wild parties on the beach, he brought lads from the town and there were problems with the boys from the village. This girl was in the middle of it all and her father wanted to get rid of him."

"What happened?"

"The father told him to clear off. But it didn't work and Cliff turned nasty. The girl was besotted, thought she was a gangster's moll, and was enjoying playing with fire, defying her dad, taking drugs. Cliff liked playing the big hard man and went after the girl's younger sister and her father found him trying to force his way on her, she was only 14." Gwilym paused and took a slurp of his beer.

"Go on."

"The father was a small man but he tried to hit Cliff who turned on him and beat him up. He was badly beaten, broken jaw, ribs. But Cliff left saying he would be back."

"Did he come back?"

"Yes the next night. With a carload of heavies. But we were ready for them"

"And?"

"The girl was horrified what had happened to her dad. She told him that Cliff had been trying to persuade her to bring her little sister to meet him. So trying to please him she had taken her along and Cliff had tried to rape her. He thought that she was his by rights. Nasty Bastard. Cliff thought he could do what he wanted and told her to come down to the beach car park the next night and bring her sister again or her dad would get worse the next time and Cliff's friends would watch."

"Did you go to the police?"

"What good would they do? At the time there were rumours flying around about how the Williams family were protected by the police. The girl told her mam that she was scared what would happen and her mam called a meeting."

"What a women's institute meeting?"

"No, we all knew what was coming and this Cliff was lording it over us. He was a danger to our village and we had to deal with him ourselves. Your Taid was there, he agreed that we should stick together. Almost all the men of the village were there, thirty of us. All farmers and fishermen, strong, good with our hands and all with families to protect. That night Cliff came with his friends and drove into the car park at the end of the road. Eddie Bont Farm blocked the entrance off with a tractor and we surrounded the car. They came out fighting but we gave them a proper hiding. We told Cliff to stay away and let them drive off. We knocked all their windows out first."

"Now that's a story you haven't told me before. Did they come back?"

"No, they didn't. It never reached the police, or if it did, nothing was said. Not long after, Cliff was caught near Manchester with drugs and was sent to prison. There was a rumour that his brother Brian grassed him up. Cliff was out of control and was bad for business."

"You've seen them off once, why not again?"

"It's a different world now, a different community. I wouldn't know how many would back me up?"

"And you are still scared of them?"

"Annie said it to me today. I am older and not wiser. I shouldn't have picked that argument. I was lucky you were there."

"Gwilym, bullies make threats they don't carry out. This guy didn't even make any threats. He was too busy rolling on the ground puking up his cider. What is he going to do anyway? He's not a gangster, he's a spoilt kid. If he needs cutting to size then I will do it. I have seen so much badness in people Gwilym. If he wants to come back at me then I will deal with him."

"Sometimes in families a black sheep will resurface somewhere along the next generation. Stephen is like Cliff, he will nurse a grudge."

"So they are not all bad in the Williams family then."

"No, they are not all bad."

Then after a moment's consideration Gwilym said, "I think we deserve a whisky." He coughed "Go on it's your round, I will have a large Laphroaig. It will get the petrol fumes out of my throat."

When Dan came back to the table they raised their glasses in salute, "Iechyd da."

4.

Dan woke refreshed. The alarm had not yet gone off and under the duvet it was warm. The morning light was breaking through the panes of the small bedroom window. He could see the marram grass on the dunes swaying gently. Beyond the dunes, the sea was calm. The day was going to be bright, sunny and cold, high blue skies with wisps of white cloud.

The only solid constant fact in his life for the last three years was that the tide would be an hour later than yesterday. High or low, neap or spring, the sea governed by the phases of the moon. He had sat in the small cottage through these monthly cycles, the fire burning with driftwood from the beach in the winter or the windows and door open to let fresh air into the house for the summer. The thick walls and slate roof built to keep the elements out and the heat in for the winter and the heat out in the summer. He did not know how old the cottage was perhaps he should look it up. The cottage needed some care and attention perhaps he should do that too.

He had gone through the motions, feeling the spirit of his Taid whose advice for Dan would have been to take it easy. To take time to recover and to build his reserves back up again. His Taid had overcome his own demons, leftover from his experiences of battle during the Second World War.

The spirit of his grandfather had watched over him and to secure the bond Dan had worn his Taid's yellow gold signet ring. The only other items of importance had been the old man's war medals, which along with Dan's own, were kept in the cottages place of safekeeping.

Dan as a boy had been told tales of smugglers and fishermen and of the village folk helping the smugglers to escape the excise men. Dan had listened avidly and the young boy's eyes had opened wide as saucers when he had been told about the hiding place.

One prolonged holiday his Taid had slowly built up to his big reveal. Playing the children's game, a hint of hot or cold as to where the secret

spot would be. Disclosing that there was something else hidden away that Dan would be very
lucky to some day see.

It had been sunny the day that he was shown
the secret. The young boy and the old man had
been out in the varnished clinker dinghy. An old
seagull engine clamped on to the flat transom
board, the black motor started with the thin rope
tightly wound around the flywheel and pulled hard
to start. They had taken their lines out and had
spent a contented couple of hours fishing with
hooks hidden in bright feathers to catch the mackerel. They had six fish in a bucket when they had
come home. Dan had gutted the fish and his Taid
built up the fire in the range stove. The mackerel
with their black and green stripes had sizzled and
spat in the black cast iron frying pan. The smell of
the fish had filled the kitchen, and although most
of the smoke went up through the chimney, there
was a grey fug that the grandfather and his grand-
son ignored.

The scrubbed oak table was set with two sets of
bone handled knives and forks, two white enamel
plates with blue rims and two mugs filled with well
water. A saucepan of boiled potatoes was taken off
the stove. Green samphire, an edible seaweed grass,
which they had picked from the shoreline of the
estuary, was placed into the frying pan where it
soaked up the butter and the juices from the fish.

To top it all young Dan was offered a drop of his grandfather's whisky in a small glass tumbler. It literally was a drop, more of a dribble but to Dan it truly was the water of life, which his grandfather told him with reverence, was the original translation of the traditional Gaelic word 'Uisce Beatha'. His Taid told him to sip it and to savour the taste on his tongue. It burned his throat as it went down.

After dinner, Dan washed up the plates and the pans while his Grandfather sat in the lounge chair and listened to the radio while he sipped on another whisky and smoked a woodbine. The harsh smelling cigarette smoke mixed with the after effects of the fried fish, but with no woman around to tell either of them off they neither noticed nor cared. Dan would have moaned to his mother for having been forced to do the washing up at home but the old man had him well trained. There was normally a reward or a story that was just enough to keep Dan on the right side of surly teenager before his Grandfather left him to go to bed and strolled down to the pub.

With his chores done Dan sat down next to his grandfather, who ruffled his hair and looked thoughtful. The evening was still light and the room was bright. The grandfather looked out of the window. To heighten the atmosphere of excitement he made a play of pulling the thin curtains across the window, locking the cottage door, and then switching on the light

"Right Danny bach, its time to show you where the family treasures are kept. It is not to be told to anybody else unless it is a matter of life or death."

"Yes Taid."

"Now this place has been used by smugglers as a hiding spot for jewels and treasure for hundreds of years."

"Yes Taid."

The old man pulled himself from the chair and motioned Dan to join him. He went over to the old Welsh dresser against the inside wall of the kitchen and said for Dan to give him a hand to shift it over a couple of feet. They should probably have moved the china plates, kept for best and so never used, but they were careful in their actions. There did not seem to be anything underneath apart from the kitchen floor, just smooth blackened slate tiles about 12 inch square and laid tightly together.

"Can you see anything?"

"No Taid."

The grandfather pulled his penknife from his cardigan pocket and opened the blade. He bent down and ran the knife along the edge of a square tile closest to the skirting board. Using the blade, he levered up the thick tile to reveal a shallow recess. Beneath the tile was a dark green metal box about 18 inches long and 6 inches deep. On his hands and knees, Dan looked closely down into the hole. It was about 10 inches deep and another foot under the wall. The floor tile rested around the edges on a seal of old felt.

The old man gently pushed Dan aside and pulled an old box from the recess. They sat at the table to open it.

"This is an ammo box, When we used them during the war I knew that it would fit this hole. So one home leave I brought one back with me. Your great grandfather was not easily impressed but he liked this when I showed it to him. There had been an old tin there before. It had Redcoats with white hats fighting the Zulus on it. Like that film of Rourke's Drift, where Ivor Emmanuel sang Men of Harlech. Good film that!"

"Yes Taid."

The clasp was undone and the lid flipped back. Inside was a red leather presentation box. Dan had seen that before, it held his Grandfather's medals,

worn on Remembrance Day in the parade in the
town. The veterans marching shoulders back,
chests out, with their poppies and medals proudly
displayed. There was also a brown manila envelope,
thick with yellowing documents lying across the
bottom of the box. Resting above it a heavy object
wrapped in a cream coloured cloth cash bag with
brown stitching around the outside and Midland
Bank stamped across the fabric.

His Taid looked around at the windows, checking the curtain was still closed, before putting his
hand inside the bag and pulling out a gun. It was
black and shined, glistening with a thin layer of oil
under the electric light

"This is a revolver. A Webley .38"

"Wow!"

The old man delved into the bag and produced
a close wrapped cleaning kit and a small square box
of thick brown cardboard. When the box lid was
pulled off and the greaseproof wrapping was
opened out the snub noses of twelve small bullets
could be seen. His Taid picked one out and passed
it to Dan who held it in the palm of his hand. The
bullet head itself was grey lead and the casing was
a dull brass. It had a small rim on the base and was
shorter than Dan's thumb.

His Taid took it back. "The rim holds the round in place and when the trigger is pulled the hammer strikes the centre and the gunpowder is set off and the bullet fires down the barrel."

He passed it back and Dan looked at it again. Rolling it round between his forefinger and thumb. The old man then picked up the revolver, clicked open the catch and the barrel hinged forward to expose the six chambers of the round magazine. Now separate from the trigger grip, hammer and the butt. He showed the young boy the workings of the pistol, how the round would be fired and then the magazine would revolve to place the next chamber under the hammer. He then closed the two parts and passed the weapon butt first to Dan.

"You have to respect the power of this gun Danny bach. It is a killer. You like watching the cowboy films with John Wayne but this is a real six-shooter. You must always handle this gun and any other with great care. It is very dangerous. You must never point it at anybody, even unloaded. A gun will give you power but it is also a responsibility."

Dan tested the weight of the pistol. "Has it killed anybody?"

"No, it hasn't."

Dan was relieved.

"An officer of mine was killed on D-Day and I thought it might come in useful so I took it from him. He wouldn't have needed it anymore. I kept it in my pack and when I was demobbed, I brought it back home. Your Nain hated having it in the house, but I didn't want to part with it and it was safely out of the way."

Together they stripped the pistol down and opened up the cleaning kit. There was a small bottle of gun oil and a length of string with a brass weight that was dropped through the barrel and then a small piece of cloth was pulled through after it. This left the inside of the barrel free from any dust and they did the same with the chambers of the revolver drum. There was a slight patch of rust by the raised gun sight and they gently scoured it off. Dan was shown the rifling inside the barrel and told how the twisted grooves spun the bullet as it was fired making it more accurate.

There was also a lanyard, which went round the soldier's neck and then attached to the ring on the butt of the pistol. There would have been a khaki canvas holster, which fitted on to the webbing belt. However, that had not been kept.

It had been a secret that Dan and his Taid had shared. It was never mentioned to Dan's mother and if she did know about it, it was never discussed. There was seldom much to talk about with her anyway, light and easy chit chat, but never anything serious. Like a hidden revolver.

5.

Dan drank his early morning coffee and looked out of the cottage window at the sand, the sea and the blue sky. Gwilym and he had talked about it last night and this year's fishing season was over. They would go out today, collect the pots, bring them all in and sell the last of the catch. The sea was getting colder and the whelks would not be as eager to climb into their pots. The weather forecast was turning worse for later in the week and they would lose more days on the water struggling to haul up the lines. It was time to call an end to their fishing season for this year.

The cottage's secret hiding place and its contents had weighed heavily on Dan's mind. His eyes wandered to the base of the Welsh dresser, knowing it was there. He had never fired the gun himself and there were still twelve bullets wrapped in greaseproof paper in the small heavy cardboard box. Yet he had been tempted. When he came back from Afghan with the pain in his leg nigh on unbearable, he knew his service career was over. The ghastly image of the young marine in his death throes who had taken the full force of the blast was so vivid in his memory. He had been the colour sergeant, he wore the crown above the stripes, and the boy had been his responsibility. The mandatory official report said it was not his fault and he had been given a medal but his career was over. His leg had been broken and he knew he had been lucky for it not to be amputated.

He moved the dresser and opened up the recess and the ammo box to pull the gun out. It would be better out of his life. The knife waving at him the day before had reawakened his taste for life. There might have been a time when he stepped into the knife attack, welcomed it, his death by somebody else's hand would have been a release. That Stephen Williams, the stupid little bollocks, would have made a mess of that too.

After a couple minutes of preparation, he was ready to go and meet Gwilym to go out on the fishing boat. He pushed the dresser back into place and put the gun in the waterproof duffle bag along with his Tupperware lunchbox. He walked along to

Gwilym's house and the yard where the Landrover was waiting and as he always did put his bag in the cab.

"Bore da, Gwilym." Gwilym, hungover, grunted back at him. They hooked up the trailer and threw in the oars, boathook and fuel. Annie waved to him from inside the kitchen window and he waved back at his friend's wife.

They drove to the car park and pushed the dinghy into the river channel, rowing for the boat. They didn't speak much and from the dinghy Dan passed his bag up to Gwilym on the boat and they headed west out to sea.

When they reached their small field of floating flags, they started hauling up the lines of pots. This time emptying out the whelks but stacking the pots and not baiting them. Line-by-line they pulled them up and the deck behind the wheelhouse filled up like a mini container ship with white and yellow square barrels.

They pulled up the last line and stacked it. The water was slack and the boat bobbed gently on the green sea. They stopped for a breather and to have their lunch. Gwilym was in the wheelhouse and Dan placed his bag on the loading shelf by the stern to pull out his lunch box. Dan looked around and hidden by the pots checked that Gwilym was not watching. He looked around at the empty sea and the thin line of the shore over a mile away. Holding on to the muzzle of the revolver he dropped the box of bullets and cleaning kit inside the cloth moneybag into the sea. It sank instantly, disappearing into the green depths releasing a stream of bubbles on its way down.

He stroked the barrel and then held the butt of the revolver in his hand one last time. He aimed it downwards and curled his finger round the trigger before dropping the gun into the water with a dull splash. He watched the bubbles break the surface as it followed the bag and bullets into the depths.

6.

Dan had managed a lie in, then a cup of coffee and a piece of toast before a walk on the beach. His leg was mending well, it only bothered him in the cold. A couple of days ago he had tried to go for a run. After years of early morning runs and forced marches, he had missed the strict training regimen of the Marines. Lifting the whelking pots had made his upper body stronger than it had ever been but he knew that drinking beer with Gwilym was taking its toll.

Two days before he had headed off on a long run. The path at the end of the road outside his cottage took him through the dunes to wooden steps down to the beach and he ran along the shoreline. About half a mile further along he had been out of breath trying to climb the steep sand dunes, the soft sand slipping away under his feet. He didn't push himself hard and had taken the easy option and walked back. Yesterday he had done a brisk walk and today he had fallen into the military stride of the Royal Marine's 'yomp'. The beach was flat and he had avoided climbing the dunes, the long stretch of his legs with each pace had been more fluid than the day before.

He had climbed a low hill and had viewed the amphitheatre of the Snowdonia mountain range stretching to the south. The sky was blue, it was cold but dry and the vapour trails of the planes crisscrossed the sky heading out to fly over Ireland and across the Atlantic. In the sharp morning light the peaks had looked clear, close and enticing. He had climbed them all. To the south east the three Carneddau mountains, then there was the cleft of the Ogwen Valley Pass to the Glyders, Fawr and Fach and the gherkin shaped plug of Tryfan hidden behind the smooth slope of Y Garn. Down again to Llanberis town and up to pyramid peaked Snowdon and its horseshoe ridges he had climbed during training. Down again to the Beddgelert Pass and West along the Nantlle ridge to the lower pups of the three Rivals at the start of the Lleyn. He always relished discovering the false horizons, the flat plateaus and lost valleys that you came across in high mountainous country.

The exercise, the sea breeze and the time to

think beneath the open sky did him good. He had gone back to his cottage and having switched the immersion heater on before his walk ran himself a scalding hot bath. He scrubbed himself down, careful of the scarring on his leg. As the steam rose around him and fogged up the bathroom, he laid his head back on the edge of the bath. He had read somewhere that these short deep roll top bathtubs were fashionable. This one was from a period long before interior design concepts. On parts of the tub, the enamel had worn away through to the black metal.

Dan had remembered being bathed in here by his Taid as a boy. He had a vivid recollection of the time when Gwilym's formidable wife Annie had held him by the ear, filled this bath, thrown him in and scrubbed him so hard that his skin had been nearly bleeding. The shampoo had stung his eyes and great clumps of hair had come out in her comb.

He levered himself out of the snug fitting bath and using a threadbare towel dried himself. With the razor he scraped a few days stubble off his chin and started looking around for clothes to wear out to lunch. It was harder than he thought it would be. The life of a fisherman did not call for stylish dressing. He had plenty of work gear but there was little in the inherited dark mahogany wardrobe that was much smarter than a pair of jeans and a polo shirt with a Royal Marines crest on it. He had a couple of dress shirts, but when he inspected them closer they were frayed at the collar and faded with use. Gwilym and Annie wouldn't care or comment, they had invited him to their home as a friend but he realised that he was turning into a tramp. Truth be told he realised he had probably been looking like a vagrant for a while. His clothes were clean, but they were past well worn and were wearing out.

He checked his funeral suit inside its protective hanging wrapper. It looked fine on the hanger. When he tried the jacket on over the polo shirt, his arms wouldn't fit in the sleeves. He tensed his back and shoulder muscles and he felt the fabric stretch tight. If he flexed then the seams would rip, the result of the many hours on the whelk pots. The trousers were alright and if anything looser. Whatever he had been doing to his upper body the last few years he had certainly changed shape. In the end he chose to wear the suit trousers with the least old of his shirts. All his warm jumpers had holes in and smelt of fish so he went without, wearing a greying white T-shirt under his shirt instead. A quick buff of the black shoes and the polish shone brightly, not to parade ground standard but enough for a Sunday lunch out.

Dan looked for a smarter coat than his combat jacket or oilskins. There was a woollen reefer jacket tucked away in the back of the wardrobe. He had been issued it when he had served with the Septics on the USS Midway and that would do. He had brought it home to his Taid when he had been sent back to his unit after Desert Storm and had been due some leave. Doing up the thick buttons of the jacket and thrusting his hands in the pockets he stepped out of the cottage door and headed down the sandy lane towards the village.

He was a little early and took a detour to the pub on the way to his Sunday lunch. He knew it was good manners not to turn up empty handed so he popped in to the pub to buy a bottle of wine. He did not keep spare alcohol in the house. That was a slippery slope that he had pulled back from, which could be why he had started to spend more time in the pub.

Dan walked in and Anwen was behind the bar. There were a couple of the usual regulars in but there would be more for the Sunday afternoon session. Gwilym was not allowed to the pub on a Sunday. Annie didn't mind during the week but not on the Sabbath.

Barmaid Anwen brightened when Dan walked in and pulled herself up to stand straight, perked up her cleavage to best advantage and flicked her hair.

"Haia Dan, Sut mae? You look very smart."

"Iawn Diolch, Pretty good. You look good yourself Anwen." The deep valley between her breasts was having an effect today and Dan was finding it hard not to stare.

"Diolch yn fawr a ti. Croeso Dan. What can I do for you today? Anything you want?"

"Yes please, a bottle of red wine to take out and some cans of bitter."

Anwen made a play of turning around and bending down to pull the cans from a low shelf.

He was being treated to the girl's well-rounded buttocks clad in black leggings. It was hard to ignore the sight of her thong riding up between the rim of her leggings and the bottom of her white top and the smooth skin underneath with the slight ridge of her spine. The thong was a turquoise lace and the two lower sides curved downwards, pointing the way to hidden delights.

Carol came down from her upstairs flat.

"Anwen, pull yourself up," she snapped, aggrieved at Dan for looking.

"Er, Haia Carol."

"Hello Dan."

"Carol, can I have a quick word please?"

"Yes sure, its quiet at the moment. Come in the back room, there is nobody in there."

"You ok? you look tired."

"Thanks for that Dan, you know how it is, the last two drinkers nursed their pints and were talking malu-cachu and wouldn't go home."

"Let me guess, Billy, Dai and Derek?"

"Yes that's right. Then I come down and you are all dressed smart and having an eye full of Anwen's arse. I'm all frumpy in jeans and sweatshirt and haven't had a bath yet."

She took a breath and carried on. "Oh never mind me, James has been playing silly beggars and the brewery are making loads of changes and I'm fed up today that's all. Now what do you want?"

"Er. Can you show me how to use the Internet please? I need to look up a few things. I was shown how to use it but technology has moved on so fast. Each time I look again I am trying to play catch up and its all jumped on again."

"Yes sure. I use the Internet all the time; I even place the beer order on the brewery website now. James uses it for his homework, when he is not playing games on it."

"I never had much call to use computers driving boats up and down rivers. The young recruits who came into the platoon were totally clued in and it passed me by. I need to sort myself out and need to look at the possibility of finding a job."

"A job? I thought you were going to keep on fishing with Gwilym."

"Keep it to yourself for the moment, I'm not rushing but 'I want to explore my options'."

"Happy to help. Come round and I will see if I can sort you out. Let me know if you find a good one on a desert island, I will come with you."

"You can't leave all this," he teased her. "I need your advice on something else too if you wouldn't mind. If I am looking for a job, I'm going to need a new suit and I need some good advice. Could we buy a suit on the Internet?"

"Tell you what, we could buy clothes online but I think it would be better if you try a few on. Its coming up to Christmas soon and I need to buy some stuff. Why don't we both go across to Chester this week and you can try some suits on. We will catch the train along the coast and go for the day."

"Sounds good, I will buy you lunch."

"Great. Perhaps we can go to the cinema, while we are there. How about Tuesday? Anwen can open up and James can help her until I come back to lock up and it won't be busy this time of year."

"Sounds fine to me. Thanks that will be really helpful. I will speak to you later and we will sort it out. What's the time?" He looked at the clock behind the bar. "I'd better get going. Now go and have that hot bath and get that loofah out and relax. I won't offer to scrub your back for you."

"You can if you want to, but James is still in bed so you might give him a shock. I will look forward to Chester. It will do us both good to escape from this place."

7.

Dan went through the yard to the back kitchen door and hung his coat on the rack. The bottle of red wine was well appreciated and Annie gave Dan the corkscrew to open it. There were already wineglasses set out and he left the bottle on the table to breathe as he had seen the stewards do in the sergeants' mess dinners. He was in plenty of time. Annie was setting the big kitchen table and he offered to help but she shooed him away.

"Go and sit with his lordship in the parlour, Rhiannon and Emyr will be here soon. Take him his beer in."

He left the warmth of the kitchen and the delicious aromas of cooking meat and went through and sat on the comfortable sofa. It was covered with throw rugs and he sank backwards as he sat down. The television was on, showing motorbike racing. They sat in friendly silence. Dan's cottage didn't even have a television. His grandfather used to have one but when it had packed in Dan hadn't bothered to replace it. He listened to the radio and read books and the newspaper.

Gwilym opened his can of beer and took a swig. He raised the can in salute.

"Iechyd da."

They sat for a few minutes with the droning of the motorbikes twisting round the circuit until the race was won and the ads changed the volume. Gwilym pressed the mute button on the control.

"You still not have a television then boi?"

"No, I don't miss it. When I was a kid my mother's boyfriends used to lie on the couch watching it so I went to my room to keep out of the way. So I never caught the habit of sitting in front of the box."

Gwilym looked at Dan over the top of his reading glasses. Dan didn't usually share information of his childhood.

"Annie wouldn't let our boys watch too much television. They used to moan about missing out on the programmes their friends watched. She watched that Grange Hill once about all the badly behaved kids at school so she gave them chores every night so they couldn't watch it."

"My mum would have let me watch anything. But I stayed in my room out of the way."

"Your Taid missed her when she left and your Nain fell ill."

"We never used to talk about it. Never talked about much really."

"Did she ever mention your father?"

"Hell no. He was long gone by the time I was old enough to remember him. She never kept them very long."

"She was at school with Annie and me. They were good friends for a while but your mam was wild and then she went away."

"One of the boyfriends was alright. I was about 13 and a mass of hormones and he took me to the boxing club so I could use up some of that energy and stop being a surly sod around the house. He was one of the better of mum's boyfriends."

"What happened to him?"

"He disappeared. Mum didn't keep the ones who treated her well for very long."

"Your Taid used to tell me about your boxing. You did well at it."

"For a while, before I discovered drink and girls."

"Ah that comes to us all."

"It helped though. One night I was walking home from the boxing gym through the estate and there was a gang of lads on the corner. I was minding my own business but the leader stood in front of me and pushed me and I laid him out. I had been training for a bout and going through the first fifteen seconds in my head. When he pushed me I unleashed those first fifteen seconds on him. At the end he was lying on the ground and I just walked on. I was expecting them to follow me but they didn't and when I turned the corner I legged it."

"A bit different to growing up round here."

"Just a bit. That's why the Williams are no threat. One of the local gangsters heard that I was good with my fists and approached me to do some running round for him. It was after a charity fight and they were wearing black ties and tuxedos. I remember the fog of cigarette smoke above the ring. I guess you don't get that any more. My trainer at the gym looked out for me and kept me busy away from crime for that time at least."

Dan had been watching the images on the television. They made no sense without the sound and he thought back to the northern city he had grown up in and sat back watching the pictures flash by.

"Gwilym, I need to talk to you, I'm not sure how much longer I am going to be around."

"I know boi, don't worry now. I am thinking of pulling back on the whelks anyway. I am told there is some survey work for cables to the wind farms coming up in the Spring and they want some boats to help them out. It will be less stress on my back. Anyway, I've had a good run, will keep up the summer stuff, and put a few more lobster pots down. Even look at doing some more dressed crabs. Annie thinks they could make us a bit of cash if we sell enough. What have you got planned?"

"Not too sure yet. I'm going to look at what I am good at. I was offered a career counselling service when I left the Marines but my head was wrecked so I never took it up."

"Pob lwc boi."

The doorbell rang and Gwilym's face lit up. "Ah my baby's here."

He raised himself on the arms of the chair and went to the front door, giving his daughter a big fatherly cwtch. His daughters belly was nearly as big as his own and they leant over to hug each other.

"Sut mae cariad. Haia Emyr."

"Da iawn Da."

Gwilym shook his son in law's hand and they all went through to the kitchen where Annie was waiting and she hugged them both.

"Haia Dan. Come here and give me a sws and a cwtch," said Rhiannon as warm and friendly as when she had been a child. She gave him a kiss and a big hug, her bump pressing into him.

He shook Emyr's hand and Annie chased the men back into the parlour out of the way. Rhiannon went into the kitchen to help her mam with the preparations for the roast.

"Do you want a beer Emyr?" Gwilym offered his son in law a can from his stash. "Dan?"

"Yes please Gwilym."

The three men sat back on the armchair and the comfortable sofa and sipped from their cans. The television was still on, a soap opera now and they watched the images without the sound.

"Annie didn't let the boys watch this either," said Gwilym to Dan.

"Emyr has a great big plasma screen television, very nice too. Dan here doesn't own a television," he said crossing the conversation to his guests.

"You ready for the baby Emyr? Getting close now?" asked Dan

"Yes due the week before Christmas so we will save a fortune on presents if it comes on time, Rhiannon is busy nesting so the nursery is all ready but she won't have the pram in the house yet. Says it is bad luck."

"I've never had much to do with babies so I don't know the protocols," said Dan.

"Keep your head down around pregnant women is my advice, you will find out over dinner.

She will try to organise you if you are not careful," warned Emyr.

"ITS READY," came the call from the kitchen.

They went through and Rhiannon sat them all down at the table. Wine was poured and Annie served the meal. Gwilym at the head of the table was making a show of sharpening his carving knife on a hand held grindstone. Pulling the long thick blade diagonally along the stone with a flourish and a screeching scrape.

"Da, you will wake the baby up," Rhiannon said.

"Will he be out ready for Christmas dinner?" her father replied.

"Ah I hope so. He, or she, is killing my back."

Hands in padded oven gloves Annie had placed the sizzling lamb on a counter top for the meat to rest and the juices to settle. The smell was gorgeous and all of them were salivating. She pulled the roasted potatoes and parsnips out of the oven and transferred them into flower patterned crockery bowls. She placed them on the mats on the table. They were crispy and blackened in parts, just as Dan liked them.

"They are hot, don't touch."

She placed the vegetables on the table, mashed carrot and turnip in one bowl and green cabbage in another.

Then the piéce de resistance, the leg of lamb, was put in front of Gwilym for him to carve. The twigs of Rosemary from Annie's herb plot gave a special flavouring and he lifted them off and holding the lamb with his two-tined fork he cut his first slice. The outside of the meat was brown and slightly crackled but the inside was pink and perfect. He placed the sliced lamb on the first of the stack of plates and holding it with a tea towel, ready for the purpose, passed it to Emyr, the guest to the family home.

"Careful the plate is hot."

The rest of the meat was doled out quickly with Gwilym carving round the bone and the vegetables and potatoes being passed around. Before they tucked in, they paused, stopping for Annie to say a quick grace in Welsh.

The taste lived up to the look and the smell. There was freshly-cut mint in vinegar and a thick gravy made from the escaped juices of the lamb and given a rich brown taste and flavour with a dash from an ancient bottle of gravy browning that still stood on the worktop. The lamb was from a local farmer whose wife went to chapel with Annie and him to the pub with Gwilym. The vegetables were mainly from their own well-tended plot although the potatoes had to come from the supermarket.

It was a great meal and Dan revelled in the food and the atmosphere. He was fond of Rhiannon, whose husband Emyr was protective of his wife and her cargo and was well able for Gwilym's ribbing.

Annie was pleased to have her kitchen table full of chatter and laughter again. Although careful not to talk about any gruesome details on the upcoming birth to disturb Gwilym's sensibilities she teased out the latest details.

"Have you your bag ready yet Rhiannon? Did you buy those new slippers ready for the hospital?" Annie asked her daughter.

"No mam, I'm getting the last bits next week. Then I will be ready."

"That's good, it might come early. Now try this mint jelly. I've made a batch to sell at the Christmas farmers market with Winny Hughes and I've made some marmalade. Would you like a jar Dan?"

"Yes please Annie, It didn't last long last year."

"You enjoyed that market last year didn't you mam?" said Rhiannon.

"I did, we had great fun. We were next to the stall that did the sloe gin. We were quite pickled when it was time to come home."

"They were singing hymns in the Landrover when I picked them up. Disgraceful I say" said Gwilym.

"Don't you start on me for one day of being a bit merry. The state you came home in last week and keeping me up all night with your snoring."

"Yes Dear."

"I bet Dan doesn't snore like you do. Do you Dan?"

"Not that I know, Annie"

"Are you seeing anybody Dan?" Rhiannon jumped in.

"Me? No."

"Why not? A good looking man like you."

"Don't know, not met anybody for a while?"

"So you are single then?"

"I guess so"

"Open to offers?"

Gwilym butted in. "Leave the poor man alone cariad."

"But you are taken, Rhiannon my sweet." Dan sparred back.

"I might know one or two suitable ladies. Both work in uniform so you would like that?"

"Who are you talking about?" asked Emyr.

"Well there is Sue, the sister on my ward, who's just divorced and needs a bit of fun. Then there is Delyth who you work with and she needs hitching up?"

"Oh well Delyth certainly looks good in a uniform," he teased his wife.

"Oh so you think she does do you?"

"But I only ever see her in her stab vest."

"So you don't notice that tight little bum in her black combat trousers?"

"No I don't. I only have eyes for you and your nice little bum."

"Its not nice and little anymore. Its huge."

"Yes but that's because you are pregnant and it will be nice again when the baby is born."

"So its not nice now?"

"You ever been married Dan?" asked Emyr

"No, never had the time or was in the right place or met the right woman when I did."

"Never?"

"There was a Scottish girl once, called Kirsty, when I was stationed in Hong Kong. We got on really well. It felt good but we both had to leave quickly. We thought we would have more time together but circumstances meant that we lost touch."

"That's a shame."

"Yes it was, but was not meant to be. I was seconded to duty with the American fleet just before

Operation Desert Storm and then I went somewhere else and never had the time to look her up."

"You can look her up now on the internet. Lots of people go on a website called Friends Reunited or there is a new website called Facebook that people use and is supposed to be a big thing."

"Ah... time has moved on, it was a long time ago. She will be married now with kids and won't want me back in her life twenty years later."

"You might be surprised. Well you can always try to google her."

"Google? Is that on the internet as well?"

"Yes that's on the internet. It's a search engine?"

"Right, ok," said Dan.

"So nobody else since then?" probed Rhiannon.

"I saw my friends pairing off and having weddings and then kids but it didn't happen for me. I met girls but I was always on the way to the next secondment and my colleagues were upset leaving their wife and kids. Any relationship I did have didn't last longer than a package holiday and it meant that I wasn't leaving a wife crying at the dockside as I sailed away to war. Or a weeping widow for my body to come back to. I have been at too many funerals of fallen comrades to want to do that to a woman."

"But you are out of all that now so plenty of time to settle down."

"Rhiannon here wants everybody to be happy and have babies," said Emyr.

"Well do you like women in uniform? Because when I am back at work then I will set you up with Sue. She would be perfect for you. Delyth is too flighty. I wouldn't trust her."

"Ok then I will look forward to being set But she better be good looking."

"She is very good looking, blonde and curvy."

"Will she wear her nurse's uniform for me then? I would like that."

"You men are all the same. When you see what we nurses have to do every day then you wouldn't find it sexy then."

"Well I do have a thing about uniforms actually. Do you want to hear why?"

"Yes go on," said Rhiannon.

"When I was a young Royal Marine we were coming off a joint training exercise with some Navy Recruits on Dartmoor. We had gone back to the main Royal Navy training base at HMS Raleigh in Plymouth and were sitting around waiting for transport back to our barracks. There had been very little sleep for 48 hours and certainly no shower so I was covered in sweat and muck. I was dozing with my head on my pack in front of the stores block. It was a warm summer's day and a squad of Wrens had come marching up and been halted in front of me," Dan paused for effect.

"I opened my eyes to a vision of these girls in white hats, navy skirts, black tights and shoes, best of all where the white blouses stretched by various sizes of bosom. So yes I like women in uniform.

Rhiannon liked that story and giggled.

They ate their pudding of rhubarb crumble with cream. They talked on about other subjects until Annie ushered them out to the parlour so she could clean up the plates. Rhiannon stayed to help and chat.

Emyr wasn't a bad guy for a policeman. He spoke to his father-in-law.

"I heard on the cop grapevine that there was an incident with Stephen Williams by the quayside."

"Yes he tried to bully me but Dan stepped in."

"Be careful, he's a little runt and I don't want anything to happen to my child's Taid."

"Dan taught him a lesson so he won't be back."

"They are a bad family, be careful and Stephen's pride is damaged. They call him Steve Drwg. That means Steve the bad. He calls himself that. I can warn them off if you want?"

"No just leave it; I will call you if I need to. But thanks," said Gwilym. "Where you involved with that crash last week with those teenage boys"

"Yes they were very lucky. Middle of the night, been drinking and crashed into the wall. One of them was thrown out of the car and skidded along the road on his back. He's had a skin graft and will have scars but by rights he should have been dead."

"You'd think they would learn. Nothing better to do with their time I suppose."

"They moan that there is nothing to do but if you do try and organise something they don't want to know."

"We used to say they were 'too cool for school.'"

"Yes that's right there are initiatives but they don't want to be involved. There is a guy I know who organises boxing lessons and tries to take the kids on the mountains but he struggles for numbers."

"Dan was telling me that he was into boxing," said Gwilym

"Yes it kept me out of trouble, taught me how to box properly, gave me some self respect. I still went off the rails but that was when I was a bit older."

"Frank Delaney is always looking for helpers if you were interested I could arrange for you to meet him. He owns a security company if you were looking for work."

"It has been a long time since I worked the doors. The boxing got me into that. It was a different world then, you didn't need a badge and most of the lads I worked with were just out of jail and straight back working on the doors. Came out on the Wednesday, party with a stripper on the Thursday and bouncing on the Friday."

"They couldn't do that now its all licenses and criminal record checks. It has cleaned up the industry. We don't have as much trouble now and Frank is one of the best around. Our inspector closed down the Disco under the Bay View and its all legitimate now. The college even does a course. Door Supervisors you are called now, Bouncer is not classed as politically correct."

"There you go Dan, you were saying you wanted to do something new." nudged Gwilym.

"Wasn't what I was looking for but might be worth having a chat with Frank Delaney?"

"Wouldn't do any harm and with your experience in the Royal Marines you might do some good. There was funding for a coordinator for the young offenders scheme, but it comes and goes."

"Give me his number, I'm not sure what to do next and it would be good to put all my years of training to good use."

It was dark and cold when Dan left and he put his hands deep in the pockets of the reefer jacket as he walked home

8.

Carol picked Dan up in her battered white French estate car on the bend at 0800. He jumped in and they sped off.

"Very cloak and dagger," said Dan

"It keeps the wagging tongues out of it. The net curtains will be twitching. I'm fed up of them knowing my business. I'm single so they think I'm going to steal their husbands. Its hardly as though any of them are a great catch."

"You could have your pick of all those joscyn farmers."

"I know the history of every single one of them. All their ailments down to their cow's udder's mastitis. That's all I ever hear about. And the sad thing is they know all about me. That deadbeat ex husband of mine was back last week looking for a hand out and Gwyneth Parry stopped me in the street to say how well he was looking and was I having him back. Have him back my arse. Her dirty old fart of a husband was looking down my top on Saturday night I nearly told her she should lock him up. I'm sure he touched up Anwen the other day."

"He'd have the wrath of the village lads down on her if he upsets Anwen."

"She can take care of herself. She has to the way she dresses. She has her eye out for you, you know Dan."

"Me, I'm as old as her dad."

"No she was asking after you came in the other day all spruced up. It was my little secret that we were coming to Chester today. She has all the men wrapped round her little finger that one."

"She is always friendly and has a smile"

"She knows what she wants. She's not as innocent as she makes out. Watch yourself there."

"My days of grappling with young girls are long over thanks Carol."

"My son James lights up when she's around. She gets more help out of him than I do."

"She does have certain charms. Well let's have a good day away from the village and your regulars and their nagging wives. You look nice today."

"Oh don't mind me Dan. Thanks for the

compliment. So do you. I was thinking if we drop this beast in the station car park and catch the train along to Chester. Then we can relax along the way and saunter into the city rather than the stress of driving in and trying to find somewhere to park."

"Sounds good to me, remember lunch is on me."

"Do you know when I first came up to North Wales from Swansea I thought nothing of driving anywhere. It must be living round here. I've lost the confidence to drive any further."

"Trains are fine with me."

A few minutes later the train pulled out of the station. The train was empty and they had four seats and a table to themselves and pretty much the whole carriage as well. A man pushed a trolley with tea and coffee, they sat back, and with steaming paper cups in front of them, they enjoyed the view, mountains to the right and the sea and beaches to the left. The sky was grey and heavy and there were white horses dancing on the crests of the waves.

For her trip out of the village Carol had made an effort. She was wearing a black skirt, the one she usually wore to funerals, sensible shoes, a green blouse and a long grey coat. Her hair was down and she had brushed and blow-dried it. A spray of perfume on her throat before she had wrapped a scarf around her neck. The special effort also consisted of her one set of matching black bra and pants and thick black tights. Dan was wearing suit trousers, a shirt, a pullover and his navy reefer jacket.

"Right then Dan, what do you need to buy?"

"Well, I need a suit and a couple of shirts and I need to go to the bank and I have been thinking of buying a mobile phone."

"Don't you have one?"

"No, never needed one."

"It will change your life. Everybody will be calling you."

"I've lived without one for long enough, who will want to be calling me?"

"I will."

"At least one call then."

"Oh yes every day, just to make you feel loved."

He smiled at her and replied, "Thank you."

They disembarked from the train and stepped out of the station. They walked past the taxi rank and along the road into the town centre. The busiest they were both used to was the harbour town and even in the height of the summer that was never jammed with people. There had been an article recently in the local paper about how one in three shops in North Wales was empty and their town's high street was emptier than most. Chester had no such problems, at least not that they noticed. They walked past hotels, restaurants and bars, furniture, clothes and electrical shops, before they came to the main shopping area that was already packed with people, bustling, hurrying and pushing their way along. There was a branch of his bank on the corner and Dan said that he would start in there. They agreed to meet in an hour or so under the town clock.

Just as he was about to turn away Carol said something to him in Welsh under her breath. In the bustle, he wasn't sure what she said and he ducked his head for her to speak into his ear. She reached up and her lips brushed his cheek in a kiss as she just said, "see you in a bit" before turning and heading off into the crowd.

Dan was left standing there, with her warm breath fading. He wiped his cheek of the speck of lipstick that he could feel and was aware of the scent of perfume on Carol's scarf. He sniffed the air to catch more but it had faded. The scent was overtaken by the more invasive aroma of frying bacon coming from the open door of a nearby café.

He walked towards the bank entrance. Like much of the shopping area of Chester, the front of the building was under the Tudor effect of black crossbeams and white painted plaster. The coherence of the black and white mixed with the sandstone medieval walls and the sympathetic modern signage gave the city an attractive look. When he stepped in through the doors of the bank, he part expected there might have been a portal back to another age. He had a vision of banks filled with men in tailcoats and stiff collars on high stools behind tall desks. He was disappointed that the interior décor was modern corporate and the bank tellers were behind armour-plated glass. He stepped into the allotted space for queuing guided by the nylon webbing and waited patiently till he reached the front.

He was surprised with his bank balance. He lived off the cash he earned from the whelks and that kept him going from day-to-day. He hadn't needed to dip into his bank account and over the months that he hadn't touched it the payments from his war pension had accrued nicely enough. It gave him a bit more stability. He withdrew £1000 in cash for expenses and turned down the requisite offer to arrange a review with the financial products sales manager.

His next stop was at a mobile phone shop. There were plenty to choose from and he walked into the one that was closest to the bank. There was a dazzling array of handsets and packages available and the shop assistant was very helpful in explaining the range that Dan could pick from. He even stayed helpful when Dan said that he didn't have a clue. In the end, he chose a basic phone on a pay as you go tariff. The assistant helped Dan to set the phone up, put £20 worth of credit on the account and explained how to top it up. Dan thanked the young lad profusely even though he had described how he had helped his own grandfather who also wasn't up to speed with technology.

He went to wait for Carol underneath the famous big clock perched high on a bridge over the old city gate. Hunkering down into the collar of his coat he stepped back into the shadows against the wall and watched the world pass by. There were all types of humanity going through. Teenagers in hooded sweatshirts, baggy tracksuit pants and baseball caps, mothers pushing crying babies in prams, men of commerce and law in suits with crombie overcoats, silk scarves and briefcases, office workers on breaks hurrying past with branded cups of coffee. In the village if he stood for long enough, a group of walkers might go past or Tomos Rhos Farm on his tractor. Not used to the bustle he was enjoying watching the ebb and flow of the tide of people.

One figure didn't move and that was a man in a suit and raincoat just along from the smart Grosvenor Hotel. Like Dan, he was stepped back to one side watching the world go by. He was standing trying to look unobtrusive but was failing. There was a uniformed commissionaire in a green coat and a black top hat opening doors for the hotel's customers, but the man in the raincoat was separate.

Dan watched him for a while and noted the stance, ready for action and the shift of the head as he stood guard. The man lifted his hand and spoke into a microphone in his raincoat cuff. A minute later a big black Mercedes saloon car followed closely by a black Range Rover pulled up outside the hotel and the hotel doors opened. The commissionaire stood back as a small woman in a big fur coat strode out in the middle of four bodyguards. One held the back door of the Mercedes open for the woman, closed it and sat himself in the front. The other men who had fanned out around the car, jumped into the Range Rover and both vehicles drove off. The man who had been outside on guard went back into the hotel ready for his next burst of excitement.

Still standing back, he watched Carol walk towards him with a couple of new shopping bags. She looked happier, more free than she did behind her bar. She was an attractive woman. Her legs looked fine sticking out from under her grey coat and her hair was longer than he had seen it, but then he hadn't often seen it down over her face. She was smiling and it made her look younger. She looked around for him and he stepped out into her vision. Her smile grew and her eyebrows rose, pleased to see him.

"I've found exactly what James wanted, now I can relax."

"Fancy a coffee?"

"Not yet, let's look for your suit and take it from there."

"Great."

They walked up the hill from the clock and towards the top of the pedestrianised area, where a man was loudly quoting from the bible as the passers-by ignored him. There were plenty of shops to choose from both at street level and higher up on the first floor covered balcony level that were called the Chester Rows. There were shop signs everywhere and the big shopping arcade next to the Grosvenor gave plenty of choice. Too much choice for a couple unused to the huge variety of shops, it was daunting. They went up to the first floor of the rows and along the worn wooden walkway. There was the sign for a gentleman's outfitters with plastic models in suits in the window. They looked at each other. Dan nodded and they stepped inside.

The shop assistant was dressed in a blue and white stripy shirt and a yellow tie. It was a quiet day and he looked up when the couple entered the shop.

"Hello Sir, Madam, how can I help you?"

"Hi, I'm looking for a suit and a couple of shirts."

"Certainly sir, I am sure we can help you. Do you have anything particular in mind?"

"No just a suit."

"What will sir be wearing it for, a wedding?"

"A job, an interview, that type of thing."

Carol had her own ideas on Dan's suit. "Black, possibly navy. Single breasted?"

"Certainly Madam. What size?"

"Not too sure. My last suit doesn't fit!" said Dan.

"Well let's measure you then." He flicked out his tape measure.

"Lets get your coat off you and your jumper."

"I know my inside leg is 31."

"Perfect and your waist?"

"Er not sure."

"Well lets be having you then?" said the assistant as he put his hands around Dan's waist and pulled the tape measure tight. Carol gave a little chuckle at Dan's discomfort.

"34 inch waist, 46 inch chest and 18 inch collar," he reeled off. "Great proportions. Aren't they madam?"

"Yes they are."

He looked through his rails and pulled out a hangered black jacket. Dan tried it on.

"It's a bit tight around the shoulders and the arms. Lets try a different make shall we."

The next one was too big and with another the arms were too short.

"This is a German make, a bit broader around the shoulders and under the arms."

The shine of the new cloth of the suit showed up the shabbiness of the old shirt that Dan was wearing.

"Would Sir like to try on a sample shirt to give the full effect?"

"Er... ok?"

Dan was despatched to the changing

rooms to change into the shirt and the matching pair of suit trousers. The assistant and Carol followed him up into the rear part of the shop. On coming out for inspection they both approved of the suit trousers and the new shirt. Dan looked different to the scruffy fisherman that Carol knew and when he put on the suit jacket as well, there was almost a complete transformation. The sample shirt was a light blue under the black suit jacket and the assistant pulled out a dark red tie with spots.

"They always say that if you want to give a good impression at an interview then you should wear a red tie. Here try this on."

Dan took the jacket off again and tied up the tie leaving it slightly crooked. Carol stepped up close and straightened it, her knuckle brushing off his Adam's apple.

Dan put the jacket back on and stood up straight, looking at himself in the tall mirror. The last time he had looked smart in front of a mirror had been in his black parade uniform receiving the medal from the Prince of Wales. There were no sergeant's stripes with their colour sergeant's crown above them and no medals on his chest or shiny brass buttons. He felt his head was bare without the white cap and its globe and laurel badge above the shiny black peak that he had worn with such fierce pride.

He shuddered. The memory of that day and the reason for the medal filled his head.

Both Carol and the friendly shop assistant saw him pause, his mind elsewhere. Then his eyes refocused, coming back to the present and zoning back in on his reflection.

"You ok Dan?"

"Yes I am fine." He said it automatically.

"I think the suit fits well sir. Very handsome if I might say so."

Carol agreed and held on to Dan's arm steadying him.

The suit was taken and put to one side, while they picked out two dress shirts. The shop assistant also persuaded him to buy a pair of canvas chino trousers, a casual shirt and a brown tweed sports jacket. He finished the ensemble off with a pair of classic brown brogues. Dan put on the sports jacket to wear over his old shirt and put the old jumper, which under the shops bright lights turned out to have a hole on the elbow, into the bag with the purchases. Added extras were two new pairs of underpants in a box and a triple pack of socks. With his reefer jacket back over the top, Dan was ready for food.

"You look very dashing," Carol said to Dan. "Time for lunch."

The shop assistant was showing them to the door. "Do you have a restaurant in mind?" the assistant asked Carol.

"No, we were just going to pick one we walk past."

"My favourite is a wine bar a couple of streets away. It's in the lobby of a boutique hotel. The food is superb and it's a nice relaxing atmosphere after a stressful day shopping."

"Thanks, sounds great."

"The hotel rooms are lovely to if you were to come again and wanted to stay over. I can highly recommend it. Very ro-mantic."

"Er, Thanks" Dan replied"

"Thank you, we will look for that res-taurant." said Carol dragging Dan through the   door.

9.

They passed a sports shop and Dan asked if Carol would mind if he stopped in there. He needed a pair of trainers and a tracksuit. They went in and bought what was needed, as well as a sports kit bag that he put the suit and other purchases into before they left the store. They turned down the side street and found a wine bar, which they entered through the hotel lobby.

The restaurant manager found them a table by the window and gave them freshly printed daily menus. The diners at the other tables were a mix of businessmen in suits and ladies of a certain age who lunched often. It was tasteful and contemporary.

"This is my treat? Thanks for helping me choose my suit."

"It was no hardship, believe me."

"No, thanks anyway. Do you need to buy anything else?"

"Well I need some underwear but here I think it is called lingerie."

"Well I will help you choose that if you want me to?

"Dan!"

"Yes Carol?"

"Should we order?"

The menu was small but perfectly formed. There was a £20 table d'hôte lunch menu and they both ordered from that, pate and soup, salmon and steak. They also decided to go for a bottle of wine, a chardonnay to go with Carol's salmon. It was her treat and although the steak Dan had chosen would probably have been better with a red the waiter had the good training to commend them on their choice.

"Its good to be away. I keep expecting somebody from the village to walk through the door."

"I don't think this is the type of place Dai Tractor would come to. He's more of a pile your plate high man."

"Its been so long since I've eaten in a proper restaurant that I've forgotten which knife and fork to use."

"Just use your fingers, nobody will notice."

"Yes they would. No I'm enjoying myself. Watching you have your waist measured was worth it in itself. Nice boy that assistant."

"He thought we were a couple"

"I know, its not that strange is it?"

"No of course it isn't. I think we both look pretty good today."

"Did you notice? He looked us up and down when we came into his shop. I don't think he was too impressed with me, like I wasn't smart enough. I liked your suit. You are a very handsome man."

"And you are a good looking woman Carol. Now would you like some more wine?"

"Yes please," She looked around at the other

diners. Ladies who lunched were the main clients. Dan was attracting admiring glances. He didn't notice but Carol did.

"You forget there is a big wide world out here don't you. I've ploughed a rut behind that bar and its difficult to get out. James is going through an awkward stage and I can't be there for him. If I open the door a minute late I have Twm Bach hammering on it for me to open it up."

"Is it girls that are upsetting James?"

"Everything at the moment. His dad was over last week and that unsettles him. I kicked him out five years ago for having an affair but I can't tell James that so he blames me for the break up. He used to like school but now he doesn't. I don't know if he is being bullied. He moaned that there is nothing to do in the village and I can't argue with him about that but I don't want him hanging around street corners in the town. God knows what he will get up to."

"Try to persuade Anwen to give him a kiss. A good roll in the hay will sort him out. That will cheer him up."

"You ask her, she wants a man not a boy."

"And I wouldn't know what to do with a young

girl like Anwen, Carol. I don't have the stamina these days."

"Nor me." She took a while to compose her next words and then forged on. "Dan can I ask you a question?"

He nodded in answer.

"When you are trying on that suit you had a wobble. What was it?"

Dan took a moment to answer. Then waited as the waiter delivered their starters. They were impressed and savoured the tastes and flavours.

He took a taste of the wine before answering. "I spent sixteen years in the Royal Marines and have nearly always been in uniform of some kind. The last time I dressed up I was at Buckingham Palace being given a medal by the Prince of Wales. My leg was still healing and I was on crutches going in but I was determined to stand. Trying on the suit made me realise that I am out of uniform, out of the Marines."

"What happened?"

"I was blown up, we were on patrol and we walked into an ambush. There was an IED, an improvised bomb and it went off. It killed one of the lads and then we were attacked. I was wounded by the blast but we all kept on firing until help came and saw them off. My leg was shattered and they helicoptered me out and then back to Britain. They saved my leg and there are still pins holding the bone together. It hurts when the cold wind gets to it on the boat."

"They gave you a medal?"

"Yes they did, for saving the platoon, but I still lost one of my lads. I was the colour sergeant. He was my responsibility. They gave me a medal but I would have preferred him to be alive." He took another sip of wine. "I was treated in Haslar, the Naval Hospital in Portsmouth for nearly ten months. They were great there but the government closed it down to save money."

"They just left you to it?" Carol asked

"No, chwarae teg," Dan smiled at his own use of the Welsh phrase. "To be fair, they wanted me to go to Selly Oak to the new military medical centre but I didn't want to start all over again. My leg was much better although not strong enough for active duty so I accepted the medical discharge and came back to the village and my Taid's cottage. That was four years ago. I spent a year locked away and then Annie persuaded me to help Gwilym on the boat with the whelks and I've done that for three seasons."

"Did you receive counselling?"

"I did at Haslar and they were very good, but when the hospital was closed then the psychiatric team was split up and I stopped. They wanted me to go back regularly to talk about things but I wanted to get away and my Taid had left me the cottage so I had somewhere to come to."

"I saw you wobble today and sometimes you are in the pub and I see you very withdrawn. Can you go back to see somebody?"

"In the pub its just that I've heard all Gwilym's stories before."

"Dan, I'm being serious, you can't just brush this under the table."

"Carol, when I feel bad then I close the doors. I don't sleep great so the shaking the whelk pots in the fresh air tires me out. Each time I buy the newspaper there are more casualties in Afghan. Young lads with girlfriends or wives and young babies. I'm an old sergeant from the Royal Marines. I would only be a nuisance, let the doctors concentrate on the ones with their lives ahead of them."

"Ah bechod. Dan, you are not that old. You are

not even forty yet. Don't give up on your life"

"I haven't Carol. I actually feel a lot better recently. I've started running again. My leg is sore but its getting better."

"Gwilym told me about Steve Drwg and that you went very calm when you dealt with him"

"Gwilym talks too much."

"Yes he does but he said you saved him from trouble."

"I am trained to react to bad situations. Gwilym had started the argument and it was in danger of getting out of hand so I finished it."

"He had a knife!"

"And I had a boathook. If anything it did me good. I just reacted to a silly young fool. It felt like something came loose inside me and I feel more alive. Perhaps that was why I feel it is time to move on. A bit of action, it proved to me that I am still good at something. Shame its conflict resolution rather than making money. I wasn't in danger he was just a young thug."

"He's a nasty bit of work. They talked about him at the last Pubwatch meeting I went to. The police wanted to put him on the banned list but a couple of the publicans argued against so he can still go in pubs in the town and surrounding areas."

"Why did they stop him being put on the Pub-watch list?"

"Because they are friends with the family, you know how it is."

"I used to. Back where I grew up I did the doors and worked with proper gangsters. Not like the Williams here."

The main courses arrived in appropriately sized portions for lunchtime. The salmon was presented on a piece of polished slate, the skin crispy and the carrots and courgettes were finely shredded. The steak was served on a wooden chopping board with the steak knife placed alongside. There was a small fortress of eight oblong chips, a mushroom and a cherry tomato.

"It looks lovely but can you imagine what Dai Tractor would have to say at the size of that steak."

"Yes and eating the fish from a bit of roof tile."

They laughed easily together.

"Can you imagine me serving this at the pub to

the joscyn farmers? They would be asking for a plate of chips separate."

The food, like the restaurant was contemporary and turned out to be very tasty. The salmon melted in the mouth and the light touch of the spices, in which the fish had been cooked, was just right. The steak was cooked to perfection and could have been cut with a teaspoon never mind the serrated knife blade.

"You won't have to drive for another few hours. Another glass won't harm you."

"Champion, lovely, thanks. Dan why did you join the Marines?"

"That links to working with the gangsters. I used to be in a boxing gym and fought and won some junior fights. I could have gone on but it needed dedication and I wasn't dedicated enough, I didn't think I had it in me to go professional so I gave up. It all merges together but I'd met a girl and she wanted to be taken out and bought things so I needed money. Through the boxing I knew the boss of the local door firm and he offered me a job. I was only seventeen but didn't look it. It was all cash in hand so nobody asked me my age. And by the time I had sorted out a few fights in the night-club then it didn't matter."

"When I started going out in Swansea the bouncers were very scary. A couple of my pals went with them after work. In fact I probably did too. It was the pull of the bow tie."

"There was a lot of that. I had this girlfriend who worked in the club so I wasn't as bad as the other lads, but there was a lot of easy sex available if you wanted it."

"Did you get fed up of all the easy sex then and joined the Marines?

"Ha. No. I got cocky. I had bought a black leather jacket to fit in and had helped with some repossessions and some tax collecting. It was a buzz to be with all these hard men and I was going down a path into doing worse crimes. One night we had been drinking at the club after it was shut and I walked home. We were all warned to be careful but as I said I was cocky and walked into a gang of lads who we had been thrown out earlier. There were five of them and they were drunk so they didn't give me a proper kicking but they cracked ribs and my eye swelled up. Andy Hilton who was the head doorman at the club told me to go away for a couple of weeks and leave the girlfriend behind so I went to see my Taid."

"I knew Will Traeth, your Taid, when I first took over the pub. Will the beach they called him. I never knew if they called him that because he lived by the beach or because he was on the beaches at the D-Day landings."

"Both I think. Taid had been in the Royal Marines during the war. He told me off for not bringing the girlfriend to see him. She wanted to be a model and I had a photo of her in my wallet. I thought she was gorgeous but when I showed my granddad I saw that in the photo she looked cheap and tacky. I had a wad of notes in my wallet and he saw them but didn't say anything. I was embarrassed. When we went to the pub later he wouldn't let me buy a drink, although I tried to.

"Most of the old men in the pub now would be happy to let you buy them a drink."

"My Taid would too, normally, but he was trying to make a point that I had not earned the money. He told me about his experiences in the Commandos and how proud he was to wear the Green Beret. I was proud of myself with winning scraps in pub car parks and being a gangster but I couldn't tell him that."

"So you joined up?"

"Pretty much. When I went back I found out that Andy Hilton had been having a fling with my girl. She wanted to move up the food chain, she liked taking the whizz and tried to persuade me to take it with her but I wasn't into it. He gave her free drugs and took her to wild parties. I had seen some of the videos from these parties. He was an evil bastard Andy Hilton and she got more than she bargained for. But I was well rid. So then I went to the recruiting office and joined up. Best choice I could have made. Escaped the estate, saw the world, lots of new experiences, and learned a trade"

"Was blown up."

"Yes that too. But I miss it now. I thought I had another few years and that was taken away"

"Thanks for telling me. What do you want to do this afternoon? Take in a film."

"At the moment I want to sit here and have a pudding and a coffee and just relax."

Dan's chosen pudding was an Eton mess, a mix of winter fruits, marshmallows and meringue, sweet and sticky but not cloying. Carol's was an assiette of chocolate, three smart little shot glasses with different types of chocolate mousse in.

"It looks posh but this is easy to make," Carol said. "It makes a change from using my shot glasses for sambucca that makes the youngsters sick. The farmers would expect it served in pint glasses."

"I will stick to pints of beer and a good whisky. My Taid taught me how to appreciate a whisky. When I came back after my basic training. He was so proud of me. You are given the Green Beret at the end of your training after completing the thirty miler across Dartmoor in eight hours. I couldn't wait to bring it up to show him. He let me buy the drinks that night, even though my wallet was nearly empty. He died while I was in Bosnia and I couldn't come home for the funeral."

"I know I was there. They held it in the pub and we all raised a glass of whisky to him. He was a character, always had a sparkle in his eye."

"Thanks for that."

"I've seen you come in and out of the pub for years. I always looked forward to you coming in. I wanted to help when you came back all pale and wounded but you didn't want any help."

"Gwilym and Annie kept me going. I had lots of friends trying to keep in contact but I froze them out. Life moves on. I'm a lot better now."

"So what are you going to do next?"

"Good question, have a suit so ready for an interview. But not sure what for? I need to ease my way back into being near people rather than jumping full on into something new."

"Are you alright for money?"

"Yes. I am, pleasantly surprised with the state of my bank account today. I was given compensation that I haven't spent and I receive a pension every month. I don't have any dependents so I don't need to spend anything. Probably need a car."

"Don't buy a pub. It will drain the lifeblood out of you."

"You said that with feeling."

"I've had enough at the moment. I've been surviving but not much more. James has another couple of years at school then I will make a move. Pubs are what I know. I have been working in them or running one for twenty five years so it will probably still be in catering. I'm told that if you get paid by somebody you can have a day off."

"And paid holidays?"

"And no brewery rep on your back trying to squeeze more money out of me. I'm not sure I can last another couple of years"

"We are not there today. Lets enjoy our freedom."

Their coffees came and the waiter came back with the bill. "The restaurant is closing now but if you would like to have more coffee then we can serve it in the hotel lobby?"

"Thanks but not sure yet. Perhaps we will go through and sit there while we think on what to do next."

The waiter left. Carol rolled her neck and stretched her back and shoulders. "I could do with a lie down after that meal? How about you?"

Dan looked at her. She wore a thin gold chain with a C on it round her neck. The chain dipped down the top buttons of her blouse, it rested just above the V of her breasts. They looked plump and full and swelled against her blouse. Her skin under the chain looked slightly flushed from the wine. His own cheeks were burning and he wouldn't take much persuading. He was still wearing the new sports jacket. It made him feel debonair.

"Are you sure? A bit of fun."

"The rooms are very good here I believe," she mimicked the assistant in the gentleman's outfitters.

"I'm game if you are?"

"Yes!"

"Come on then."

He paid the bill in cash and remembered to leave a decent tip. He straightened the lapels of his jacket and picked up his bag full of purchases.

With a sense of going over the top of the trench with trepidation he approached the reception desk of the hotel. A pony-tailed girl with a tight fitting black blazer smiled at him. It was easier than he thought.

"Yes, sir could have a double room. Just for the one night?"

"Yes please!"

"Would sir need a hand with your bag?"

At least they had a bag!

10.

The room was what would be described in a luxury magazine as sumptuous. There was a high bed with a leather headboard and big white pillows. Across the bottom of the white duvet cover was a foot wide brown satin rug. Dan couldn't see the point of it, too small to be warm and not very practical at all. Behind the bed was a 'feature wall' of chocolate brown wallpaper covered in swirls of big silver flowers. There were tasteful brown curtains and at the bottom of the bed a cream two-seater sofa set in front of a flat screen television that could also be seen from the bed. When they looked behind a door, they found a bathroom tiled in beige marble squares, no bath but a large complicated shower behind a glass partition. All very sophisticated. A rectangle of afternoon sun shone through the windows on to the bed.

Now they were both in the room together there was an awkward pause. Both were unsure where to start, there wasn't a raw passion that was burning to rip their clothes off. This was a slow burn and they both needed tenderness and compassionate loving.

"Cup of tea?"

"Yes please."

Dan opened a door to the wardrobe and found a stainless steel kettle and other necessary tea making facilities, including posh looking biscuits. He filled the kettle from the bathroom sink and switched it on.

"Do we need anything else?"

"Erm, I don't have any protection. Do you?" Carol replied.

"Erm... no, I wasn't that prepared."

"You didn't think I would be this easy then?" asked Carol

"Tell you what," Dan said, "We walked past one of those Metro supermarkets just up the street. I'll go down and buy what is needed. Is that ok?"

"Yes good idea. While you are out I will call James, he should be finished at school now. Then I can switch the phone off. I promise."

"Do you want anything to drink?"

"No thanks, but could you buy some tooth paste and a tooth brush please?"

Dan pulled on his reefer jacket and went out of the bedroom door, into the corridor and down in the lift. He nodded self-consciously to the girl behind reception, who just smiled back at him and he went through the doors into the cold fresh air.

In the small supermarket, he picked up a basket. This place had everything that a city dweller could possibly need. The toothpaste and toothbrushes were easy and he added a can of deodorant spray, which he needed anyway. There was a display of Durex products and he was shocked by the choice. He inspected the range, his eyes roaming the shelves. He settled on a pack of Elite condoms, they hadn't changed and had worked alright for him in the past. Fortified by the wine he also added a plastic bottle of stimulating lubricant and there was a small package with something called a fingertip vibrator. He put them into his basket. To hide them from general view he placed a broad-sheet newspaper over the top and added a women's magazine for Carol. At the checkout, the Asian checkout man didn't care about what his customer was buying. He scanned the items and asked for the money.

Dan returned to the hotel, strode through reception and into the waiting lift. He hit his floor number and a couple of minutes later he entered the room.

"Your tea is in the pot on the desk over there if you still want it?"

"Thanks." He poured himself a panad and took a sip. It was only tepid warm by now but he was thirsty.

"Well what have you bought me then?"

He delved into his plastic bag and pulled out the toothpaste and brushes, then the magazine and the newspaper, which he placed on the desk. Then came the more important items, the condoms, the lubricant and the little cardboard packet.

He took them over to Carol lying on the bed and passed them to her one-by-one. The condoms she looked at briefly, she was more interested in the other products. She opened the lid of the bottle and took a quick sniff, a synthetic raspberry. She squeezed a bit out on to her fingertips and rubbed them together feeling the texture of the gel.

The little packet was even more interesting. When she opened it, there was a white silicone ring inside. It was like a present from a Christmas cracker with a hard white plastic lozenge, inside a silicone bubble. The ring would slip over her finger. There was a purple button on the lozenge and when she pressed, the whole ring buzzed quietly. She pressed it between the same forefinger and thumb still with the gel on and it sent a ripple through to her brain.

She looked up at Dan who was standing above her. He was as nervous as she was and she reached out her hand. Their fingers touched and intertwined.

"Lets take this nice and slowly," she said. "Should we brush our teeth first? And see where we go from there?"

He pulled her up and they hugged each other. Then kissed. A cwtch and a sws. It was a good start.

"Dan, I would love to see you in that suit again. It's a bit of a fantasy of mine."

"Is the fantasy the suit on its own or me in it?"

"Taking you out of it would be good. A bit of both, I don't see many men in suits and the brewery rep doesn't count."

"Later."

They both went into the bathroom. The mirror above the sink was wide and showed them clearly. They leant their heads together as they brushed their teeth. Their eyes met in the mirror, both amused at the mundane courtesy. It was their first intimacy but seemed the right thing to do.

"Come here."

This time it was a proper snog. Lips bruising, tongues curling round.

Dan turned Carol away from him and standing behind her, they looked at themselves in the wide mirror. His chin was at the level of her ear. His hands reached round her waist, he held her for a while, and he reached his head down towards her neck. When she put her head to one side, her hair fell to one side too. He kissed the bare flesh of her neck and she pushed herself back into his body.

She lifted her own hands and undid the buttons of her blouse showing her black bra. Dan released his hold on her, pulled the blouse off her arms and threw it through the door into the bedroom. Her bra held up her heavy breasts and the straps cut into her shoulder. Still looking in the mirror, he moved the right hand strap off the shoulder so it fell loose down her arm. This time he kissed where the strap had been. His teeth biting gently onto her collar bone. He raised his hands from her waist and cupped her breasts. They were full and soft. As he squeezed over the bra cups, his hands pushed the excess flesh out of the lace cup. Inside their confinement her large crinkled nipples hardened under his touch.

Without Dan letting go she leant forward, squeezed her hands between their bodies and undid the back of her bra. It fell off pinned between Dan's hands and her breasts.

"I'm glad you did that. I was never very good at those bra straps."

Dan smiled down at her, released his hands and let the bra fall to the ground. His hands came back to her breasts and this time his hands covered the whole of their heavy flesh. He squeezed and the crinkled nipples slotted between the knuckles of his middle and index fingers. He kissed her neck again and lifted his eyes to the mirror. He could see her eyes were closed tight as she revelled in the feelings from his hands and lips.

"No marks!" she warned.

He straightened up and let the bulk of her breasts fall from his hands. He moved the hands down towards the top of her skirt and moved them around to the side until he found the zip. The skirt fell off and she was there in the final layers, her black knickers underneath her tights. Bending her knees, she pulled the tights down her legs and left just the knickers.

Looking back in the mirror Dan could see that her tummy was soft and dimpled with stretch marks on either side. The top of her panties showed but any lower was blocked by the sink. He held the convex swell of her tummy and stroked his hand over her deep belly button. His fingers roamed inside the elastic of her black panties and felt the top edge of her pubic hair. The fingers moved down the triangle, squeezed in between the top of her thighs and parted her lips. She was warm, wet and silky.

She was bending over towards the sink and Dan was covering her back with his own body. She pushed him back with her bum then turned herself around and lifted her chin up to kiss him. She moved back and lifted her fingers to undo the buttons of his shirt. With the buttons open, she pushed her hands inside and scratched her nails across the hair of his chest and the firm pectoral muscles underneath. Then moved her fingers down to his stomach and to the belt of his trousers. Wanting to speed up she yanked at the buckle.

Dan stopped her, "here, let me."

He undid the belt and the button on his trousers. As he dropped them to the floor he whisked off his unflattering briefs, taking the decision to be naked, rather than provocative in his worn out, albeit clean, underwear. She looked down at the scars on his right leg. She stroked down from the side of his rib cage, down, to his pelvis and over the scar on his thigh. The skin was rough and uneven with indentations where bits of muscle had been cut away in the operations to save his leg. She moved her fingers back round to his front and weighed him in the palm of her hand, squeezing tentatively at first and then with a firmer grasp.

The awkward revelations of their bodies were over. She looked back up at him and gave him a kiss. She pushed the shirt from his shoulders and he stepped out of the trouser legs.

"Fancy a shower?" she asked

"Yes please."

Dan kicked the assorted clothing into the dry shelter of the bedroom floor and still holding each other they frog marched backwards to the shower cubicle. It was a very modern shower unit and they had to disentangle to work the instructions out. They settled on a setting called 'rain shower' and both stepped inside. Dan squeezed the little plastic bottle of gel-de-bains over Carol. The shower gel smelt spicy and mixed with the water it created a lather. He rubbed his hands over her shoulders, her breasts and down her tummy and round to her buttocks. The soapy water made his hands slippery and warm and the sensations from all over her body shot through to the nub between Carol's legs. She could feel the length of him pressed against her back.

She hadn't planned to wash her hair but the water bouncing off Dan's chest and shoulders was making it wet anyway so she let the water wash over her head, her hair flowing down her back. The rubbing of Dan's hands was building her up towards a sensual peak. If he rubbed off between her legs again, she was going to orgasm. He did and she came. She held on to his shoulders as her body shook. She had needed that fast release.

She picked another plastic bottle from the soap tray and reciprocated the washing action back to Dan. She held the bottle up, squeezed the gel out on to Dan's shoulders, and rubbed hard as it ran down his chest with the shower water, foamy and hot. He held his hands out against the wall of the shower to steady himself. He was caging her in. She was trapped in his personal space. She ducked under his arms and turned to concentrate on his back. She made a special point of lathering down his shoulder blade and towards the invisible soft hairs of his lower back. She pressed her breasts close against his skin and stretched her arms around him. She held him close, stroking further down his stomach until her hands touched his erection. She groaned as she squeezed and felt his hardness. He groaned too, he was pleased she couldn't see his face.

In an effort to distract himself from his own building tension, he was reading the instructions on the shower dials. This was a very fancy shower unit, he thought to himself. There was another dial, he twisted it, and water shot out of the waist high nozzles on the side of the unit. The water fountained between his and Carol's private parts. She gave out a squeal and dug her nails into his flesh with the shock. He switched the extra nozzles off.

Satisfied he was cleaned with the suds Carol bent down to inspect him closer. She went down on her haunches and took half of the length of him into her mouth and sucked and kissed before letting it drop out. Dan's toes curled and he sighed as he looked up into the shower head. He held one hand tight on to the back of Carol's head as she took him all the way down her throat, then out again. He released her head and she pulled back and kissed the tip then used her right hand to feed him into her mouth. The water was a distraction and he switched it off. His own build up would not take long and he gave in to the rhythmic motion.

He had heard once that it wasn't good manners to come in a girl's mouth unless she had given permission. He had no idea where that relevant piece of moral information came from but it must have been picked up somewhere along the way. He let go of Carol's head, pushed her back slightly, and let himself go. He pushed his aim down away from her mouth and face and released himself over her chest. She looked up at him, giggled, and stood up.

"Thanks for that. Can you switch the water back on please?" she said

He turned the shower dial and the hot water cascaded down again. She pushed out her chest and the water washed off the creamy globules of semen, which sluiced around the bottom of the shower tray before disappearing down the plug-hole.

Dan stepped out, picked a thick towel off the shelf and dried himself before tying it around his waist. Carol took longer to wash herself and to shampoo her hair. Dan held a towel up for her when she switched off the tap and came out. He patted her down quickly before handing her the towel to give her some privacy and went to the wardrobe in the bedroom to find the matching dressing robe. He passed it to her and she put it on. She emerged from the hotel bathroom with a towel wrapped around her hair and with a big smile. Dan had also found a pair of disposable slippers that she put on her feet.

"This is fun," she said.

Dan smiled back and she appreciated the way the light glistened from his bare and still wet shoulders.

"Go and lie on the bed and I will dry my hair," she said looking through the drawers for a hair-dryer and finding a new one in the second down along with the Gideon bible.

"Would you like another cup of tea?" she asked him as he stretched out on top of the crisp duvet cover.

"Erm... I think a coffee this time."

She checked there was enough water in the kettle and pressed the button. Then turned her attention to finding her hairbrush in her handbag and went back to blow-drying her hair.

Dan lay on his back under the covers. The crisp white duvet came up to his chest and, resting on a plump pillow, he held his hands clasped behind his head and closed his eyes. The cacophony of the hair drier and the kettle wasn't ideal but he was satiated enough not to care.

After a couple of minutes drying her hair, it was still slightly damp and Carol wrapped the towel back around her head in a turban. She stood up to climb into the bed and let the dressing gown fall off her shoulder and slipped under the covers. Dan was watching her the whole time and even after their shower together she was still self-conscious enough to hold the duvet over her breasts.

The light was fading from the day and they had already closed the curtains. Carol had put on the main light to dry her hair, but now twisted around and with thanks to the wonders of hotel design and the small bank of switches she switched off the main light and experimented with the lighting. She managed after a couple of attempts to set the mood with discreet lighting from a standard lamp in the corner of the room. The lamp was not too bright to pick out all the details yet soft enough to illuminate their faces, like so much else this afternoon just right.

The digital clock on the television said that the

time was 4.47. She had to be back at the pub for closing time at 11. If they were to catch the 8.30 train, they would have to leave the hotel by eight. That still gave them nearly 3 hours to relax together. With that mental calculation done, she turned to Dan, rubbed her hand over his chest and leant in to kiss him. He kissed her back and moved his hand over her soft plump breast. Her nipple hardened and taking his time he moved the hand down over her tummy and down between her legs, which she parted to allow him easier access.

After a short appreciation of his ministrations, she asked to take a breather. She turned again and picked up the supplies of Durex products from the bedside locker.

"Lets find out how these work should we?"

She pressed some lubricating gel out of the bottle and on to her finger. After a few more rubs from both sets of fingers in the very specific area, she realised this was good stuff, giving her a slight burning sensation. She lifted her hand, slipped the silicone ring over her fingertip and pressed the purple button. The lozenge started vibrating with a quiet but steady buzz. She moved it down over her stomach to rejoin Dan's fingers that were dipping inside her. It touched the right spot and the buzz conducted through the stimulating gel to hit her clitoris, which sent a rush to her brain and back down again.

Dan placed his hand over hers and pressed down feeling the buzz on his own fingertips. This intensified the feelings for Carol and she closed her eyes, licked her lips and lay back to enjoy herself.

11

The pub was heaving and Dan was fighting to be served at the bar. Carol and Anwen were busy pouring pints and James was picking up the empty glasses from the tables and refilling the fridges. The village chapel's Christmas Eve service had been well attended and minus the kids most of the congregation had come back to the pub. Carol had provided mulled wine and mince pies but these had evaporated a couple of hours earlier. In the side room the youngsters of the village were playing killer on the pool table.

"Two pints of Winter Warmer please Anwen and two port and brandies?"

He had to shout over the sound of Christmas music on the jukebox.

"There is some mistletoe here Dan. Are you going to take advantage of it and give me a sws?"

"Sorry Anwen, I'm getting old. Can't hear you above all this noise," the pretty barmaid stuck her bottom lip out at him and he relented.

"Oh come on then," he leaned over the bar and gave Anwen a peck on the cheek. He winked at Carol as he caught her eye."

"You are both looking gorgeous tonight. I love the Santa hats. Nadolig Llawen."

"Nadolig Llawen Dan," Anwen was disappointed the kiss had been on the cheek.

"Don't I get a sws too Dan?" asked Carol.

"Oh it's a hard life this Christmas. Two beautiful women to kiss in this pub. Come here Carol."

Anwen watched as they gave each other a quick smacker on the lips.

Carol whispered in his ear, "Will you stay to help me lock up?"

Then she looked to the next customer wanting a pint.

"No I will not give you another kiss under the mistletoe Billy. You've had two already," heard Dan as he took the tray of drinks back to his table. Gwilym was holding court with an English family group at the next table and Annie was sitting next to her friend Winny. She had noted the familiarity between Dan and Carol but didn't pass comment.

"Thanks for the drink Dan, Iechyd da."

"Cheers Annie. Here's to Rhiannon and Baby Bethan."

Gwilym turned round in time to pick up his replacement pint and join in the toast to his new granddaughter. He slurped the head from the dark frothy pint.

"These people have bought Tony Pritchard's cottage on the headland road. They might want to come fishing with me in the summer."

"Well don't bore them for too long will you."

"Hush woman, we are having a great chat about the history of the place," he turned back to his new English friends.

"He will be telling them old Eifion Pritchard's ghost still haunts the place and they won't have any sleep," she said to Dan.

She passed a few words in Welsh to Winny who answered. "Another house in the village gone to outsiders. It's a shame."

"Yes, these incomers like me taking over the village," teased Dan.

"You're not an incomer Dan. Your family has been here for generations," replied Annie

"Yes Taid loved it here. I'm starting to wonder what life would have been like if Mum hadn't gone to England and stayed here instead. It was so different to where I grew up. I suppose I wouldn't have been born."

"No you were on the way when she left," said Annie sipping her port and brandy.

Dan did a double take. "But I thought she met my father in England and he left her and she stayed."

"No Dan, she left here when she was pregnant with you. That's why she argued with your Nain and Taid and he threw her out," replied Annie. "He regretted it but by that time she was gone."

"But she made me believe my father was English."

"No he was Welsh."

"Annie, I've not heard this. Do you know who he was?"

"Not one hundred percent. Your mam was a very rebellious girl and she wanted to party all the time. Your Nain and Taid were from the different generation who fought in the war. Their first child a boy, Daniel had come along after the war and he was a young teenager when your mum was born."

"I remember him," said Winny. He still went to the village school when I started as a little girl, before your time Annie."

"Yes Winny, I forget you are older than me"

"Go on Annie I didn't know this," said Dan

"When your mam was eight or nine then Daniel was hit by a car. He had been to a dance in the town and he was on a bicycle and cycling back along the coast road. He was knocked off and killed."

"But there are no photos of him."

"It devastated the family. Your Nain's health

suffered and Will hardened himself to his son's death. Your mum suffered too and as she grew up she was headstrong and always argued with her parents. She was wild but great fun. It was the late sixties and all the rock music was coming out and she wanted some excitement."

"So why did she leave?"

"She used to go to all the dances in the town and would sneak away and cause terrible trouble with Will. I was starting to see Gwilym then and wanted to spend time with him and your mum wanted to party and meet boys."

Annie looked at the broad back of her husband and patted it. He swivelled round and squeezed her knee then turned back to the English family.

Annie carried on. "She fell in with a bad crowd. One of the boys was older and went to university. She thought he was the bees' knees, as we used to say and the next I heard she was pregnant. The boy didn't want anything to do with her. Your Nain was ill and Will handled it badly. Your mam went away. I think the boy gave her some money and she never came back."

"So she called me Dan after her brother, who would have been my uncle?"

"Yes I always thought you would know that."

"Nobody told me. Mum never wanted to talk about her home and I was dropped off with Taid and then was picked up. They hardly spoke."

"She went looking for excitement in the big city, dances, music, fun. I hoped that she would find a nice man and settle down but I was young and happy with this big handsome fool here. We married and then my babies came along and I wanted everybody else to be happy too."

Dan thought for a while and took a long gulp of his pint. "She was lost in the city. It ate her up and spat her out. My earliest memories are of being cold and hungry and there were always different men in the house."

"You used to come back at the holidays. I remember you once came back and I had to throw you in the bath, scrub you with disinfectant and comb the nits out of your hair."

"I remember that too. I thought my hair was coming out."

Winny passed a few words in Welsh to Annie.

"Behave yourself Winny," said Annie to her friend. "It was sad. Gwilym and I talked about inviting you to stay with us and the boys. Rhiannon was a baby herself then. We even suggested it to Will but he said no."

"We survived. Mum tried but she was easily distracted and I was glad she was out of it in the end. Growing up on the council estate made me tough and self-reliant. So it was good for the Royal Marines, when I joined up."

"Your Taid was so proud of you when you went in the Marines."

Dan stared into the fire and took a sip of his beer. There were unanswered questions but he was not sure he wanted to know the answers. He knew that Annie would tell him if he asked.

There was a disruption in the side room with the youngsters. Angry shouted voices came back. He could see Carol coming out from behind the bar to deal with it. Dan automatically raised himself to his feet.

The sons and daughters of the village had been enjoying themselves playing pool and drinking. They were of farmer stock, unsophisticated and friendly and Dan knew them all. In the middle of the room were three lads from the town. Hooded sweatshirts, shiny tracksuit pants and white train-ers marked them out from the check shirts and jeans of the farmer boys. The middle tracksuit was Steve Drwg and he was pointing his finger at the chest of Sion Tractor. His other hand pushed a pool ball out of the way to disturb the game.

As Dan came up behind Carol he heard Steve saying, "You owe me money, where is it?"

Carol marched up in front of the three tracksuits. "What is going on? Its Christmas and you are coming into my pub shouting."

"Its nothing to do with you."

"Yes it is you made it to do with me when you came into my pub." Carol was taking no messing.

Dan was at the door to the room and he felt other males from the village pressing in behind him. He put his hand up open palmed showing the back of it to the men behind him to hold them back.

Steve Drwg was concentrating on Carol, behind his back his two friends were smirking at the bravado of their leader. Dan could tell they were thinking that this was great fun intimidating the joscyn yokels. He was angry these idiots had come to this pub on Christmas Eve.

"Go on leave," insisted Carol.

"We will leave when we are ready," said Steve Drwg. "Perhaps we will have a game of pool first."

"You will leave now."

"No we won't." snapped back Steve. He had widened his shoulders and towered above Carol deliberately trying to intimidate her. He was wired, his head and upper body was moving in jerks. Dan sensed this was going to turn nasty and he stepped into the room behind Carol.

"Right now boys. The landlady has asked you to leave and its time for you to go," he said

Steve Drwg had not recognised Dan until now and he took a momentary step back as the memory of their last encounter filtered into his brain.

"We are going to have a game of pool before we go," Steve had too much face to lose to back down from Dan in front of his mates.

Dan saw one of the tracksuits pick up a red pool ball from the table and hold it in his fist by his side.

The local youngsters were pressing against the wall away from the aggression and the local men were still in the main bar behind him but the

whole pub was watching their backs. Dan had a
vision of the new English family seeing this drama
so close to their dream holiday home. His temper
was boiling under the surface. The Winter Warmer
was a strong Ale and the alcohol in his blood-
stream was clouding his judgement. He was aware
of this and took a deep breath to clear his head.
Sion Tractor was staring at his feet, embarrassed.
Trust Sion, son of Dai to mess up an easy drug deal
on Christmas Eve, thought Dan. Why did he have
to bring it here?

Dan tried to be nice. "Boys, Its Christmas Eve.
We are all enjoying ourselves here and its time that
you left."

Steve swaggered his shoulders and took a step
closer towards Dan. Carol moved to one side before she was pushed. Steve's pupils were dilated
and his eyes were black. There was white spittle on
his lips. He was as tall as Dan and leaned his head
towards him.

"Are you going to make us leave then old man?"

"If I need to."

"What are you going to do then?"

Dan leaned in so that only Steve could hear
him and possibly Carol.

"I'm going to rip off your head and then piss down you throat." Dad said it with quiet venom and to accentuate his words he banged his forehead sharply against Steve. The minor butt did the trick and woke Steve up to his situation. He stepped back from Dan's hostility.

"Oh yeah" Steve held his hands out by his side as though goading Dan on to fight. But then he dropped them.

"Come on boys lets go. It's a shit pub anyway." There was a pint glass of lager on the side of the pool table and Steve knocked it onto the green baize where it ran towards the middle pocket.

Dan stood to one side as the three tracksuits walked past him. Dan knew that the last one still had the red pool ball in his hand and as the lad brushed past him, Dan grabbed his wrist and prised the ball from him. He dropped it back on the table where it bounced on the baize-covered slate. He followed them out and watched them get into their metallic blue hot hatch car that was waiting for them outside the door. Another tracksuit was in the driving seat, this one with a white baseball cap. Steve ducked into the front passenger's seat and as the driver revved his engine Steve stuck his middle finger up at Dan and they drove off.

12.

In the second week of January Dan pulled up in his new car, bought for fifteen hundred pounds from Richie F1 and parked on a strip of wasteland next to the boxing gym. The weather was grey and damp but not cold. It was a few streets away from the main part of town. The houses were run down and there was litter on the ground. Dan didn't care too much about the local youths trashing his car. It was the advantage of buying the old navy blue Ford Mondeo Estate versus a sporty BMW. Dan was pleased with his New Year's purchase from Gwilym's mechanic mate. It had leather trim and top range Ghia specifications, even if it did have over 115,000 miles on the clock. It was the first car Dan had ever owned. An expensive pick up truck in shiny black with chrome bull bars was already parked outside. He presumed this monster belonged to Frank Delaney.

The boxing gym was in an old schoolhouse with high roof and big windows. The door was a plain steel plate while the windows outside were covered in wire mesh. There was a yellow sign "protected by Pentagon Security" with a five-sided diagram logo. The door was locked and when he banged hard a broad chested man opened it, head shaved bald wearing a red hooded sweatshirt.

"Frank Delaney? I'm Dan Richards.

"Ti'n iawn boi."

"Sori dim siarad Cymraeg. Dwyn dysgu Cymraeg, Tipyn bach."

"Da iawn boi, Dim problem, No problem. Fair play to you for trying to learn Welsh. Come in. Let me just lock it again." Frank rattled his keys in the lock and put them down next to a big padlock and a bolt. "I have to take the bolt off the front door or the little buggers lock us in. There's nothing in here to steal but they like to wind us up. Sure weren't we all little scallywags." Frank's strong North Walian Welsh accent also had a twang of Irish and Dan had to concentrate to understand him.

"Yes we were," Dan agreed.

With the heavy door locked they went into the hall. The walls were painted an institutional yellow and festooned with the occasional poster of ancient fight nights, signed pictures of once famous boxers and group photos of local lads in amateur boxing vests grinning out at the camera.

In the big room were punch bags of differing sizes and lengths, small round Speed bags and big thick tackle bags of leather, with indentations where they had been pummelled over years of training assaults. Pushed into the corner was a half-size boxing ring complete with ropes and corner pads. In a smaller room adjoining the main hall were weight benches, iron plates and bars to put them on. There was a double shelf of dumbbells and behind it a wall of mirrors. One mirror had a large crack.

"This is a working gym. Not like the posh place on the edge of town. No babes in tight fitting leotards, to preen themselves in the mirror, or distract the lads from the serious workouts," said Frank.

Dan believed him. The magazine poster pinups of female bodybuilders bluetacked to the wall attested to the lack of females. There was a smell of stale male sweat mixed with disinfectant. It was the same smell as the gym that Dan had spent so much time in back in his home city. It awakened a nostalgic sense of belonging.

Frank Delaney was a barrel of a man with his arms sticking out at angles from his broad chest. He was shorter than Dan and older, perhaps in his late forties. He had a permanent, open smile. He had grasped Dan's hand and squeezed. Not in an effort to assert his dominance or to put Dan down but that was his natural grip. A strong hard man who had little to prove.

"You said on the phone that you have done some boxing?"

"Yes it's been a while since I was in a ring but I boxed as a kid and in the forces."

"Who were you with?"

"Royal Marines, I was a Bootneck for 16 years."

"Seen some action too by the look of it."

"I've seen my fair share," said Dan.

"Good on you, and survived. What are you doing now?" asked Frank.

"I came out three years ago and have been working on a fishing boat potting for whelks. My Taid left me his cottage and I've been living there."

"Fed up of smelling of fish?" Frank laughed. "I don't blame you, I helped out on a trawler out of the harbour for a season before I went to work on the tarmac with my old man and worked around in security after that."

"Felt it was time for a change. I need to have some more human contact. Plus I have a lot of training and experience, which I've realised recently, is going to waste. I heard you work with the young offenders' scheme and thought I would give you a call."

"Sounds great. We are always looking for fresh helpers if you can manage to keep up with all the rules and the politics. There's no funding at the moment. It comes and goes."

"Its not for the money. I'm not sure how long I'm going to be around but I have some time so thought I could be useful. I've been sort of buried away since I came back and its time to step up a gear. Anyway you said to come over for a workout."

"Yes sure. The lads mostly come training in the evening so I have the place to myself if I want to work out during the day. Most of the lads who work for me on the doors have day jobs so I'm usually on my own. I've joined them all as members but they don't always turn up. Every couple of months I do a fresher course of restraint techniques and I put them through their paces. Plus I can claim it back on tax. I take it you know your way around a gym."

"I've been once or twice"

They started their workout with a warm up of circuit training with lighter weights, then pushed heavy on squats and chests. Frank was strong and although Dan spotted for him, his assistance was not needed. Dan was strong himself and held his own but was a couple of plates lighter than Frank could push or lift. Although Frank didn't push him hard, Dan enjoyed pushing himself and they fell into working out together with an easy cohesion. His leg wound hurt on the squats but he ignored it.

After the weights, they moved onto the bags. Dan held the first big bag while Frank laid into it, Dan's bodyweight absorbing the blows. On his turn he was given a pair of old gloves that he strapped on and started on his routine. The gloves were sweaty and he could feel the internal fabric was ripped against his knuckles. He thought he would need to buy his own pair, the old skills coming back to him.

'One, two, one, one, two.'

He aimed his fists and pummelled into the hard bag as he worked some of the tension through his shoulders and out into the bag. He was sweating hard, the moisture soaking into his t-shirt and tracksuit. He would need some more training kit as well.

"You leathered those bags," said Frank as they sat down to catch their breath.

"I had a lot of frustration to work out. About four years worth."

"But you said you had only been out for three. Not that I'm pushing for information or anything."

Dan paused before he answered. Frank was a decent sort of guy. Dan had learnt to tell the difference and had warmed to him.

"I was blown up on my last tour and spent a year in hospital and rehab when I came back from Afghan. I came back to my grandfather's village and locked myself away. The wound's healed but it has taken a long time to feel normal again."

"I saw you wince on the squats. But you kept going so I figured that you had been injured."

"Yes wounded and discharged on medical grounds. A bit of compensation and a pension."

"You have kids or are married?"

"No. I was always away on postings and never settled. Told myself I didn't want to leave a widow behind me."

Frank nodded, "sounds sensible, there was a lad from the town who didn't come back a couple of years ago. Left a young wife and a baby."

"Yes it hits home when you carry your mate's coffin and see the Padre comforting the wife and kids."

"So what plans do you have for your next job?"

"I have no idea. There's not much around here so will have to travel away. I went to the job centre but because I'm not signing on then they couldn't really help me. There are plenty of jobs gutting chickens in the meat processing plant but I don't fancy that. There was an older careers adviser there, coming up to his pension probably and he was straight with me and said that not many companies want squaddies as we would be too rigid in our attitude and not adaptable enough. I'm not a squaddie I was a Bootneck Royal, which is a hell of a difference but I took his point."

"That's a bit harsh"

"I preferred being told the truth rather than being fobbed off with a load of useless interviews. It doesn't help with my next step on the job front though. I've had a friend helping me look on the Internet but nothing interesting yet."

"I've employed a few ex-squaddies on the door and for static guarding. I've never had any problems. But then I suppose I'm looking for somebody who can stand as a sentry or deal with hassle where most jobs are not looking for that."

"True, its difficult to come out of uniform back into civilian life. It is hard to readjust. That's always been the same, from the days of Waterloo but now everything is so close because of the television there is no escape from the daily news. Apart from not having a television like me."

"Yes there was another casualty on the news today. We have the young squaddies coming into the club. Only kids most of them and they don't always behave. I stopped one of them last week from arguing with his girlfriend. He went to hit her and we put him out. Then he wanted to fight us. Then he was in tears and she was in tears and he was telling us that we don't know what its like out there."

"You don't. You can't unless you've been out there. You can't expect civilians to understand and the old soldiers just kept quiet and bottle it up. I've seen a lot of that. When I first joined up the Falk-land veterans didn't talk about it. They didn't have mobile phones and the Internet then. I don't think they were tougher but they knew to keep their experiences to themselves. You only talk about it with your mates."

"Do you talk about it?" asked Frank.

"Me? Never. I guess its all locked up inside of me. I'm an old sergeant. The young lads need their help not me."

Frank's phone rang and Dan motioned him to take the call. "Pentagon Security" said Frank into the phone.

"Yes hello. Sure I know the Bay View Hotel. Yes I can come and see you this evening. Great see you then, Brendan." Frank took the phone from his ear.

"Softly, Softly, Catchee monkey," he said to Dan with relish.

"You look happy."

"Yes, I've been waiting for that call. There's a new owner at the Bay View Hotel. He's reopening the disco underneath the hotel and wants to see me. The whole place needs a lot of renovation but the disco was closed down due to bad management by the police. Now my new friend Brendan O'Casey wants me to speak to him about the security. There's a new crowd trying to push their way in but my name is the best the man said. That will do me boi."

"Well done," said Dan

"It's a shot in the arm. But I will need some extra staff. You ever done the doors?"

"Yes before I went into the Marines, when I was young and stupid."

"We were all young and stupid once, you can take on the world when you are eighteen. I like older boys who have been around the block with more life experience. Nothing to prove and less trigger-happy. I'm good at sussing people and I reckon you would be good at it. Fancy a job?"

13.

A couple of days later Dan was back at the gym with Frank.

"Ah you came back for more. I thought you would," said Frank.

"Arms and chest are a bit sore but it won't take long to get back into it."

"Great, shall we start?"

They went into the same routine of warm up and circuit training with light weights on different stations. After twenty minutes they stopped to catch their breath, it was colder today and their panting produced a mist of condensation from their mouths.

"Its good to do this with someone who just gets on with it," said Frank. "The young ones keep stopping and starting and forgetting where they go next. It makes a difference to your routine."

"I've had years of training. I started boxing when I was fourteen and then the Marines took me and stripped me down and built my techniques up again. I've been running along the beach into the forest for a few weeks and my times are speeding up."

"How's that leg of yours on the run?"

"Its ok, 'no pain no gain' the Americans say."

"Maybe or pain is the way your body tells you to stop before you damage yourself."

"I'm not dead yet Frank. Come on lets work these shoulders."

At the end of the workout Frank produced a thermos flask full of coffee and after putting on a clean t-shirt and his royal marine hooded sweat-shirt Dan appreciated the hot sweet coffee. There was an unusual kick.

"I put a shot of whisky in for a taster," said

Frank with a smile. "Weather is turning colder. I need a boost for my old bones."

"Shouldn't we be eating bananas and drinking protein shakes."

He raised his plastic flask top cup, "we probably should but I'm too old for that healthy living stuff. Iechyd da."

"Cheers," said Dan amused at Frank's maverick attitude

"We don't have showers here as they were never cleaned so we closed them off. Most of the lads live in the town so they are close enough."

"What is the smart gym like?"

"Full of poseurs. Not my type of place. Some of my staff go there and they like it, but probably for the girls in tight Lycra, if I know my lads."

"You don't fancy a swim or sauna afterwards then?"

"I've heard some of the things they get up to in that sauna so I will stick to the council pool."

"You don't like the place then?"

"I don't like the owners and some of the clientele. The Williams family owns it. Have you come across them yet?"

"Yes I've had dealings with Steve."

"Little prick isn't he?"

"Yes I hit him with a boathook and he doesn't like me very much."

"So that was you? I heard about that. Well done, boi. He needed that. Too big for his boots that one. I've dealt with his uncle Cliff for years and just as he calms down Steve Drwg pops up trying to run the town playing the big I am."

"Yes I've heard that. He was trying to bully a friend of mine on the docks and pulled a knife on me. So I hit him with the boathook pole."

"Right between his legs, it was the talk of the town when it happened."

"Great and here's me trying to keep my head down."

"The old man Owain is still alive but has passed on control of the businesses to his son Brian. Brian is ok. I was at school with both his younger brother Cliff and Steve's father John who runs the trawler.

I've had a load of run-ins with Cliff. Brian is a businessman through and through, came back here after University full of ideas. The gym was set up by a national health club chain. They thought there was more money in the town than there actually was. There was a story that their computer system thought we were closer to Dublin, it missed out the Irish Sea or something. I love these big companies coming in from London and getting us wrong. Anyway the club was doing badly and Brian Williams offered to take it over and his son Phil runs the place now."

"Are they making money at it?"

"Lets just say that the place is no busier than it was but they are raking it in. The Williams are like that. They have to clean their money somehow. They've got a building company, waste disposal, road landscaping. Anything they can put in for a council contract. There are some very wealthy councillors who have speedboats and villas in Spain thanks to their friendship with the Williams family."

"They get away with it?"

"Yes Brian is clever and plays at being legitimate. If Steve Drwg causes problems then he better watch out for Brian. Cliff was a silly boy and there was a story that Brian told the police that Cliff would be driving back from Manchester with a boot full of drugs and what car he would be driving. There is no love lost between the brothers after that. But it kept Cliff well away from the business for a few years and Brian really grasped control then. Cliff is paid to keep quiet now and keep out of the way. He does some small time dealing and trains hard, which is why I don't like the place. He's into the steroids and has taken too many. Starting to look a bit strange these days. You know, muscley but skin all stretched and spotty and not normal. He's going bald and has a tuft of blonde hair on his head. You can tell he's juiced up on the steds."

"Sounds charming"

"Yes, a proper toe rag. Brian's son Phil is ok. I heard that Cliff had been inappropriate with a young girl at the gym and followed her home and Phil put him in his place. Phil was a karate champion and went to the Commonwealth games. He went to university like his dad and I thought he had escaped but he was persuaded to come back to run the gym. He's bored and likes the women so he trains hard. He keeps it natural and has his own mixed martial arts school and has moved up into cage fighting. He's supposed to be good at it. He was on a Welsh television programme recently and came over very well. He's a bit of a local celebrity. My lads did the security for the shoot and rumour

was he went back to the hotel room with the pre-
senter from Cardiff and she couldn't walk the next
day but had a big smile on her face."

"As long as she was smiling afterwards."

"She was, but she was going back to her famous
boyfriend the next day so I hope he didn't leave
any marks. Phil's a good-looking lad and now he's
pumped up and has had loads of tattoos. She must
have liked them."

"How was your meeting with the hotel guy?"

"Very good. Brendan O'Casey, nice bloke, very
Irish, like my old man. Made money in a communi-
cations company. Said he is looking for a different
lifestyle choice so he bought the Bay View Hotel.
Must be mad. But fair play to him, he has lots of
ideas and energy. Will need a lot of money as well.
Said he always wanted his own hotel and saw the
Bay View on the internet and bought the place.
You will like him."

"I will?"

"Yes I want you to take over the place when it
opens in three months."

"I don't have a badge yet?"

"Well I've sorted that for you as well."

14.

Dan parked in the community college car park and followed the sign to the reception. With all the eager young teenagers running around excited after their weekends, he felt old. He was smartly dressed in his black trousers, one of his new shirts and his reefer jacket. He reflected that he looked more of a teacher than a student. Indeed, in his last time in a classroom he had been the teacher of young recruits rather than the pupil himself. He felt the urge to straighten his beret but he wasn't wearing one. The reception area had a big notice with the different vocational courses that were running and he followed the sign that said, 'Door Supervisors Course BTEC Level 2'.

He was the first to arrive. When the door had shut for the last time and the attendees settled down the class had five other students in it. There was a lady teacher in her late twenties who introduced herself.

"Bore da, Good Morning, my name is Annette Davies. Croeso, Welcome to the Door Supervisor's course. This course will be five days long to cover the mandatory time for you to learn and on Friday there will be an exam with multiple-choice questions. We will cover all the answers so no need to worry."

Dan wasn't worried and he thought about the likes of his old head doorman Andy Hilton and some of the lads he had worked with back in the city when he had been young and stupid. The thought of them in the classroom doing multiple-choice questions made him smile to himself.

Annette Davies was attractive, tall, slim dark hair pulled back in a ponytail. She was wearing black trousers with inch-heeled boots that showed off the shape of her long legs and her shapely bum. On the top she had a fluffy purple and black sweater with a baggy collar that hung round her chest like a scarf. Dan was impressed. He picked up the local Welsh accent although it was softer than most.

"Right if we can go round the room first and introduce ourselves?"

"I'm Huw Evans, I've been in the Welsh Guards and came out three months ago. There are no jobs but my girlfriend works at the chicken factory and says there is a security job coming up if I pass the license." He was a big lad and Dan could see him sitting upright as he would have done with the Guards regiment.

"Good, next?" She indicated the first of four tracksuits who had been chattering to themselves. .

"I'm Dafs. The job centre sent me."

"I'm Emyr and the job centre sent me."

"I'm Paul and the job centre sent me."

"I'm Osian and the job centre sent me. Miss"

Dan could see Annette Davies close her eyes and take a deep breath. She obviously knew she was going to have to work hard to motivate these four.

"It's not school lads. You don't have to call me Miss. Do you want to work in security as a career?"

"If the money was ok then I would. I can work up to sixteen hours before I lose my benefits," said Dafs, the leader of the pack.

"Well I hope you will learn something from the course and hopefully there will be a job at the end of it when you get your license. And you?"

Dan was the last to say his name. He had never been good at sitting in classrooms and was tempted to say that he was from the job centre too but he threw the teacher a bone of enthusiasm. She was good looking and it was going to be a long stretch if he was going to watch Powerpoint presentations all week in a classroom. The heating was well up and he would be in danger of drifting off.

"I'm Dan Richards. I've been offered a job with Frank Delaney and I need the badge."

"I know Frank, he is going to come in on the fourth day to teach Physical Intervention techniques."

"Yes he said that he helps out. Would you like to tell us a bit about yourself Miss Davies?"

"Call me Annette please Dan. Certainly, it's only fair. I am a member off the Catering and Tourism Department here at the College and I mainly lecture on customer service and the college thought that the Door Supervisor's course should come under that. I worked in restaurants and bars locally. Then when I went to university to study

Psychology I worked as a restaurant manager in the city centre so I have dealt with many drunks and situations involving alcohol," She looked at Dan who smiled at her and she carried on. "I came back after university and applied for a job lecturing here. I do have the SIA License and so am able to work as a Door Supervisor. Frank Delaney keeps asking me to work for him but so far I keep saying no."

Dan nodded back at her in thanks.

"Right. First I have to go through the administration. You should have all brought identification with you. A passport or driving license and a utility bill or dole book and two passport photos?

"We weren't told to bring anything Miss.," said Dafs the tracksuit.

"Ok, there's a surprise. Technically, you should not be allowed to start the course but I will bend the rules so as not to disrupt the rest of the trainees. Will you make sure you bring something tomorrow?"

"Yes Miss," the row of tracksuits chorused.

There were all sorts of issues to go through and they sailed through the first three days. There were Powerpoint presentations with cartoons and pretty pictures designed to keep even the shortest attention span on board and a matching textbook. The course was one designed by an SIA approved training body and was split into four modules, which Annette taught one a day.

All that Annette had to do was follow the structured presentation, which worked towards key tasks and learning outcomes. There was plenty of time for going over the points again and again. This was learning by parrot fashion. Even with the loudest mouthed tracksuit, most of it sank in. They had long lunches and coffee breaks and the days still finished early.

The subjects came and went within the modules. How the Private Security Industry was regulated. Awareness of the law, health and safety, what colour fire extinguishers to use and how to deal with bomb threats. Annette repeated often that the main purpose of all these points was to keep within the laws of the land and generally call the police if anything happened.

They were taught the levels of seriousness for crimes, the role of a door supervisor and how they should be nice and friendly to customers at all times. How to avoid, prevent, manage and respond to conflict. Cover and switch techniques and a bit of the psychology when dealing with aggression.

They debated some of the points, especially

about issues with drugs. How the right to search was limited to when permission had been specifically asked for and granted. It was stressed that a search without consent could be classed as a personal assault.

Dan put an end to that discussion about refusing to be searched. "They don't come in."

Dafs the tracksuit wanted to labour the point, "I know my rights I don't have to be searched if I don't want to be."

"You do if you want to come into licensed premises. Its simple, if a customer is refused then they can't come in. It is still the case of 'The Management reserves the right to refuse admission'."

Annette grateful for his intervention finished off his point by adding, "Unless they are a warrant holding member of the licensing authorities."

On the Thursday afternoon it was the Physical Intervention Module and Frank came along before lunch and they pushed back the tables to clear a space ready to start when they came back.

As Annette, Frank and Dan went into in the canteen Frank said. "Dan this is the best bit the lovely Annette buys me lunch."

"Yes and you get to pick the best of my students."

"Anybody decent this time?"

"Well Dan here seems to know what he is doing." Annette teased them both.

Dan knuckled his forehead, "Thanks Miss"

Dan went first and picked a bottle of water and a plastic wrapped sandwich from the display fridge. Frank matched his sandwich and raised him a slice of chocolate cake, which Annette paid for. She made sure to get the receipt for Frank's meal to claim back later while Dan and Frank went to a table by the window.

"I have to squeeze the most out of this place. I would buy her lunch but she can't accept, as it would be classed as a bribe. After some of the stuff that goes on round here its bloody daft."

Annette came over to join them and sat down.

"Good to see I'm with the grown ups today, are you sure I'm allowed to eat with teacher." said Dan.

"I'm sure we will be fine, as long as you don't make any inappropriate suggestions then we will be within the guidelines."

"Try me?" said Dan with a twinkle in his eye.

Annette lowered her gaze but Dan saw her lips move upwards in a smile.

She coughed and answered Frank's last question. "The ex-squaddie Huw is good, his girlfriend wanted him to come out of the army but now he's out he misses the life and there aren't any jobs around. Says he's got a security job at the chicken factory."

"He hasn't, its already gone to Tony Hughes. He used to work for me but was unreliable so I let him go. His brother works in the factory and he got him the interview. I heard yesterday but he mightn't last the month. Ok so one possible. What about the others?"

"Erm, not great. One didn't come back to the course on the second day and the others are a bit full of themselves. But the college needs the job centre training to pay for the majority of our courses. What do you think of them Dan?"

"Dafs, who is the loudest, was a pain but he could probably do with a few nights working. I've told him doing the job will knock a few rough edges off him."

"What did you say to him? To make him shut up on the first day." Annette asked.

"Oh just a word to the wise, whispered in his ear. He's been fine after that."

"I can fight my own battles you know."

"I'm sure you can Annette but I thought it was going to be a long week if those idiots were going to mess around all the time."

"True. What do you think of the course?"

"Its been a long time since I did the doors but some of the stuff is still the same. When I worked in the nightclubs there was not much customer service around then and most of the guys I worked with wouldn't pass the criminal records check. I think the main point I would make is that in the field or on the door then the reality is different to a class room."

Frank came into the conversation, "I agree I lost some good lads who didn't pass the checks and probably wouldn't have passed the exams, but they were good doormen and could handle themselves. Now we have these jacket fillers who have a badge but no presence. I know who I would prefer to stand next to in a ruck."

"Frank you can't say that the old days of thugs on the door who beat up customers was better than now?"

"As I keep telling you Annette you have the badge and doing the job will make you a better teacher of the subject."

"You always say that Frank."

"I need a switched on girl and you would be perfect. Back me up here will you, Dan?"

"Not sure I want to get involved between you two but I agree with Frank. You are a good teacher but some of the points are academic and if you do the job then you can pick and choose between what to advise your students. It's the type of job that you can only learn when doing it, even with a bit of plastic to say you have passed a test.

"Maybe you are right," said Annette

"Work with me one night. I'm sure Frank can arrange it. Then you can teach me how to be nice to people."

"Ok you win, my boyfriend won't be happy about it but he's not happy about anything much at the moment. So I will think about it."

They went back to the classroom where the others were waiting.

The training went fine and it was stressed that any physical intervention should be as a last resort. Dan found that the SIA approved manoeuvres were stylised and sterile. There was a lot of talk about presenting two open hands to gesture non-aggression, then to not retaliate if somebody threw a punch. There was a lot of teaching about how to break a grab hold from an assailant and then to step back into a non-aggressive stance, which just gave them a chance to have another go at you.

Frank summed it up. "Listen in lads. It is all about justifying your actions. Head butts, punches and strangleholds are difficult to justify in the cold light of day in front of a judge."

Dafs, the loudmouth tracksuit who had calmed down over the week fancied himself as a bit handy. When it came to the role-playing exercise for ejections, he asked to have a go with Miss Davies putting him out. Annette was tall and slender and the loudmouth could have fought her on strength alone. Dan offered to do it with him instead but Annette said she was ok.

Dan looked at Frank who shook his head and winked back at him. He need not have been worried, when loudmouth tried to struggle out of a hold Annette tightened up and applied pressure and the lad fell to his knees.

"Didn't Miss Davies tell you that she is a Karate black belt? A National champion." Frank said to the classroom in general.

15.

The habit of early morning runs had kicked back in and Dan was pushing himself hard. There was snow on the mountaintops, the air was crisp and the sea was flat. His boots broke the thin layer of ice on the sand as he pushed himself up the dune and into the forest. He ran in a green woolly hat, surplus hair sticking out from the fringe. His scrim scarf tied around his neck kept out the cold. Long hours in cold climates had taught him to keep his neck warm.

When he came back to his cottage Pat Post's red van was pulled up in the lane and the postman was pulling himself out of the driver's seat.

"Haia Dan, Bore da. Letter for you."

"Bore da Pat, diolch," the postman drank in the pub and everybody called him Pat, but Dan didn't know his real name.

Dan put the letter on the kitchen table and turned the taps to run a bath. The letter said he had passed the exam and attached the plastic blue identity card. The card fell on the table with a small picture of his face staring upwards in the bottom right hand corner. He picked it up to examine it more closely. There was a date three years ahead to show how long the license was valid for and a 16 digit number along the top next to the SIA logo. On the right edge there was an orange strip denoting he was a Door Supervisor.

He looked at his photo. He saw the same face every day but he doubted that his previous incarnation as an eighteen-year-old bouncer would recognise his future self. Tanned and weather beaten, scars and hair with grey flecks He rubbed his hand through his hair in reflection, it was wet after his run and it clumped in his hands. It needed cutting. That would be a job for today, smarten himself up a bit.

He lay in the bath contemplating his new badge. He wondered what Andy Hilton was doing now twenty years later. He could probably 'google' the name on the Internet and wondered what he would find. Head of a crime family with lots of little shaven-headed Andy's running around, in prison or dead, shot in a drive-by on a club door. . Andy probably wasn't as old then as Dan had thought he was, late twenties, thirty. He had a shaven head then so could have been any age. Dan wondered what had happened to the blonde who had been the first to make his toes curl and then passed him up for bigger fish. He rubbed the soap over his body and across his face then sank himself beneath the water to sluice it off and raised himself again above the waterline. He felt arousal at the memory of the blonde and counted off the women he had been with since then. Some memories were stronger than others. A parade of women of different shapes, sizes, colours and creeds, quick drunken fumbles, package holiday romances that faded into the past. The strongest memories of sexual encounters were those he regretted leaving behind. As he often did he thought back to Kirsty in Hong Kong and the way her body had moulded to his own. It was enough to put him over the edge and he put himself under the water again.

He lay back in the bath reflecting on missed opportunities. Through confused circumstances he had lost touch with his Scottish girlfriend Kirsty who had been a bar manager in the colony and that had hurt him. Since then he had kept what he had thought was a healthy detachment from love. He had enjoyed the excitement and function of romance and had been complimented on his performance. However that was not the same as involvement and entanglement, which he had not been complimented on, as attested to by thrown drinks, plates and salty tears. The heat from the bath worked its magic on his brain and he contemplated the parade of women. He knew deep down that the latest squeeze in the line up, landlady Carol was not high up on his list.

After his recuperative bath he called Frank.

"That's great. Just in time. It's the England v Wales match this Saturday and its one of the biggest nights of the year. If Wales win there is a happy atmosphere in town. If England win then there could be murder. Its a busy night all over the county so all hands on deck."

"So you are expecting a lot of trouble?" asked Dan

""Not too much, mainly the effects of all day drinking but I have seen the Cross of St George burnt when England won. That was along time ago."

"Sounds great."

"You'll be fine and I will give Annette a call she might as well start by being thrown in at the deep end. If she can cope with Wales versus the Sais then she can cope with anything. I'll put you on the chain pub with Robbie and Alan. They are good lads, Big Robbie is a builder and Alan is a farmer. I'm pleased you are coming on board Dan. Look forward to working with you."

Buoyed up by the prospect of his new job he walked into the village. Apart from the pub the only surviving business in the village was a blue rinse hairdresser and he needed a haircut. He wasn't sure if Mrs Roberts was open but was in luck. One of the matrons from the village was sitting with her head underneath an ancient drier as her perm was set and reading a celebrity magazine. Another lady was sitting with a cup of tea with no pretence of hair being cut and Mrs Jones was standing chatting holding a long handled floor brush.

Dan's shadow blocked the door and towered over Mrs Roberts who sat him down.

"Short back and sides please Mrs Roberts."

"Yes Mr Richards," said the old lady chopping away at Dan's locks with a pair of scissors.

After a few minutes she held up a mirror to show him the nape of his neck shorn of hair.

"That's great thanks Mrs Roberts, Diolch yn

fawr"

He paid with a few coins and went out into the street. His neck was cold and he rubbed his hand over the remains of his hair and round the back where the tightly ends hair prickled his fingers.

He was a Bootneck again. He even stood with a straighter back and swung his arms and marched along the street. He knocked on the pub door and Carol let him in. She looked tired.

"Come in Dan, you've had your hair cut. You look well."

"Thanks so do you." Dan said it automatically.

"No I don't Dan I look like shit." She hesitated and pulled back to civility. "It's been a bad week. Do you want a coffee?"

She took him upstairs to her flat and when the kettle had boiled they sat on the sofa sipping at their mugs.

"Sorry, it's not your fault, I shouldn't have snapped at you. The brewery are on my back and James is playing up."

Dan listened as Carol unburdened herself.

He had no understanding of running a business and certainly no experience of bringing up a teenage boy in a rural community. He could not suggest that James should join up with a branch of the Services. He knew that young lad's mothers don't want to think of their sons possibly going to war. Dan thought to himself that a roll in the hay with Anwen, the bar maid would make a man of young James. Despite his own sexual adventure with James' mother, that suggestion mightn't go down too well either.

Carol and Dan were not going anywhere romantically it was not spoken but he presumed they both realised that. He was sure their secret interlude hadn't dented their friendship and he was there to talk to when required. Another shopping trip to the hotel in Chester had been discussed but a fixed plan hadn't materialised. He thought that both of them were aware that the connection that they had forged that late afternoon on the shower was slipping away.

The dealings with the brewery were a worry. Before the credit crunch, the Brewery had borrowed lots of money to buy out a smaller rival for what was, with the benefit of hindsight, a foolhardy expansion. The banks wanted their money back and the brewery had cut back where they could and disposed of some of their more desirable properties. The Management were now looking to in-

crease the rents for their existing tenants at the
same time as squeezing through a price increase on
their beer. In the cutbacks the established area
manager who had known Carol from before her
divorce and knew her history and her struggles and
successes at the pub, had been made redundant.
The new area manager had survived because he
was a company man and a supporter of the management's policies. He was happy enough to put
extra pressure on Carol and had driven up in his
shiny new BMW to tell her of the rent review and
increase on the beer that she was tied to buying
from them. Matched with the Government's so-
called beer tax escalator and the rise in the Council's business rates Carol was uncertain she could
carry on and ultimately was unsure whether she in
fact wanted to.

She had told Dan about the brewery man with
the sharp suit and his new car.

"I can tie him to Gwilym's lobster pots if you
want me to. Just give the word?"

"I might just do that," she smiled for the first
time. "You are joking aren't you?"

Dan smiled back and put his empty coffee mug
on the floor. "Come here and give me a cuddle"

She gave him a thin smile. "I'm sorry just a

cwtch."

"That's ok," replied Dan holding out his arm.

She lay across the sofa and he pulled her into his chest. She had survived in this rural pub, where others had failed around her, through hard work and being canny. She was unsettled and since her trip to Chester she had become more restless. That trip had reminded that there was a wider world out there with more opportunities for James and for her own future.

"I can't keep going here Dan, " said Carol

Dan squeezed her shoulder in tacit support. "Something will come up babe, just hang in there."

16.

Saturday afternoon found Dan standing on the door of a big national chain pub with his new license in a plastic pouch tied around his arm. It was the crunch six nations rugby match between Wales and England and the town was heaving with red Welsh rugby shirts and one or two brave souls who were wearing the English white. It was a four-man door and Dan joined the two regular lads called Alan and Robbie. The fourth member of the team was Miss Annette Davies who had been persuaded to do the job rather than just teach it.

Frank had given Annette and Dan black ties with the Pentagon logo in red and the word 'security' embroidered in white letters underneath. They were clip on, like the prison warder issue so that if they were pulled in a fight they would snap off without strangling. They all wore white shirts, black trousers, and black coats. There was a layer of snow on the ground leftover from a cold spell of weather and frost was forecast. Annette wore a black North Face puffer jacket, a pair of black combat trousers and black boots. The puffer jacket bulked out her shoulders and she was tall so she didn't look out of place. Her dark brown hair was tied back in her usual ponytail and she wore a slight dash of lipstick.

Dan was wearing his reefer jacket, black trousers and his army boots. The trousers fell over the high leg eyelets of the boots, which had seen a coat of polish. His face had been close shaven to match his cropped hair cut. Apart from the badge on his arm framed with two fluorescent strips and the word security on his tie he looked smart. The last time he had worked on a door the uniform had been a tuxedo jacket and a bow tie. Unmistakable. No badges. He remembered that his bow tie in the old days had a Velcro fastening on the back to pull off easily and the second hand tuxedo still had the bloodstains from previous usage.

As the big pub filled up there was no sign of a recession or credit crunch. The manager, Tom was English but hid that well enough with plenty of Welsh flags and the staff wearing rugby shirts, none of them white. He had been in the town for over a year and had been caught out by the England v Wales Rugby match in his first month of the job. He had not seen the need for door staff during the game until a barstool had been thrown through a window when England had beaten Wales and certain elements of the crowd in the pub had turned nasty. He was pretty sure that the rugby result had been nothing but an excuse to cause trouble by those he now knew to be the usual idiots but it had been an early black mark on his record with the police who had taken him for a young mug.

The four door staff had turned up for duty and Tom had passed them the council registration book to sign in. The pub was starting to fill up and he already had ten bar staff working behind the long bar and a further six waiting-on staff to serve food and collect glasses. Soon there would be very little space to serve the cheap food that his pub was known for.

Robbie did the honours with the first coffees of their long shift and the pub became a sea of red shirts and blow up daffodils given out for free in a beer promotion. The national anthems were sung, the crowd joined in with the Welsh anthem with passion 'Gwlad, GWLAD.' Some booed the English anthem of 'God Save the Queen' and the match commenced. There were verses of "You can stick your sweet chariot up your arse" and chants of

"Oggie, Oggie, Oggie" and generally there was a good-natured ambience and a huge cheer when Wales scored a try.

Their main job on the door was to check the ages of customers and to stop trouble brewing. The only place to smoke was to the side of the main door. This caused a few problems but Robbie and Alan had it pretty much sorted on their own. Dan and Annette were not really needed.

They all had radios and Frank had given them a cheap plastic earpiece. Compared to military life, radio protocols on the door were basic, as was the quality of the radios. Dan had never used radios on the door before and the calls were going to be simple. If assistance was required then call to the area help was needed. At all times two of them would be spread inside and two would stay on the door and they would rotate around to keep it interesting.

Dan slipped back into the job easily enough. Alan and Robbie were friendly but he knew they wouldn't treat him as an equal until he had proved himself to back them up and not leave them for a kicking. Technically Alan was the head doorman, having worked for Frank the longest but as the night progressed Robbie and then Dan shared the duties. Dan started inside and ended up watching most of the rugby match on one of the ten television screens. The atmosphere was loud but remained good-natured. Wales scored another try and the crowd erupted, as they did when Wales went on to win the match.

Inside the pub, Dan walked his rounds, pushing through the packed crowd of drinkers. He would go into check the toilet or would ask an over-excited punter to calm down. The most excitement during the match was to tell one customer to put his shirt back on, pull his trousers up and step down off the table. Dan did it quietly but effectively and went back to stand by a wall where he had the best view of the door and his colleague at the other end of the bar.

The red shirts started filtering out and there was a lull before the night started properly. The team of four took it in turns to sit down drink coffee and eat some cheap food.

As the night went on the clientele changed. During the match and soon after, three quarters of the customers were wearing the red shirts of Wales in differing generations of styles and sponsors names. The modern shirts with the tight fabric were unforgiving to some of the belly shapes on boys and indeed girls. Most had been a long way from a rugby field, gym or even a stretch of pavement for some time. The older retrospective styles were a little more acceptable. There was even a lad in a kilt with a Welsh brown and green tartan underneath his red rugby shirt. It was a great chat up line and Dan watched him work his way around the pub offering to show what he wore under his kilt. He tried it on most of the females including Annette. Dan watched to make sure he didn't upset any jealous boyfriends but after the Wales team win the boys didn't seem to mind.

As the percentage of red shirts clicked down, leaving only the hardened drinkers who were in for the long haul, the normal Saturday night partygoers started to come out. Girls in short skirts and tight tops and lads in fashion brand embossed shirts or tight t-shirts, all ready for their Saturday night out. They would probably go on to the town's one and only nightclub in the old cinema later. Annette commented that hardly any of the Saturday night clubbers had coats

Alan and Robbie knew most of the regulars and Annette knew a few familiar faces, a couple from her schooldays, rugby playing friends of her younger brother and some students from the college. In her black puffer jacket with just the white collar of her shirt showing then not many people recognised her and if they didn't spot her then she didn't acknowledge them, it was easier. One of her brother's friends tried to chat her up. She said it was nice to see him. Then deflected his attention by putting her finger to her earpiece and pretending there was a call she was listening to. Robbie had suggested that trick of the trade to her early in the shift.

Frank Delaney drove down the High Street in his big black pick up truck and pulled up opposite their door. He chatted to Tom the manager who was happy that his tills were filling up with cash.

He then spoke to Annette who was on the street catching some fresh air, "How's the night going?"

"I'm enjoying it, the boys are keeping an eye on me."

"Well keep an eye on Dan, in case he needs looking after". Dan was inside, she was happy to keep an eye on him for Frank just in case.

"Is it like you expected?"

"Busier, noisier, you don't have time to catch your breath."

"Welcome on board. I always thought you would enjoy doing the job. What did your boy-friend say about it?"

"Don't ask? We had a row before I came here. He didn't want me to work, but he won't find a proper job himself so I have two jobs now to keep us going."

"Is he coming down to see you at work?"

"No he has gone all Welsh Nationalist on me again. Won't come to a pub owned by an English company. It suits me fine, he will be pissed when I go home. Working here is a welcome distraction."

"Plenty of other fish in the sea," said Frank.

"I'm starting to think so," replied Annette.

Frank drove off to check the other venues in his care.

Annette did look over occasionally at Dan. She was the proper new kid and although it was Dan's first night since his badge came through he looked as though he had always been there. She noticed a few admiring glances in his direction from other women, which he seemed oblivious to. He was an attractive man and had an air of steady confidence and she noted that the young boys coming in were more respectful to him. He didn't say much but every so often gave a nod of his head to check she was all right. She nodded back keeping her face as stern as his, not wanting to seem flippant.

She was standing by the dance floor. As she was watching Dan, he moved into a crowd of lads by the bar, two of who were squaring up to each other. As she watched over they started pushing and just as one started to throw a punch Dan arrived in the middle of them. He used the momentum of the punch to knock the arm down and pull the lads wrist round and behind his back. It was all completed in one smooth action. The lad was propelled out of the middle of the group towards the door. His opponent was left with nobody to fight. It happened so quickly and efficiently that Dan was at the door before Annette realised that she should have been helping him. The lad was passed on to Alan and Dan came back inside as she came hurrying up.

"I'm sorry I missed it," said Annette

"Don't worry, Lets go and see what it was about." He walked back into the crowd, which had quietened down. They were only young, late teens or early twenties. Annette went behind Dan.

Dan looked at the other fighter and stared at him giving him an opportunity to come up with an excuse.

"Sorry, sorry thanks. He used to go out with my cousin and he cheated on her. Our families don't get on."

"Ok, well don't bring that trouble in here. It's

been a good night so far," Dan insisted.

"Ok thanks, Diolch."

Dan glared round at the others. "Anybody else got a problem?"

"No, he's always an idiot when he drinks," one of them said.

"Ok then, stay happy," Dan retreated to a distance where he could watch.

Annette went over with him.

"I'm sorry Dan I didn't see it."

"Don't worry; it was easy to deal with. Watch people's heads. When they all turn in to watch something it could be an argument or a fight. Step in quickly and remove the trouble maker."

They both watched as a crowd of girls came through the door. One tall thin girl was wearing a bright pink tight tube of a dress. The boobs were pushed together and were popping out at the top. The bottom hem of the dress barely covered the girl's knickers.

It was hard not to notice and Annette looked up to see Dan watching her with a smile. He winked at her. She had seen that there was a lot of eye contact, winks, nods and hand gestures between the team. There was very loud music playing so it was difficult to hear and the small signals kept the night ticking along. She had been watching the girl and Dan had been watching her. She would have to be careful of her expressions.

When the girl had walked past them she gave the open mouth signal for 'Oh my god!'

Dan nodded back. He leant into her ear and whispered, "You can see what she ate for her dinner in that can't you."

Annette giggled and then put on a serious face in case anybody else was watching.

About eleven o'clock, at the pubs busiest part of the night, she did spot her first fight on the dance floor and went straight in to stop it. The dance floor, cleared of the daytime food tables, was packed with writhing bodies with a lot of bare flesh on show. There was a forced clearing by one wall and Dan was right, everybody who had noticed was looking in that direction. There were three males laying into another with a red rugby shirt on. She had seen the guy in the Rugby shirt all the shift and he had been drunk but happy. His girlfriend was also in a red shirt. She was trying to stop the three lads, who were skinny with weasel faces and all looked the same. The Rugby shirt was big and had been jolly but his night was spoiled as the three thin lads circled him tightly and took pot shots with their fists at his head. He was taking the punches well but he was lumbering and slow in return.

As Annette fought her way through the crowd, a voice crackled in her earpiece.

"Dance floor, Dance floor."

As she came into the clearing, the Rugby shirt had backed himself into the wall and was going down on his hunkers with his hands about his head to protect himself. She went to drag off one of the assailants who turned round to push her away. The pupils of his eyes were almost totally black and he stared wildly at her as she moved in.

He went to punch her and she knocked the punch away instinctively as her years of karate training took over. She pushed him backwards and he teetered off balance before trying to hit her again. She used the weight of his punch to twist him into an arm lock to disable him. The SIA regulations said she should now release the little shit and step back to a non-aggressive stance. Stuff that! She was not going to let him try to hit her again. So she twisted his arm and he cried out in pain.

His two friends were still attacking the big guy in the Rugby shirt. Annette had one but couldn't tackle the other two as well. Then Dan arrived, followed within two seconds by Robbie. Dan just steam-rollered straight in. He went in like a Rugby centre and handed off one weasel with an open palm. The little scrote bounced off his hand against the wall. The second one he shoulder charged and sent him flying into the Rugby shirt's girlfriend. It wasn't pretty but it was effective. Robbie picked up one of them in a bear hug, lifted the lad off his feet and with his arms pinned to his side he half carried, half walked the guy to the door. Dan motioned Annette to take her one out first and he followed with an arm hold on the third. At the entrance, they were sent hurtling out of the door, where they turned to give abuse.

Alan called up on the Pubwatch radio and asked for assistance. The radio went to the town's CCTV system operator, who liaised with the police. The three weasels were across the road now offering to carry on their fight. They were ranting, trying to goad the door team to cross the distance. The full door team were ready to block their way back in but it was all bluster. Within a couple of minutes, a police van came up, blue lights flashing. Alan stepped out to tell the four police officers what had happened. The three lads were still high with whatever was in their systems and the adrenalin from the fight. As the police approached, the yobs continued to shout abuse and tried to swagger. One told the policemen to "fuck off pigs." He was promptly picked up, thrown against the side of the van and handcuffed. His friends started to sober up and had the sense to keep quiet.

Annette and Robbie went back in to check with the guy in the Rugby shirt who had been attacked. He was bruised embarrassed and had a bloody lip, he had sobered up and was holding on to his girlfriend who was stroking his hair.

"She wanted to go home hours ago but I wanted to stay out, those three were trying to wind me up when we were dancing and I rose to them. I'm sorry."

"One has been arrested outside; do you want to press charges?"

"No, I shouldn't have reacted to them and I should have gone home like she said, they didn't hurt me. They wouldn't try that with me sober would they? Pricks."

Annette could see the beginning of a bruise on his eye and thought that he might feel differently in the morning.

His girlfriend was holding his hand and said to

Annette, "He stood up for me, when they were be-ing nasty" Then she burst into tears and he gave her a big hug.

17.

The night went on without further trouble and they closed the doors a little after midnight with all the customers going home or on to the town's nightclub. Tom had offered them a hard earned drink after work and they sat down on four high stools around a tall table and took the weight from their feet. It had been a long shift and a busy one.

The bar staff were tidying behind the bar and restocking fridges and the glass collectors were picking up the last of the empty bottles and plastic glasses from the floor. Tom asked what they wanted. Dan had to drive home so ordered a pint of bitter shandy. Alan had a bottle of Bud and big Robbie opted for an alcopop, red, sweet and sickly. Annette thinking of her mountain trek the next day asked for a fruit juice.

She had drunk a lot of coffee through the shift and with the excitement of dealing with her incident and relief for surviving the night was a touch wired. Dan took a deep swig of the shandy and grimaced, the pint was in a plastic glass that had just come out of the glasswasher. Shandy was bad enough but the warmth of the plastic on his lips made the experience worse. Alan and Robbie raised their bottles to Dan in salute.

"That's why we drink bottles from the fridge." said Alan. "A couple of years ago before Frank took over the door, a bloke was glassed in the face and its part of the license that they use plastic glasses after 6pm."

Dan looked around at the empty pub that only an hour before had been full of young people laughing, dancing and shouting. This wasn't a place to come to enjoy a nice drink or food but there was evidently a market for the low end of expectations.

"Did you enjoy yourself?" Robbie asked Annette

Yes I did, it went quickly. Sorry I missed the start of the first fight."

"Don't worry, it wasn't a bad one and you did

well with the dancefloor later on. That's what counts. Last lad that Frank gave us to train up spent most of the night chatting up girls. We told Frank that we didn't want him back," said Alan,

Annette guzzled down her fruit juice. Well I didn't chat up any blokes."

"No but we saw you being chatted up by those lesbians with the tattoos."

"Yes I saw you laughing at me. You didn't come to help me did you?"

"They were very scary women those two and you managed to escape them without us."

"Yes no thanks to you three." She took another swig of her juice. "It was good result in the match the Welsh boys played well."

"Made our night easier. The mood would have changed if the Welsh had lost to the Sais. Would have felt a long shift," said Alan.

"It was great to be part of it, everybody proud of their Welsh shirts and their language. It was fun."

"How's your Welsh coming on Dan?" asked Robbie

"I understand enough to get by, usually I just nod and say 'Iawn boi' as they come in. It seems to get me by. I didn't want to be too English tonight with you lot crowing about the wheels coming off the English chariot."

They all laughed and shared the camaraderie of a hard shift well done.

"You did well Annette, you ok to work next week?" asked Robbie.

Annette was relieved that they wanted her back. Alan nodded at her for a job well done. Dan nodded his approval too. Praise indeed.

Alan and Robbie were going on to work for the last couple of hours at the nightclub where Frank ran the door. They all finished their drinks and made ready to leave. Tom thanked them from behind the bar and they headed for the door.

Alan and Robbie were going to walk down to the nightclub that Frank ran and they invited Annette and Dan to go with them but they both said "not tonight."

Dan asked Annette where she was parked and it turned out they were both in the same car park a couple of hundred yards away so they walked along together. Their cars were the last two left in the car park and were only a couple of spaces from each other. She noticed that Dan was watching around him aware of his surroundings but nobody jumped out of the shadows at them.

It was a cold night with a clear sky above. The yellow sodium lights of the street lamps dimmed the stars. They were wrapped up tight in their coats, their breath frosted as it left their mouths. They stopped to chat halfway between the two cars.

"That's another thing to tell your students on the next course. In the military we call it 'Op Sec'. Stands for Operational Security. Always be careful when you leave the venue, where you park your car and that you don't walk home alone, especially if you have had trouble." Dan told her.

"I will add that to my list."

"A long time ago I was beaten up on the way home from working in a club."

"I thought you were indestructible," said Annette

"It taught me a lesson that nobody is indestructible. I was young and stupid. Thought I could take on the world."

"Was that were you got that scar under your eye?" The streetlights were not strong enough to see the scar but Annette had noticed it during the training course and had seen it again during the shift.

"No that was somewhere else and that's another story?"

"You will have to tell it to me sometime," she said. "Tell me did you fancy any of the women out tonight?"

"Strange question."

"I'm trying to guess the type of woman you go for."

"Ah. Tall slim about five foot ten, dark hair tied back in a pony tail and a black tie on that says security."

She punched him on the arm then snatched the tie from her throat and undid her top button. "I'm being serious."

"Oh apart from you. Let me think? Not the girl in the pink with her fanny hanging out who thought she looked gorgeous. There are lots of princesses but not much class around here. There were one or two women who were more sensibly dressed. Not exactly nuns, but a bit more sophistication. They wore less make up, showed less cleavage. Nicely curved bodies were hidden, waiting to be revealed at a later time and not all on show. Nice eyes. I like eyes. Does that answer your question?"

"Yes, I liked that you liked me

"Good, I hoped you would. You did well tonight Annette. Were you nervous?"

"I was at the start but as the night went on I forgot to be nervous."

He smiled back. "And you looked after me. It's been a long time since I was a bouncer."

She retaliated with a quick, "Its not 'Bouncer' its 'Door Supervisor'."

"Yes Miss Davies, Sorry Miss Davies."

She poked her tongue out at him.

She could not think of anything else to say. Not wanting to make a fool of herself she made up her mind to go. Before she did, she bit the inside of her lip and breathed in quickly, before reaching up to give Dan a kiss on the cheek. Her lips lingered on the slight re-growth of stubble. Her nostrils blew out a stream of air towards his ear before she stepped away.

"Nos da Dan."

"Nos da Cariad," he replied.

She stepped away towards her car. She switched on the engine and as she warmed up the car and wiped the inside windows, Dan was watching her. She knew he was waiting for her to leave safely before he went himself. It was good to feel protected.

He was unlocking his old car with the key and she rolled the window down.

"Dan, what are you doing tomorrow?"

"Nothing planned. Why?"

"I am going for a walk in the mountains if you fancy it? Possibly up Snowdon if the weather is bright enough."

He didn't take long to reply. "Ok, what time?"

"Not too early, leaving about 10.30."

"Do you want me to pick you up?"

"No I will meet you. Do you know the lay by next to the Bedol pub?"

18.

Annette was waiting where they had arranged and they decided to leave his car in the lay-by and drive on into the mountains together. The views of the mountaintops were fantastic, a crisp and clear vista of snow-covered peaks with blue sky above.

Annette offered to drive in her car, a black sporty hatchback and Dan squeezed into the passenger seat.

"We are late starting so if we take the easy route up Mount Snowdon from the Ranger Youth Hostel. The track leads up to the peak and we can take the Rhydd Ddu path back down again. We will avoid the crowds walking up on the main Llanberis route. If we don't dawdle, we should be back down well before dark. Are you up for that Dan?"

"Sounds fine to me. Will be good to be back up the mountains again."

"I love my car," said Annette with pride a few bends later.

She drove fast down the windy country road along the valley between the rising mountains. Dan rolled from side to side with each bend, he was acutely aware of his thigh hitting off Annette's hand as she changed gear. His head brushed against the fabric of the roof. He was regretting the whisky nightcap he had taken before he went to bed just a few hours before. He had dreamt of Annette's green eyes and the body under her work clothes but he didn't pass on that piece of information on to his driver.

Getting ready beneath the bare trees of the car park Annette's walking gear was far more modern than Dan's and a lot more multi-coloured with a bright pink and grey daypack and red gaiters. She wore her black North Face puffer jacket and had a purple sweatband around her ears. The finishing touch was a pair of wraparound Oakley sunglasses. She slotted an ice axe securely in the side of her pack. She had brought along a spare ice axe, along with a spare pair of adjustable crampons set to a man's size.

Dan in his army surplus rig felt under dressed and under prepared. His one concession to colour was an orange fleece that Annie and Gwilym had given him for Christmas a couple of years ago, it smelt of fish. His clothes were warm and functional, he even had an old pair of shades but he was conscious of being older than Annette and looking older. She was nearly thirty and looked younger, he knew he looked old and was turning craggy. Gone was the carefree young Marine and he knew that the weight of his failed responsibilities had weathered him.

He felt a generation gap between her bright colours and his drab greens. She was an attractive intelligent girl with a good career. He was a washed up retired Sergeant, who had little to offer her. She didn't seem to care, had been pleased to see him and had chatted away brightly in the car. Dan had noted that she didn't mention a boyfriend or partner to him and he had clocked early on that she was not wearing a wedding ring.

They crossed the road and walked upwards on a farm path to the left of the hostel. As she climbed over the top of a stile she looked back at him and the low sun caught her face sending a long shadow behind her as she opened her arms.

"How do I look?"

"Gorgeous."

She liked that and beamed a smile back at him.

They set off up the mountain at a steady pace and zigzagged up the first mile of the slope before coming out on to a plateau underneath the main peak of Snowdon. They met small groups of walkers, who had been up early and were now on their way back down. The path up ahead was waymarked by fluorescent dots of other walkers at different levels above them. Annette set a steady pace and Dan kept up.

The flat ground gave them a chance to speak as they walked along together side by side.

"I wasn't sure if you would bring along a boyfriend today?" Dan waited for her answer.

They walked along a few paces before she replied.

"I do have a boyfriend who I live with. His name is Daffydd but I haven't been happy for quite a while. He's a surf dude. I've been with him for six years. I thought he was the one I would marry and have kids with but now I can hardly be in the same house as him."

"That's pretty serious."

"Yes it is. We got together when I came back from university and at the start it was fun. We'd go down the coast and catch the waves. You know the sort of thing. Camp on the beach next to a fire, then up at dawn to hit the surf."

"Sounds a great life."

"It was for the first few months but you can't live on a beach and I had my new job and I wanted to get my teeth into my career. I passed my psychology degree then did a postgraduate certificate in education so I could teach. I did the teaching course because I knew I wanted to come home to Wales and live near the sea and the mountains but there are so few jobs. So I had a plan."

"And your plan worked?"

"Yes it did and my work life is fine. I lived at home with my mam and brother to save the deposit for a mortgage and I bought a terrace house in the town and I've done it up and Daffydd lives with me."

"Does he pay you rent?"

"Sometimes when he has money, which is becoming less and less. He wants to set up his own surf school so he says he is saving for that. There are grants available and I brought the forms home for him but he still hasn't filled them in."

"Is there enough surf on this coast to make money at it?

"Not really, its not constant like in Cornwall or the Atlantic Coast in Ireland and its difficult to guarantee surfing lessons if there are no waves but he could make a go of it if he wasn't so lazy. He could do kite surfing or kayaking as well, there is loads of potential. When there is surf he prefers to be out on the water than teaching others who will pay him."

"It must be difficult for you."

"Yes it is. I don't mind paying most of the bills and he is a nice guy but a few weeks ago, when I first met you, I went home for lunch to find him opening yet another cardboard box, this time with a fin to make his surfboard go faster, or to let him hold closer to the wave or whatever it bloody did. If I hadn't turned up then the packaging would have been hidden and I would never have known.

Dan kept quiet. It was a story Annette wanted to tell him and he hoped her boyfriend's transgressions would be to his benefit.

"One of the problems is that Daffydd is a fervent Welsh Nationalist and he turns the issue of not having any money round into how he doesn't want to be subservient to the English tourists who would be his customers. He has a theory that I am selling out by teaching local Welsh young people to be servers to tourists in the restaurants."

"I've heard the arguments before. My Taid used to laugh about them and he was a very proud Welshman."

"I believe in an independent Wales. Look at the rugby match last night, everybody proud and singing the national anthem and speaking our language. We went to Sligo in Ireland three years ago and it's not unlike here but being on the Atlantic shore the waves are bigger. The Irish know how to take tourist's money with a smile on their faces. We talked about it to our hosts in the bed and breakfast. They have the balance right and nobody thinks the Irish are subservient. Daffydd just wants visitors to leave their money at the end of the A55 on the Welsh border."

"Perhaps tourism isn't the best business for him to be in then."

She smiled, "no its not, I'm just more realistic about life. There was talk of a new customer-service call-centre being built locally by a multinational company. My college had been asked to help with the training if it was built. Some of the councillors were arguing that they were not proper jobs. You saw those lads on the training course. We need the jobs. The Welsh accent is classed as warm and trustworthy. Surely, those employees who would be answering callers would be better able to deal with customer's problems if they could look out of the window and see the sea and the mountains. Anyway they realised they weren't being welcomed and went elsewhere."

She carried on, "he always has an excuse as to why he should put off doing a more lucrative job. He's very bright. He monitors the internet for the strength of the wind and knows where all the best surf beaches are. He knew all about the frequency of waves and that the best surf is two days after a big storm when the rollers have built up out in the ocean and settled down to a long swell up the Irish Sea and to crash onto a facing beach. He knows all that. I just wish he would put some of his energy into being more productive. It doesn't help that he likes smoking dope. I've tried to persuade him to cut back on the cannabis. He now very rarely rolls a joint at home but I'm sure he still smokes around his friends' houses.

"Are you ok?" Dan said, "you don't have to tell me all this."

"I want to tell you Dan. I've bottled it all up. You know us Celtic girls, with all our emotions bubbling away under the surface ready to explode."

"I thought that was all women. I've had the odd plate thrown at my head."

"Yes watch yourself Dan Richards." She pointed her finger at him in mock warning.

"Anyway yesterday Daffydd and I had a row before I went to work. Then I had a great time and enjoyed working with you and the boys," she walked on a few more steps before continuing.

"Do you know Dan, Robbie was telling me that he has four kids at home and the money from working the door pays for him to take them all on holiday."

A few paces further on Annette continued with her torpedoes aimed amidships at her fast sinking relationship.

"I respect Robbie for that. Then when I arrived home last night after our chat in the car park and the house was filled with the smell of dope, how am I supposed to feel? There was a half eaten donner kebab all over the kitchen table and his trousers and underpants were on the landing. I slept in the spare room and then came out to meet you."

"Perhaps you should have stayed to sort it out with him?"

"I didn't have your phone number so I couldn't have left you waiting for me."

Dan was about to reply but she cut him off. "No, I know when a relationship is broken beyond repair. I'm a grown-up girl Dan, I wouldn't have come if I didn't want to."

"I'm glad you did turn up."

"So am I, Dan, very glad," she looked around at the snow-covered mountains and the blue sky and opened her arms again to showcase the expansive views. "Besides, where else would you want to be on a beautiful day like this?"

They had reached the next incline and the exertions of the steep diagonal climb meant they needed to save their breath and they stepped on in an amicable peace. As they climbed higher, the snow was becoming deeper and they followed in the well-trodden footprints of previous walkers. The sky was still bright blue and there were a few high wisps of clouds. The views opened up as they climbed higher. As they stepped above the plateau at the top of a rise there was a fence and they came to a stile, which exposed a new horizon to the East.

They stopped and looked down on the opposite valley leading down to Llanberis. In the distance there was a steady stream of humanity going up and down the wide path. They were both pleased they had the unfashionable Ranger path mostly to themselves.

They paused to prepare themselves for the next stage of the ascent. A slip in the snow would send one of them hurtling down to Llyn Ffynnon hundreds of feet below and they fastened on their crampons and pulled their ice axes from their rucksack holsters.

They carried on up the slope as it became steeper and they followed the path in another wide zigzag to gain height. Dan and Annette with the ice axes in hand and the crampons now bolted on to their boots were surefooted and steady progress was made higher and higher.

As Dan followed Annette up the steep path, the patches of rock and grass turned to thicker snow. At one deep drift they stepped off the path to look around them. As they walked Dan had told Annette about some of the cold weather exercises he had done in the Royal Marines.

She pointed at the snowdrift "Is that deep enough to make a snow shelter"

"Just about, if we get stuck I can burrow out an ice cave," said Dan. "It would be cold but we would survive."

"Would we have to share the bivvy bag to preserve body warmth?"

Dan couldn't see Annette's eyes through the reflective sunglass lenses. Her cheeks and the tip of her nose were red with the cold. Her white teeth showed as her lips parted in a smile.

"Yes," he said, "Royal Marine protocols for hypothermia are to keep warm any way you can. If necessary by taking off wet clothes and preserving body heat."

She licked her chapped lips, they were red with the cold and Dan behind his own shades focussed on the tip of her tongue.

He carried on to rescue the conversation. "Of course it could be extremely embarrassing if somebody sent the mountain rescue team out for us and found us with no clothes on tucked up in an orange plastic bag."

"Ooh we would be all sweaty inside the plastic. Perhaps not today, lets concentrate on reaching the peak and then arriving back at the car park safe and sound."

Her smile teased him and she set off up the path following a line of frozen footsteps in the snow. For the first few steps her bum was on the level with his eyes and he had a spectacular view of her long legs and rear end clad tightly in her elasticised black walking trousers. She looked back and did an exaggerated step up and down on the spot making the muscles of her bottom move up and down.

"Come on slow coach," she said and set off up the hill.

They reached the junction with the main path and for a few hundred yards shared the track with a variety of people heading up and down. Some were dressed the same as Annette in modern technologically advanced hiking gear, whilst one family had come up the main track with the three kids in jeans, trainers and anoraks for warmth. Annette and Dan shared a glance at the parents' stupidity.

Annette explained to Dan that Mount Snowdon's name in Welsh was Yr Wyddfa, which translates as 'the Tumulus.' It was named for the mound that had been heaped over the body of a giant killed by King Arthur. The mighty Mount Snowdon might have been a tourist attraction, but it was also a very dangerous one. Many unprepared walkers had been caught out on its slopes.

"My dad worked with the coastguard and before he died always taught me that the lifeboat crews and the mountain rescue don't mind being called out if you make a mistake and need their help as long as you are prepared and have checked the forecast and have the right clothes," said Annette after the family had wandered past.

"Good advice," agreed Dan.

They strolled the last part of the slope to the cairn up on the summit and the clear blue-skied panorama from the peak was breathtaking. From the Isle of Anglesey in the North, to the Lleyn Peninsula, out towards the Irish hills of Wicklow in the West, the heartland of Wales in the South and towards the hated England in the East, the views in the clear air were magnificent. They could see the harbour town in the distance.

After a couple of minutes standing still the wind started to bite through their layers. Even in the calmest of days, the wind swirled on the summit and today it was biting cold. They stepped back down the mountain to try to find some shelter.

It was too early in the year for the Hafod Eyrie, the summit café. It opened when the snows had finished and the railway could reach the top every day bringing staff and supplies. The top of the mountain was too exposed to stand still and fellow walkers had taken any available spots so they agreed to walk a bit further back down to have their lunch. They had discussed this on the way up and were returning down the track to Rhydd Ddu village. They would then walk along the road back to her car.

They set off on the western path back down to the distant valley floor. They went down a few hundred feet and went off the path to stop for lunch and huddled behind a rocky outcrop in a natural shelter. They could see back up to the building at the summit café and could see how well it blended in with the granite of the mountain.

They took their gloves off to eat and burrowed in their rucksacks for their lunch. He had doorstep bread sandwiches of ham and cheese and she had a Tupperware bowl of pasta salad. They shared the coffee from his flask. Even down from the summit the views were awe inspiring and uplifting. They tidied the remnants of their picnic back into their rucksacks.

They had flirted on and off all morning and she had wiggled the admirable shape of her backside before him. He looked at her pretty face; her cheeks reddened by the cold were the only piece of flesh showing out of the layers of warm clothing. She had taken off her sunglasses while they were eating and her green eyes flashed at him, daring him on. Their heads were close together and she smiled at him.

Behind a rock, near the top of Wales's highest and most mystical mountain, he leant in and kissed her for the first time. Her lips were warm, soft and tasted of coffee. The tip of her tongue brushed his teeth; their shared breath was warm inside their mouths. He put his arm round her and felt her slender body beneath the layers of jacket and clothing.

They broke for air. He watched as she blinked in the light of the pale sun and the blue sky. As she opened her eyes, they creased in the cold then opened again as her face lit up in a cheeky grin.

She went forward for a repeat of the kiss, a shorter one this time.

"Come on lets get back down to the car."

19.

The walk back down to the valley was uneventful. Annette kept looking back at Dan as they traversed down the easy path. When they reached the bottom of the track at the small village of Rhydd Ddu, they navigated the gates to cross the train tracks of the Welsh Highland steam railway line that in the summer operated along the valley floor back to Caernarfon. Then they hit the road and started out the last horizontal trek back to the car.

After a couple of hundred yards there was a pub, the Cwellyn Arms and they walked past it for a further mile to the Snowdon Ranger. The afternoon light was darkening to dusk when they reached the car and they took off their outer gear and put it in the boot with their rucksacks. She

took off her winter boots and put on a pair of trek-
king shoes.

Dan had a spare sweatshirt in his rucksack and
he took off his damp base layers, briefly showing
Annette his bare torso before covering it again. He
put his orange fleece back on over the dry sweatshirt. He hoped the fresh air had expunged the
fishy smell.

"Lets warm up shall we?" she said. "That pub
looked nice. I bet it had a log fire."

They drove back to the pub, the cold car windows steaming up from the heat of their bodies.

There was indeed a blazing log fire and with
the Sunday lunch trade over there were just a couple of tables taken. They picked a corner cranny out
of the way. Their faces were pink from the fresh
mountain air and the heat inside the pub made
their cheeks burn.

"What would you like?" asked Dan.

"Lots of things,." she looked straight back at
him. "But I can't have everything I want so will
have to settle for a hot chocolate."

"Er, Ok."

Dan went to the bar and chose a pint of Rampart cask ale from the local Conwy brewery. The girl behind the bar was in her thirties and smiled at Dan. The pint of beer was easy, the hot chocolate was trickier and he had to negotiate the choice of plain or fancy. He opted for the fancy one with cream and marshmallows and the barmaid said she would bring it over to their table. The beer was dark and frothy and he sat down and let the pint clear before he took his first sip. It was a hundred times better than the shandy in the plastic glass that he had been given in the chain pub just the night before. He took a big gulp before placing the glass back down on the table.

Annette watched him. "My Dad used to drink his first beer like that at the rugby club. He would buy me a pack of crisps and a bottle of coke with a straw."

The hot chocolate arrived. Annette thanked the barmaid in Welsh, and they had a brief conversation. Dan felt he was involved as both the barmaid and Annette were looking at him although he did not understand much of it. Annette stroked her finger across his face and the barmaid said something else and left them alone.

"What was that about?" Dan asked.

"I said that it was lovely and warm in here and

she said I was lucky to have such a good looking man to keep me warm."

"I thought she was saying be nice to your father. How did she know I didn't speak Welsh?"

"You are not that old. You ordered the drinks in English. I will have to teach you some Welsh."

"I did hear that the best way to learn a language is from pillow talk."

Annette's green eyes stared into his. "Well I will have to have you fluent within weeks."

"I never was much good at schooling, it might take months?"

"I'm a good teacher."

"Yes Miss Davies."

He looked around, they were a long way from home and there was nobody to overhear them. She sipped at the piled cream of her fancy hot chocolate. The cream stuck to her top lip and he moved closer to her and wiped it off with his thumb. They were close but he didn't lean in to kiss her. He looked into her green eyes.

"What can I offer you Annette? What do you

want from me?"

"I want a man not a boy, somebody to look after me, to protect me, to have fun with, to make me feel like I am grown up a woman."

"I have seen a lot in my life, a lot of very bad things. I struggle with what I have had to do. I've missed out on a normal life. I've never had time for a family life, no wife or kids and that time has passed me by."

"Did you ever want a family?"

"I thought I did once, but then I went to Operation Desert Storm, when Saddam Hussein invaded Kuwait and I went from one war zone to the next. It was a buzz, an adventure. I was good at it."

"Did you kill anybody?"

"Yes I did."

"Did you have friends killed?"

"Yes I did."

"Why did you leave?"

He thought back to that patrol in Afghanistan and recalled the blast. He tensed up and she put her hand on his. He took a deep intake of breath and carried on.

"I was blown up. We were on patrol from a river base and there had been intelligence of insurgents. The intelligence was false and we were hit with a roadside IED, a homemade bomb. It killed one of my men and injured two more. The marine who died, his body took the blast and although I was injured, I survived."

"Were you badly hurt?"

"The blast broke my leg and shattered the bone. At one stage, they thought I would lose the leg but they pinned it and I have been lucky. I can walk fine."

"I have seen you grimace at times like you were in pain. Does it still hurt?"

"Yes it hurts but it reminds me I am still alive. Unlike the poor lad, whose body took the blast."

They both took a breather from the intensity of the conversation and took a sip of their drinks. Another couple had come in and sat over the other side of the bar room. They smiled over. They were walkers too. Their cheeks flushed red from the cold wind and fussing about taking off their outdoor coverings. Annette smiled back, sharing the fellowship of the beautiful day. Dan was lost in his memories and she gave him time to collect his thoughts.

"I'm going to order us a roast pork dinner is that ok?"

He nodded.

She went over to the barmaid and placed the order for food. She also ordered two pints of lime and sodas. At the bar she checked her phone. There were three missed calls and a text message from Daffydd saying, 'Where are you?' In this valley between high mountains, she was glad that there was no signal. She had heard the phone ring muffled deep in her jacket pocket at the top of the mountain. With a sense of finality, she had pulled it out, only to switch it to silent so that her day would not be disturbed.

She paid for the meals at the bar and went back to their table with the bubbling green pints of lime and soda. Dan had snapped out of his reverie and was sitting up straight. He smiled at her as she came back and half raised himself up in a gentlemanly gesture to pull his wallet out to pay for the food.

"No, it's my treat."

"Why?"

"Because you offered to pay?"

Before she sat down. She bent over and kissed his cheek and her hand went behind his neck. She released him and sat down next to him. Their knees and thighs were touching.

"Erm ok thanks, sweetheart."

"I prefer Cariad. I am Welsh you know."

"I have noticed and we are in God's own country. Cymru am byth."

"That's a good start to the lessons Dan bach. But we haven't finished with you yet." There was a pause. "When the bomb blast hit and your comrade was killed." She took a breath. "Did you blame yourself?"

"Yes."

"Why?"

"Because he was only 19. He was my responsibility."

"Did anybody else blame you? Was there an official report?"

"Nobody said they blamed me. The report came back that we had been misled about the information that had been received and had walked into a trap."

"So you couldn't have prevented his death?"

"Only if it had been me that had died in his place?"

"But it wasn't was it? . You survived."

"Yes. I did."

"So don't you owe it to your comrade who died to live your life to the full?"

"Yes, I suppose I do."

"That's good then. Let's give it a shot," said Annette, squeezing his hand.

Two steaming plates arrived. It was a full roast dinner - a big plate of pork, with roast and mashed potatoes, carrots, cabbage and broccoli, finished off with pieces of crispy crackling that were melting under the all-covering gravy. After the exercise of the day and the mental stress of this confession they both ate with gusto and sat back to let the food digest. Some local residents had come into the bar now and the noise from their banter was swirling round the room.

A big red-faced farmer was holding court in Welsh. Annette translated for Dan. "One of his sheep was knocked over by a tourist and he has just had the insurance money through. It was twice what the sheep was worth so he is happy."

Dan stretched and put his arm around Annette's shoulders. It felt natural and she snuggled in to his strong chest.

"Dan, thank you for telling me, you didn't have to be so open."

"I wanted to be open with you. It feels important that I should be. Plus I like talking to you. You are a good listener."

"It was part of my university course."

"You seemed to understand not to push that I wanted to talk."

"My father died of cancer when I was young. I learned to cope without him and asked myself lots of questions"

"I'm sorry to hear that."

"He had been very ill and when he died he was at peace. It took me a long time to realise that."

Dan squeezed her shoulders and kept quiet. They sat together for a while longer. Their plates were collected and they finished their drinks.

"Dan, as I said earlier it's over between Daffydd and me but I am going to need some time to sort myself out. I would like to explore starting a relationship with you. Can you wait until I am ready?"

Dan stroked her hair. "I am a very patient man. Let me know when you want me?"

They stood up to leave and put their fleeces back on before heading out into the cold and dark. The car was parked round the back of the pub and she clicked the locks with the key before they reached it. She turned round and put her arms around him and they kissed.

"It won't be long and I assure you it will be worth the wait."

"I am sure it will be," Dan replied.

20.

They were asked to work again the next Saturday at the big pub. They didn't have to start until 8 and this week Frank had asked both of them to follow on at the nightclub. They arranged to meet earlier and Annette sat in the passenger seat of Dan's car in the same car park they had been in the week before. It was a stormy night, the rain lashed against the windows. It was dark inside the car.

They gave each other a kiss on the lips. The touch was brief and fleeting with the promise of more.

"I'm not sure Frank would approve?" said Annette as she put her hand on Dan's knee.

"How's it going?" he asked.

"I've missed you. I want more of the kisses."

"I'm here when you want me."

"I know. Thanks for being understanding. I've had a serious talk with Daffydd. I've told him that I've had enough of his malu-cachu."

"I know that one, Bullshit, right. My mate Gwilym says that all the time. Says it and speaks it."

"Yes that's nearly right. We will be having you fluent in no time."

"How did it go?"

"Daffydd thinks this is just a blip. I've given him ultimatums before but things have calmed down."

"Are you sure that's what you want?"

"Yes it is. It has been broken for some time. My friend Carys has had a second baby. I'm not in a rush for one but even in five years I can't see myself bringing a child into a house where I'm the only responsible adult. After the row over the surfboard fin I stopped having sex with him. If we don't have the sexual part then we don't have much else. If he doesn't receive gratification from me then it won't be long before he finds it elsewhere. He holds himself up as a surf dude guru on the winds and best places to launch from. There are plenty of young willing surf dudettes around and he has enough admirers. It's only recently that I feel threatened by his access to these young female surfers. Looking back I should have been more worried there are times when he didn't come home and said he had crashed at a mate's house. He's had plenty of opportunity."

"It sounds sad hearing you talk about breaking up. You can't regret it if you are doing it to be with me."

"I'm not on the rebound Dan. I've done my grieving for the relationship. I'm ok? Should I ask what you look like in a wetsuit? I've never asked. Have you ever surfed?"

"Me, yes I've surfed in the Pacific Ocean. Hawaii and Bondi Beach?"

"Really! That's impressive."

"Yes it was. In the Royal Marines, attached to the Royal Navy, we did some joint exercises in the Pacific with the Americans and then with the Australians. We had plenty of shore leave and three of us went surfing. My core stability and balance was better then, not sure what I would be like now.

"Any other special talents?"

"Not sure I am allowed to tell you. Official secrets and all that. I'm a qualified bomb disposal diver and I'm not a bad canoeist. Have you ever heard of the Cockleshell Heroes? We used to do a kayak trip every year in their honour.

"Wow and there was me just thinking you were a fisherman who did a bit of bouncing, I mean Door Supervision." she corrected herself.

"What about your special talents Annette? I know about the karate."

"You will have to wait to find those out." She leaned towards him and positioned her mouth to inches away from his. She darted in putting her lips on his and moved away quickly. "Please keep waiting," she whispered before kissing him again, longer this time.

They left the warmth of the car and the steamed up windows and headed to work. They separated a couple of steps apart as they turned the corner onto the high street and their approach was watched by Alan and Robbie. Dan licked his lips to remove the slight taste of lipstick.

"Haia bois. Sut mae?" said Annette

"Wet and cold. It's quiet so far but will get busy soon enough," said Alan. Go and sign in the book and I will rustle up some coffees."

"That will be great."

The night went on smoothly. The Saturday night party crowd came in. Again the girls were in various states of undress.

"Aren't they cold?" asked Annette to Dan when their rotation on the door coincided.

There was a queue formed along the side of the pub and Alan called Annette to check Identification documents.

"Your eyes are better than mine and I'm not going to wear my reading glasses anywhere near this lot." Alan told her.

Dan stood slightly back from the queue on the road. The rain had slowed to a drizzle but it was still dropping onto the shoulders of his coat. He watched as newcomers joined the back of the line. Two lads tried to push through to the front. Dan spotted them, stepped in and tapped Alan's shoulder.

Alan refused them entry and they became bolshy. "Why not? We're not drunk?"

"Come on lads. Not tonight."

When they realised the refusal was permanent they upped the ante.

"Fuck you fat bastard. Yeah fuck you. Fat bald wanker"

Annette stepped in front to switch their attention from Alan and spoke to them.

"Come on lads, not tonight. Make way for the others to come in."

Faced with a female, they lowered their aggression. As they walked away past Dan, who had been ready to step in, one of them raised his voice. "Fucking Lesbian," then they staggered off.

Annette looked round and caught Dan's eye. He winked and gave a nod. She winked in reply and turned back to ask the next punters for their ID.

At the end of the shift there were some refusals for being drunk, one fake id and two minor fights to put in the incident book.

"We don't need to ID all the customers but we do it to show our presence and that we are on the ball," Robbie explained to Annette.

Alan carried it on. "If they are going to be arsey with us for asking for ID they will be worse with punters inside. Then we can always think of a reason to refuse them. Sometimes you tweak them a little bit and if they react you keep them out. If they take it in good spirits then you let them in.

They said goodnight to the Bar staff. Tom the manager came with them to lock them out.

"You coming to the club later Tom?" asked Alan.

"Yes won't be long. I'm bringing the two new barmaids with me for a bit of an initiation session. You never know my luck?"

"Ok see you later."

They walked four abreast down the street towards the club and Robbie told Annette and Dan about their arrangement that Tom and his staff came in to the club for free after they were finished.

"Tom's a decent bloke. It's a lonely life, moving from one town to the next. He chats to us because he doesn't trust his assistants and they slag him off to us. He's not supposed to fraternise with his staff but he spends so much time there how else is he going to make friends?"

"It's a strange life this bar game," said Dan. "When I did it before I lost six months of my life very easily, it really drags you into it. Then spits you out."

Annette noted that his comment was bitter, she recognised that he had hidden depths and she wanted to ask him more questions and open him up.

They turned a corner and the nightclub was in front of them. The door was on the corner of the building and the sign above said 'Roxy' in big blue neon letters with a pink surround. Frank was on the door and a short queue of stragglers lined up outside behind a fence of waist high metal barriers slotted together. Another large doorman was checking IDs. The crashing beat of dance music could be heard inside, muffled by the building, then amplified and reduced every time an internal door opened and closed.

"Great, reinforcements," said Frank. "Its busy in there so if you can all take off your coats, sign the book and pick up your radios. Then Alan take the dancefloor and Robbie stay on the door so I can show Dan and Annette around.

"This is Carl," Frank indicated the other doorman on the steps. "Annette your boyfriend is in
there. Came in an hour ago asking for you and
wanted to be passed through for free."

"Oh shit. Is he pissed?"

"He was vertical. Moaned when I made him
pay. I don't mind letting him in for free but let me
know first."

Annette looked at Dan and pulled a face, "sorry
Frank. It's a bit difficult with him at the moment."

Frank assessed Annette's face. "No worries.
Any problems with him let me know."

Frank took them in to the foyer of the nightclub. They passed the ticket booth next to the door
and on the other side of the foyer a cloakroom with
a girl attendant taking coats. Another Doorman was
on duty inside searching the customers when they
had paid the entry fee.

"This is Kev, This is Dan and Annette" Frank
pointed to each of them and they gave the raised
hand, nod and smile that says 'hello' when you
can't speak or hear properly.

Frank led them through the double fire doors and they were hit by a wall of noise and flashing lights. The floor beneath them reverberated with the music. To the right was the main bar with a low ceiling and to the left where the roof opened up there were seats and a walkway separated from the lowered dancefloor by a wall with gaps for steps at compass points around the circle. Above the dancefloor was a complicated structure of lights and lasers. The dancefloor itself was a mass of humanity. Writhing bodies with arms raised, shaking hips and shoulders to the beats of the music. In the far northwest corner of the dancefloor was the DJ box. Dan could see the white shirts and black ties of four of Frank's men stationed around the floor. Frank pointed them out and took Dan and Annette to the far side of the bar where the toilets were situated and through a door to an open roofed back yard full of smokers. One white shirt and black tie was watching over them.

"That's Jason," leading to more raised hands.

"There's your fella, Annette," said Frank. A tall slim guy with dirty blonde curly hair in a surf brand T-shirt with a beaded necklace was smoking a cigarette by the back wall of the yard. He was in a group of younger kids and was looking down the low cut top of a blonde girl.

Dan saw that Annette ducked her head. Frank

noticed it too and took them back out into the main bar and walked round the outside of the dancefloor to the DJ box. He counted off the four fire exits on the external walls.

"A strobe light will go off if they are opened and the alarm goes off in the ticket booth so we will call the number on the radio. Annette, you stay here in the DJ box, with DJ Chris. You have the best view from here. Dan you keep with me on the door.

Through the next two hours calls came through Dan's radio earpiece. 'Dancefloor', 'Main Bar', Check Exit 3', 'Gents Toilet', 'Frank to the Front Door, No Rush, No Rush'.

He helped with evictions for drug use in the toilet and a fight on the dancefloor. Frank used him and Robbie as a heavy duty troubleshooting tag team, keeping them on the front door and sending them into the club when needed.

On return from one kick out he said to Frank, "The jobs not changed that much since I did it last."

Frank replied, "No just the kids keep getting younger."

At 3am with a build up of various calls from the

DJ for 'last orders at the bar' and 'come again next week' the music was switched off. The attrition of alcohol and tiredness had already thinned out the numbers and the last dancers standing headed for the street with some gentle cajoling from the door team who ushered them towards the door. Dan had been sent inside to check that the music was switched off and the inside team were coping without any hassles.

Annette was playing her part in herding the dancers into the foyer and she gave him a thumbs up and flashed him a smile. He went outside and picking his reefer jacket from its hook in the now empty ticket booth joined Frank on the steps. Robbie and Carl were across the street. The drizzle was making the clubbers moan as they stepped into the cold wet night.

"Its good when it rains," said Frank, "makes them leave quicker."

"Suits me fine I'm knackered."

"Your mate Steve Drwg's over there, in that car" Frank pointed along the road at the metallic blue hot hatch car that Dan recognised from the run-in on Christmas Eve. "They park over there and think we don't know they are dealing drugs"

Dan indicated the parked police car on the opposite corner. "Don't they do anything?"

"Not much they can do. There is never enough in the car to say anything found is not for personal use. If they try to deal on the street then the police pull them up. It's all done by phone now. Look."

One of the occupants of the car stepped out and pulled his hood tight around his head. He swaggered up a side street and came back a couple of minutes later. He sat inside the car again before the driver revved up his engine and ragged up the street. The silver exhaust pipes emitting an aggressive snarl.

"They've sold the drugs and are daring the police to stop them. The cops know they are being wound up so don't react."

"Does Steve come into the club?"

"He's not been put on Pubwatch so depends what mood he's in. Tonight he's being a chavvy drug dealer trying to intimidate us, next week he could come in all friendly dressed up in sharp clothes playing the big 'I am' with the ladies. Depends what mood I'm in whether I let him in or not. He never quite crosses the line in here. Knows there's nowhere else to go."

The crowd was drifting away down the street

and Frank sent Dan back to check inside.

The lights were up. At the main bar Annette was remonstrating with Daffydd who was the last remaining customer. They were speaking in Welsh and Alan was watching.

"They are having a domestic. He's being a prick but I'm not sure whether to step in. It's her boyfriend. What do you think Dan?"

"Its ok, I'll deal with it."

Annette was tall but Daffydd was three or four inches taller than her and was starting to wave his arms to gesticulate whatever point he was making. They were by the wall close to the foyer door and Annette was trying to edge him out.

"You ok Annette?" He could see she was embarrassed.

Daffydd turned his attention to Dan "Siarad Cymraeg, Speak Welsh or don't speak at all."

Dan didn't bite. "The club is closed. The lady is asking you to leave."

"What lady?" Dan still didn't bite.

"Daffydd!" Annette pleaded and used open

hands to move him along.

Daffydd was refusing. His hands were raised in frustration at Annette's shoulder level.

"Come on mate its time to go."

"Sais Gont!" Daffydd spat the insult at Dan. Pulling himself taller above Dan. The vein in his neck was pulsing and his face was reddening.

"Daffydd Cae dy geg. Stop it, shut up."

Dan saw Daffydd twitch his right hand towards Annette and he stepped in.

He grabbed the wrist with his left hand and twisted it behind Annette's boyfriend's back spinning him around. With his right hand up in the back of the neck, Dan propelled the boyfriend's face against the wall. With his boots he kicked Daffydd's feet apart so that there was stability and he wasn't going to fall over. Daffydd's face was pinned and his left cheek was squashed against the painted plaster.

"Now calm down and don't disrespect the lady."

Daffydd struggled and Dan responded by putting his hand in the lanky hair, pulling the head back and giving the forehead a sharp tap against the wall. He pulled the right ear towards his mouth. The lips left a trail of spittle on the wall.

"Move again and I will take you down to the floor. DO YOU UNDERSTAND ME?" He said it slowly and clearly into Daffydd's ear.

"Yes I'm sorry."

"Don't be sorry to me. Be sorry to the lady." Dan tightened his grip on the back of the head to accentuate his point.

"I'm going to let you go now. Try anything and I will put you down. DO YOU UNDERSTAND ME?"

"Yes."

Dan slowly released Daffydd and allowed him to stand away from the wall.

"Now wait outside. Alan, will you take this guy out please?"

Alan stepped in and with her boyfriend removed he wiped the sweat from the hair on his trousers and turned to Annette.

"I'm sorry Dan. I've had a great night its so

much fun in here. Then Daffydd goes and spoils it. He's drunk he won't remember in the morning."

"I don't give a shit about him. Are you ok?"

"Yes. Thanks."

"How are you going to get him home?"

"I'll get him to the car. He will be ok now."

"Maybe. We are parked in the same place. You walk with him and I will follow behind you both. We will speak soon."

"Ok, thanks," she looked around. Three of the doormen were sitting down at a table waiting for the end of the night drink. She lowered her voice "I want to kiss you good night but I won't"

"Give me a hug. A cwtch will be just like with one of the lads."

As he held her tight, she raised her head to his shoulder and whispered, "Soon".

They broke apart and he followed her to the door. She said goodnight to Frank who was still on the steps and spied out Daffydd who was standing with his shoulders hunched, hands in his pockets and his chin on his chest.

She took a deep breath. "Daffydd dos adra."

Frank and Dan watched her telling him off. Then she stormed back up the steps.

"He's forgotten his coat, Ffwl!" She came out again a couple of minutes later. Clutching a grey surfing fleece with leather collars and cuffs.

She raised it in a fist and shook it at Frank and Dan. "That's the last present I ever buy him. Ffwl!"

They watched her departing backside as she gathered Daffydd up in her wake.

"Fiery temper that one," said Frank. "I hope you know what you are doing boi?

Dan unclipped his tie, undid the top button of his shirt and pulled the badge from his arm.

"Haven't a clue Frank. But I think I'm going to enjoy the ride. I'll follow them to check she's ok. Nos da."

"Thanks for tonight, you did well. You've still got the eye for it. See you on Monday in the gym. Nos da Dan, Dos adran saf. Safe home mate."

Dan followed Annette and Daffydd up the opposite side of the empty high street keeping a streetlight pole's length back from them. The kebab shop was closed and the paper takeaway wrappers were flattening to the pavement in the rain. A drunken couple meandered past. He walked on staying close to the boarded up windows and weathered 'for sale' signs sticking out above the shops. Annette looked back a couple of times and he saw her thumbs up signal.

They walked past the closed up chain pub, the coloured lights of the bar pumps reflecting off the back bar mirrors and soon after he saw Annette turn the corner to the car park.

He stopped just before he stepped into the road. A horn blasted behind him and a metallic blue car shot past him. The brakes slammed on and it stopped still in the road thirty yards ahead of him. The red brake lights blazing the occupants' hostility at him. The exhausts breathed smoke as the engine was revved.

Dan stood still on the pavement. He had a half axe handle in the driver's door pocket of his car, which was still a minute sprint away.

The engine revved again the horn blared and the driver tried unsuccessfully to burn rubber as the car sped off up the wet street. Dan relaxed and got to his car. Annette was pulling away and she raised a hand to wave at him as she went past.

Careful of any following headlights he headed out of the car park and along the coast road. Half-way home his phone beeped and vibrated in his trouser pocket to herald a text.

He waited to pull up outside his cottage before fiddling with the buttons and opening the message.

"Thanks again. Please wait for me. A xxx."

21.

On a Wednesday a couple of weeks later Dan was working at a music night in a rural pub with Big Robbie.

Robbie told him why they were needed. "In the summer, this pub holds a sheep shearing competition. A couple of years ago, all hell had let loose with undesirables from another village coming to cause trouble. Three ambulances were called and all the police cars from within thirty-miles turned up. The local Police Inspector was not impressed and a clause has been written into the Premises License saying that at least two Security staff must be employed for any advertised event. I came with Alan and Carl last year and there was no trouble. The fight was over which farm had won the prize bull at the County's Agricultural show."

"I don't doubt it," said Dan, "Life is like that in the country."

They had an easy night with niggles but no major issues. The most excitement was when a big red-faced joscyn farmer with hair coming out of his ears took exception to a young lad who despite the cold was trying to show off his muscles in a tight T-Shirt. The farmer was used to picking up a sheep under each arm and had a faint whiff of the farmyard about him. It was that type of pub.

The youngster was standing at the bar and had elbowed the farmer out of the way. The farmer looked him up and down and Dan and Robbie who had clocked the lad's bad attitude stepped in to cool him off.

"Look at you boi. On steroids, are you? Look at your tits. Pumped up full of water. Just like a chicken!" The other farmers around the bar burst out laughing. "Have you got a limp dick from the steroids as well have you boi" and the farmer flapped his little finger at him.

The lad was not impressed and squared his shoulders but with the doormen standing in between, he did not pursue the argument and left soon afterwards.

The farmer was pleased with his victory and later came over to Dan and Robbie on the door.

"Pumped up full of water he was. Not like us boys. We are natural," he said as he patted his ample belly and then clapped Robbie and Dan on the back. We'd make a good front row wouldn't we boys."

It was a local band playing in Welsh and the music was good and loud. Dan enjoyed himself. There were no threats, he was getting paid and listening to music. It wasn't a bad way to spend the evening.

Halfway through the band's first session Annette turned up with a couple of her girlfriends. She introduced her two friends to Dan and Robbie as Carys and Diane and she gave both of her colleagues a kiss on the cheek. She also squeezed Dan's hand as she did so. Robbie gave her a big bear hug.

"We'll call you if there's any trouble should we Annette?"

"Not in these boots. Do you like them?" She lifted her leg for the boys to see. Her long legs were in tight black jeans and she wore calf hugging high leg black boots nearly up to her knee, they had a 2-inch heel. She wore a red collarless blouse with the top buttons undone under a navy blazer jacket. She had blow-dried a curl into her dark hair, that tonight she wore down at her shoulders. She had even applied lipstick.

"I've never seen your hair down before it suits you."

"Thanks Dan."

She gave him a glowing flash of her white teeth and pushed through the thronged noisy pub to order a bottle of white wine for herself and Dianne and a juice for Carys, the driver.

As the night wore on and Annette's friends chatted about their own lives, she stole glances over at Dan. Diane, Annette's friend, was eyeing up the men in the pub and her eyes also fell on Dan, broad shouldered in his reefer jacket and smart with his white shirt and black tie underneath.

"Do you really work with him?" she asked Annette

"Yes, I taught him actually," she hesitated. "Well he came on my course."

"He is a bit of alright isn't he? Moody and Dangerous. Just my type."

"Keep away from him Diane," Annette snapped rather too sharply. Her friends both looked at her with interest.

"I've seen him before somewhere," joined in Carys. "I know! I saw him on the playback of the CCTV at the seafood factory. He had an argument with that Steve Drwg. Stephen Williams."

"Did he? What happened?"

"He must work as a fisherman with Gwilym Jones and they ran into the crew of the Mary Ann. John's son, Steve had been drinking and picked an argument with Gwilym. That guy there was in the Landrover and came out and Steve Drwg pulled a knife on him."

"That's terrible. What happened then?"

"Well that guy clobbered him with a boat hook. Left him on the floor in pain. Served him right pulling a knife like that. He's a nasty shit that Steve Drwg. Remember what he did to that girl outside the Bay View Hotel and she had to leave the town with her family? Didn't you go out with his cousin Phil at school Annette?"

"Yes I did. He was a shit too. Were the police called?" asked Annette.

"No it was on the CCTV and we all saw it in the office but the police weren't involved. I'm sure it was that guy. I thought he was good looking on the video. Better in real life. Hey Diane?" Carys winked at Diane.

"Iawn, Iawn, OK, OK. I do like him. But nothing has happened and won't until I am finished properly with Daffydd."

"He is not your usual type," Carys teased Annette.

"What grown up and independent you mean?" Diane joined in the slagging. .

"Ha, Ha, Ha. Very good. Thank you for your support of poor Daffydd who's been my boyfriend for five years now."

"And is on the way out. About bloody time. Stuff Daffydd lets go back to the hunky bouncer. Does he Siarad Cymraeg?"

"Tipyn bach, A little bit. I am going to teach him."

"Pillow talk is the best way to learn a language," said Diane with a wink.

"So I have been told? How's your Italian holding up?" fired back Annette with a sweet smile.

"Will you two stop it, I'm a mother of two and happily married. I don't need to hear about whispering sweet nothings to strange men in bed."

"Don't come over all prudish on me. What about that Spanish DJ in Tenerife?" put in Diane.

"I don't remember that." Said Carys in a huff.

"We do. Don't we Annette?"

"Don't bring me into this," Annette changed tack, pulling a 'don't go there' face at Diane. "Now how long have you left of maternity leave Carys?"

The band started again and the music banged away with a second playing of Queen's 'We are the Champions, my friends' in honour of the Welsh team's Grand Slam win, joined in by the whole pub and the girls too.

They had to stand up to see the band through the crowd. The band finished with a pumped up version of the traditional rugby standard *Sospan Fach* about "Dai Bach the Soldier" which finishes with a rousing chorus of 'who beat the English? Little Sospan Fach', to the great acclaim of the audience.

They then did an encore of a verse of "We are the Champions before packing up their instruments into the van and having a few drinks with their fans.

Carys made moves to leave, picking up her handbag and rattling her car keys.

Annette hesitated, "Er, I won't come back with you. One of the lads will give me a lift back to town when they've finished."

"Are you sure? As long as you have somebody to look after you?" said Carys.

"Yes, the very best."

While Diane finished her glass of wine, Carys went to the toilet.

"Are you sure you don't want me to stay behind with you?" asked Diane, with her tongue visibly stuffed in her cheek.

"You're a bitch Diane," replied Annette, "Don't let on to Carys. You know how disapproving she is these days."

"Yeah I won't tell her that Doctor Mike might come round quickly at midnight either will I."

"Oh Diane I thought you had given up on him?"

"Yeah well he's told his wife that he is doing a double shift so is staying over at the hospital so we have a few hours together."

"Oh Diane, Cariad, you can do so much better."

Carys was waiting for them at the door and checked that either Dan or Robbie would take Annette home.

"I'm sure we can get her back to the town ok," said Dan who had already planned the diversion with Annette earlier in the day.

The girls gave him withering looks trying to see into his soul, as good friends do when they care about the heart of one of their own. Dan survived their scrutiny. Diane gave him a kiss on the cheek to welcome him into their circle.

Dianne said something in Welsh to Annette as she skipped out of the door. .

Robbie, Dan and Annette stood outside the pub as Carys drove past and beeped her horn. It was a windy night. Tall dark trees edged the car park and the narrow road. Their empty branches shook high above. They went back inside.

The pub cleared out. Annette knew a couple of the other customers and was careful not to be too close to Dan in case somebody else knew her, as they were likely to in this district. She had already seen some of Daffydd's friends but they had left when the band finished. Dan went for a walk round the pub.

"Are you sure I can't give you a lift home I live closer to you than Dan does?" said Robbie.

"No thanks Robbie. Dan offered first."

"I'm sure he did. Nice boots by the way, you going to wear them on your next shift?"

Annette pulled tongues at him and they laughed.

"My wife likes to hear about my shifts at work and I've told her about Dan. She's tied to the cooker and washing machine looking after the kids and she likes me to tell her what's going on. I've told her that Alan and I like working with Dan. You know your back is covered and he takes no prisoners when it came to a ruck. He is proper Old School but with a badge. He has a quiet way with him and has nothing to prove to the youngsters who try it on. He has a calming influence. Frank Delaney is the same. They have both seen it all and have little to prove, especially around this part of the world. You can tell. Some guys you work with it's a busy shift and with others like Dan it is calm and there are fewer incidents."

"Yes he is good isn't he? I like him a lot."

Dan returned from his scout around and the landlady came over.

"Thanks for that lads. There was no trouble again. You can go now. There are just a few locals in and I can deal with them. Here's payment for Frank, can you give it to him" She passed a sealed white envelope with the payment inside to Dan to pass on.

She closed the door behind them and the regulars settled down for a lock in.

22.

obbie drove off and waved to Annette and Dan as they sat together in his Ford Mondeo. There were still some cars in the pub car park and there would be no privacy if any of the drinkers chose to drive home.

"Where would you like to go?" Dan asked

"Not home. Not yet."

"You could come to mine?"

"I would love to but I am sorry I can't. I will soon."

"That's fine, there is no rush."

"There is. I want to be with you."

"Sounds good."

"It will be, believe me. I have some holiday coming at Easter we can be together by then."

"I can wait."

She had her hand on his leg and he had his hand on her thigh. His touch was burning her through the tight denim. She wanted him now in the car. She ached for him. She felt like a teenager on a naughty date. She pushed the cares of adult life, a mortgage, a successful career and a live-in boyfriend out of her mind.

"Lets drive. I know somewhere to go," she said.

"Tell me where?"

"About a mile away. It's at the start of a footpath I know."

Five minutes later after following her directions Dan rolled his car to a stop on a piece of bare gravel behind a hedge. The gravel was a half-hearted attempt to protect cars from jolting too much on the rough ground of the parking area. He switched off the engine and then the lights. They were in darkness and as his eyes adjusted to the dim starlight outside he could make out the slope of a hill ahead of him. He part rolled down the window and the cold wind blew in through the gap.

"Where are we?"

"There is a hill fort up there. In daylight from the top there are great views, you can see the Harbour and Snowdon."

"Do you come here often?"

"Ha, Ha. Not usually at night?"

"You suggested this place pretty quickly?"

"I had been thinking that if I struck lucky I might bring you here."

"Well here I am? Do you want to walk to the top?"

"Yes. Here we are. Not in these boots! Lets stay in the car."

They kissed hard. There was a sour taste of white wine and the smell of her perfume as Dan's mouth touched Annette's soft lips. Again, it was a good kiss.

"Your cheek is smooth today, no bristles, have you shaved just for me?"

"I even bought new razor blades. One of a man's little luxuries is putting in a new razor blade. Its so sharp I nicked myself."

"Where?"

Dan held her hand in the dark and lifted it to the point on his neck. Annette pushed herself out of her seat and placed her lips on the minute cut.
"Is that making it better?"

"Hmm. It is" He enjoyed her lips on his neck before he moved his own lips to catch hers.

Annette settled back into her seat, which drew Dan to follow her over to lean above her and his hip pushed off the steering wheel.

They were still kissing when Dan moved his right hand inside her jacket and squeezed the soft fabric of her blouse. Annette's left breast was small but firm. He readjusted his hand and slipped it between the buttons, popping one open as his thumb rubbed the bare top of the flesh above the cup of her bra. His hand squeezed over this next layer and Annette moaned gently. It was a half-cup designed to make the best of her meagre assets and push the breasts together. The bra was in a satin material and felt silky under his touch. He again pulled his hand out and this time found his way inside the cup of the bra, there was space for his fingers and those fingers, made rough by the season's fishing, touched her nipple. It was small, hard and round like a pea. The coarseness of his hand made the effect more dramatic and Annette stopped kissing him and laid her head back against the headrest to enjoy the sensation. He squeezed the nipple between his two fingers and cupped the breast.

"They are very small," said Annette

"But perfectly formed," replied Dan. "Wow!"

"Wow indeed! Give me another sws."

"Yes Miss."

He undid the buttons of her blouse and bent his head over to kiss the nipple that was still free popping out over the edge of the bra. Annette again leant her head back and enjoyed the sensation as he first took her hard nipple between his lips and then spread his mouth to cover and kiss the whole breast. Her breasts were small and sensitive. The sensitivity of the nerve endings over the smooth skin was making up for any deficiency in size. He took a breather and she felt for the seat adjustment knobs and twiddled them until the seat went backwards a few inches.

Dan's right hand went back to the skin. It wandered down from the breasts and over the soft skin of her stomach. Dan spread his palm and his fingers took in the flatness of her tummy and stopped at a pierced ring in her navel. He gave it a tweak of curiosity then carried on around to the far side round towards her back. He dragged his nails across her skin back over her belly and this sent even more shivers through Annette's body. He did this a few times and his little finger, the lowest, started to stray beneath the waistband of her tight jeans.

He fumbled with the button and zip. Annette put the seat back further and raised her hips off the seat to give him easier access. He waggled her jeans over her bum and down to her knees, where they caught against the top of her boots. There wasn't much leeway to move his fingers now and she spread her legs slightly. His wandering hand cupped over the outside of her panties. He could feel the lace patterns under his hand, a contrast against the smoothness of the skin on the inside of her thighs.

He was leaning far over now and his head rested on her chest, his leg was jammed between the car's hand break and the gear stick but he didn't care about the discomfort. He moved his hand around the outside of the lacy pants and then pushing out the elastic with his nail tips to gain access he gently pushed his fingers inside the panties down across the soft tangle of her pubic hair and to the warmth between her legs. She was wet and his fingers sought entry and rubbed on the outside of her soft lips. He started rubbing against her clitoris. Two of his roughened fingertips were rubbing around and massaging the nub of her. Every so often, he pushed the fingers downwards and into Annette's vagina. He kept up a steady rhythm building up the tension inside her body.

Many years before a lover had shown him how to maximise her pleasure and Dan concentrated on his repetitive actions, pleased with the response. He had a quick flash of recollection. It had been Kirsty who had shown him how to be gentle, yet still insistent, with the motion he used. The smell of cooked rice that pervaded through the walls of the Causeway Bay flat in Hong Kong came into his nostrils at the memory. Now was not the time to reminisce and he pushed the vision away to focus on Annette's body and to maximise the pleasure that his touch was giving her.

His head still rested on her chest and her fingers grasped the thick hair on the top of his head, her nails dug into his scalp, which he ignored. Her breathing was becoming shallower and she was letting out gasps. Dan knew to keep going and not to change his rhythm. The thrusts of his fingers were pushing deeper each time, hooking up inside her and she willed him on. She gave a long moan and a shudder and Dan plunged his two fingers deep inside Annette's body. He pushed upwards and squeezed his thumb on the outside. At the same time, he rubbed his fingers deep inside the front of her vagina. This had the desired effect and a couple of minutes later she had another orgasm, this time giving out a little scream as she tightened around his fingers.

"Enough please enough!"

Dan was happy with that result. He pulled his fingers out and unravelled himself from his contortions across the gear stick. Annette pulled his face back towards her to force him to kiss her. They kissed deeply and he fell back down into his seat.

"Wow!" said Annette sitting back exhausted.

"Wow indeed"

She stretched her arm over and rubbed his thigh before moving up to the bulge of his crotch. She was still nearly horizontal with the car seat pushed back and was bending her body upwards to be able to stretch over.

"I'm ok, thanks. Lets get you home, it is a school night after all."

She went to protest, wanting to please him too but he leaned back over and put his fingertips to her lips. She kissed them. She closed her mouth over his fingers and sucked. He made to pull them out and she held onto them biting with her teeth, her lips closed around the first knuckle and then sucking him in, the second. He pulled them out and she licked the ends with her tongue and then let go. He pressed them again to her lips and she let the friction roll her bottom lip out before kissing the tips a last time.

They readied to drive off. He adjusted himself into a more comfortable position and she pulled up her jeans, redid the buttons on her blouse and returned the seat to its upright position. The whole event had taken place in near darkness and when Dan switched the headlights back on they were both dazzled when the twin beams bounced off a couple of grazing sheep in the neighbouring field. They looked at each other and she giggled at their matching grins.

He drove her home to the town, following her directions. As per instruction, he dropped her at the end of her street. Stopped at the junction, he watched her walk to her front door, fiddle with her key, and then give him a brief wave before going in.

He drove home rather pleased with himself.

He was definitely not so old after all.

23.

The storm had blown itself out and the next afternoon was warm for the time of the year. Dan had the car windows open as he drove up to the Bay View Hotel and could see signs of renovation and refurbishment. There was scaffolding on the front of the building and there was a large skip full of building rubble and a broken toilet on the top. Dan waited a few minutes before Frank drove up in his black pick up truck and parked next to him. Together they went into the main entrance to the hotel and into the large reception hall. There was a smell of fresh paint and drying plaster and there were old tables and chairs stacked and ready to be thrown out. Even with the fresh paint, the hotel had a faded grandeur. The reception area still needed a lot of work but had potential to be special.

A girl in a black shirt came out from the bar off to one side.

"Hello, can I help you?"

"Yes Brendan O'Casey please, he's expecting us," announced Frank.

She went scurrying off.

Brendan O'Casey was a big man, blonde red hair, tall with a wide chest, somewhere around the mid 40s age wearing brown corduroy trousers and a check farmer's shirt. His big hand crushed Dan's as he shook it vigorously.

"Nice to meet you Dan. Frank's told me about you. Lets show you around."

He had an Irish country brogue and spoke fast. The man had a sparkle in his eye and was enthusiastic about his new venture.

The hotel was on the end of the promenade from the harbour and a little away from the main drag of the town with the club and the pubs. It stood alone on a hill in grounds with the large car park to one side and lawns, paths and bushes sloping down to the end of the promenade below.

The main bar led off the reception area through double doors and in daylight overlooked the harbour and out to sea. A lot of work had already been done and there was a new carpet through the bar, which led through to the restaurant. Despite the views and the size the hotel had few guests staying and had survived on providing accommodation for visiting contractors, who worked at the few industrial factories and on the offshore wind farm.

Brendan had grand plans and waved his arms expansively.

"Some of the new leather furniture is going in the reception area and I'm going to have clusters of tables with tub chairs and sofas. Then square and round tables and new high back chairs in the restaurant. I really want to take advantage of the views. Can you imagine yourself here looking out at the harbour and having your gin and tonic?"

"When will you be ready?" asked Dan.

"I've told the workmen I'm opening in two weeks for the May Bank Holiday so we catch the full summer season. If I see them taking too many fag breaks I keep telling them to get a move on."

"What brought you here?

"My Granny had a pub in the town I grew up

in, so it's in my blood," Brendan replied. "I went off and made some money and thought I would like to have a different life and would buy a hotel."

"But why this one? Did you know the area?"

"Sure its mad but I saw it on the Internet and thought it had potential and six months later here I am," he said it with a twinkle in his eye.

"Good luck to you. I hope it works out for you."

"Sure, with you and Frank looking after me why wouldn't it."

Brendan led them through to the kitchens where new equipment had already been installed. The stainless steel work surfaces still had their protective plastic coverings on, as did the rank of commercial fridges and freezers along one wall. As he went past, Brendan pulled the white film off one of the fridges to reveal the shiny steel. It made a swishing sound as it came away from the metal.

"I love doing that," Brendan grinned like a little boy.

"How are you doing for staff?" asked Dan.

"Bar and waiting staff are ok and I have a head chef starting next week. I could do with a couple of experienced managers if you know of anybody?"

"Actually I might?"

"Great that's quite urgent. Tell them to give me a call. Soon as possible. I have a bar manager for the club who is very full of himself but I will make my own mind up how good he is."

There was a back corridor next to the kitchen and stairs, which led down to the basement club and they came out behind the bar. Brendan explained that it was the only connection between the main hotel and the club itself. At the bottom of the stairs was a triple bank of light switches and he flicked them all on to reveal a cavernous space, a low ceiling held up by pillars stretching to a far exit.

"I always wanted my own nightclub," said Brendan with glee. Frank and Dan exchanged looks. The club stank of years of stale beer and cigarette smoke that had infused into the fabric of the room. There was also the smell of damp and neglect. There were booths of seating and the walls and ceilings were painted black and red. There were strips of tarnished chrome piping in places and mirrors along a couple of walls. A glitter ball hung above the dance floor. The whole theme was dated to back in the eighties. It reminded Dan of the Triad's nightclub back in Hong Kong. That brought back other memories of a different life.

"It's a great retro style isn't it? You would pay a fortune for that style now and I already have it. I know it needs a freshening up. I've already booked to have the place steam cleaned and am going to put some big heaters in here to dry it out. I have done a deal with a beer wholesaler for the whole lot and am having new beer pumps put in next week. Look at this, will you boys?"

Brendan went behind the DJ's booth and he switched on the disco lights. The colours flashed off and on. Bizarre without the crashing beats. He did a John Travolta impersonation with his arm in the air and wiggling his hips. Frank and Dan laughed with him; it was difficult not to be caught up with his good mood and enthusiasm.

"Everything was just left here and one of the DJs who used to work here is going to do the opening night. We have a 'MySpace' page for the launch and have had over a hundred views already. I've invited members of the town's chamber of commerce and sent letters to local businesses and the council about the opening party to showcase the hotel and we will open the disco on the same night."

Frank took control of the conversation. "Sounds great Brendan, I'm not a big one for the internet and I don't think Dan is either but you bring them in and we will look after them for you."

Dan walked with them further through the club, looking for lines of sight and blind spots.

"I've never run this door. It has been done in-house by a couple of gorillas, Pat and Terry who were linked to the Williams family. I take it you are aware of how bad the reputation was for this place?

"I've heard it wasn't the best. But with a new owner and all cleaned up then it will be a fresh new start. Sure it will all be grand"

"I'm not sure it is as easy as that, we know the troublemakers who are on Pubwatch and will keep them out. Dan here is amongst the best doormen I've ever worked with and I'll give you a strong team."

Brendan was smiling at him. "Now come on now Frank, it will be grand. You said your dad was Oirish. You will all do a great job and we'll have a great night and a great summer and this place will be the best nightspot for miles around."

Frank shared a look with Dan and gave in.

"Ok, Ok, You fecking mad Irishman, full of blarney. Just like my old da. I just want you to know that this place has had lots of problems and they mightn't be so easy to fix."

"I do know that," said Brendan, "what is past is past and lets look to a bright new future."

"Ok as long as you know. Look this place was an institution in the town. It was a grotty hole but it was our hole and the town was almost proud of it. I will speak to the Police and tell them that I've taken over the security. They should treat you better then."

"I've met the police inspector, what a cow's arse. He was very negative about me reapplying for the entertainment license but I had my lawyer send him some letters and they don't have a reason to stop me."

Frank and Dan discussed the numbers of staff needed. The club was in the basement but with the hotel being on a hill the closed door was on a level with the car park. Customers entered through the main door and went into the foyer area where there was a cloakroom and the ticket office. They then went into the main part of the club.

"If we put two men on the front door and two in the foyer with one to watch the other search and then have four inside. If we are expecting trouble we can easily reinforce the door.

"What about radios?" asked Dan.

"My previous business was in communications. I'm still owed plenty of favours. Ha, I might have to go back if this place doesn't make me any money. I will get you radios and earpieces and if we put a signal booster by the DJ booth then it will cover any black spots because of the pillars and walls."

"Sounds great. Can you do Frank a deal on radios please Brendan? The ones he gives us are from the ark. It would almost be better to throw them at each other as try to speak into the ear piece."

"They are fine. They've got a few years life left in them yet. You aren't supposed to whisper sweet nothings to each other. It's a nightclub for god's sake," said Frank, miffed at the comment that he should spend money.

Brendan took them back upstairs. His dynamo mind was whirring away.

"Is there anything else I should be asking you lads?" asked Brendan.

"Not at the moment. We will put our heads together and lets meet up next week at the same time. I will speak to the police and we will give you a rota for the opening night on the Friday and then the Saturday night too. There's bound to be teething problems but we will address them as they come up. Is that ok?" said Frank

"That's great. Thanks for that. The new furniture will arrive the Monday before opening and will need to be unloaded and set up. The cleaners will go in downstairs and we should be ready. No problemo."

"I can help you unload on the Monday if you want and we can ask some of the lads to help.

"That will be great thanks Dan. It will bring you in as part of the team and I don't know that many people here to help yet. All support will be appreciated."

"It's a new project for both of us Brendan," said Dan, "I'm looking forward to it and I think you should be supported for injecting some energy into this place. I think the town will back you to."

"I do hope so."

24.

The next day, after his morning run and his bath he rang Carol.

"Hi Carol are you free? I have an idea for you. Yes sure, can I can come over now. I'll walk. It's a lovely day. No, the rain's not that bad. Ok, see you soon."

A few minutes later he knocked on the pub's door.

Carol looked tired but gave him a thin smile.

"Hi Dan, come in. You look better and better. Healthier than when I saw you last. Have you been avoiding me?"

"No, not at all. Gwilym said the same thing. I've been working a lot of nights and doing plenty of exercise. Running on the beach. Weights, boxing. I've climbed up Snowdon twice and I did Tryfan and the Glyders last Sunday. I was getting a beer belly but it has almost gone now."

Dan went to raise up his Tshirt to show his abdomen but stopped. Carol was preoccupied and he could tell she was trying hard to be interested in his stories of freedom and adventure.

"What's up babe? Come on let's sit down." They sat against a wall in the empty pub on a high backed bench covered in dark red vinyl leatherette.

Carol held her hand to the level of her eyes. "I've had it up to here Dan. That bastard from the brewery has been back. He wants to go over my accounts again to see what he can bloody squeeze me on. I've already had a rent increase and he's talking about me doing more food in the summer and then in the next breath cutting down on my staff costs. I can cook it but who is supposed to serve it to the customers and give them drinks. I've had enough Dan. This is the worst I've ever felt. Here's you coming in all fit and healthy and talking about climbing mountains and I don't have the energy to walk down to the beach. I'm so tired Dan."

"I'm sorry I didn't realise how bad it was. I could have helped."

"You've been busy, Gwilym was saying you are doing all these things to get fit and telling me how you must have a new woman tucked away somewhere and telling me that he hasn't seen much of you either."

"You know how it is working in bars and nightclubs. You finish late and don't go straight to sleep when you get in. I've not been getting up till the late morning and then I go for a run."

She cut him off. "Dan, I have to get these accounts ready. You said you wanted to see me. Have you come to tell me that you've met somebody? If you have that's fine. Just another shitty thing in my shitty week."

"Hey calm down, its not my fault the brewery are being total wankers. For the record I have met somebody. Its very early days and I have no idea how it is going to pan out. She is coming round tonight and we are going to discuss the future and if there is going to be one. She's a bit younger than me and it is all a bit complicated."

"Its not bloody Anwen is it?"

"No its not, she's someone I met while I was

doing the Door course. As I said I'm not sure if it the relationship is going anywhere, we are going to talk about it later and see where it goes from there"

"Ok, well thanks for telling me." Carol stood up to force Dan to leave.

"Sit down and stop it. I've actually come with some good news that may help you. Now sit down."

Carol sat and put her hands on the brass table in front of her and stared ahead.

"You look like a naughty schoolgirl." Carol showed the glimmer of a smile on her lips.

"Do you want me to put you over my knee and spank you," said Dan. This time the eyes smiled too.

Dan held her hands. "I'm sorry if I've upset you. We had a bit of fun in Chester and on Christmas Eve but the last couple of times we could have been together you didn't seem interested. You've obviously had other things on your mind and if I led you on I'm sorry."

"No you are right. Life's not been great since Christmas and with all this pressure then I wouldn't have been much company."

She gave him a naughty glance. "Perhaps I needed a smacked bottom"

"And I would have given it gladly sweetheart. Look I came round to tell you that I'm taking on a job as head doorman at the Bay View Hotel. Do you know it?"

"Yes the disco was closed down about three years ago. There was a lot of fuss about it at the Pubwatch meeting."

"Yes well there is a new owner who has taken over. I met him last night and he is desperate for a hotel manager. You could do the job and I immediately thought of you. That's why I'm here."

"Oh, when's it opening?"

"The disco is opening before the May Bank holiday. I think the hotel is already open but there is a lot of refurbishment going on. He's Irish, made money elsewhere and has this mad idea to buy a hotel. He is full of enthusiasm and I thought you could be really miserable and bring him down to earth," Carol looked at him.

"He's really switched on. There seems to be no shortage of money with all the work that's going on. I just thought it could be a way out for you from the brewery. Here is his card give him a ring as soon as possible."

"Thanks Dan."

"Carol you've been a good friend to me. I feel good at the moment but for a couple of years it was touch and go. You really helped me. I know you are stressed out here so what harm is there giving Brendan a call. I liked him a lot and I thought you could give it a go. Think about it but call him soon."

He stood up to leave. Before she let him out of the door they stood a foot apart and he opened his arms and welcomed her in for a hug. She held on to him for a few seconds longer than he held her.

She gave him a thin smile "She's a lucky girl. Go get her"

25.

Dan brushed around the cottage and tidied the functional furniture into a semblance of style. In a hangover from years of military life in barracks, the rooms were tidy and showed little of his personality. His clothes were tidied away into the mahogany wardrobe and the ancient chest of drawers that he had inherited. He looked around the cottage and had a vision of his Nain and Taid bringing up his mother in this small space. It was not perhaps surprising that she had taken the first opportunity to leave for the city and he felt sorry for the life of rebellion she had led in her escape. Since he had returned, he had lived the simple life of a bachelor and he had been in danger of falling into a solitary existence.

His mobile phone beeped loudly with the tone

for an sms text message. It was from Annette.

'Just leaving work, will be 20 mins xxx'

He replied back:

'*Great, Dan xx'*

The phone beeped in his hand and he nearly dropped it in shock at the rapid repetition of the contact.

'*Will stop to get wine A x'*

'*Great X'*

In the next twenty minutes Dan double-checked the cottage as though ready for a sergeant major's inspection. He straightened the towels in the bathroom and made sure the toilet roll was on its holder. He had already lit a fire in the sitting room and he made sure that there was wood and coal ready to throw on if needed. He straightened his Nain's love spoons and horse brasses above the mantle piece and mentally ticked off that the room was secure. He even went into the unused second bedroom and patted down the duvet on the single bed that had been his mother's and he had used himself during his lifesaving childhood holidays. On a shelf above the bed, there were old hardback annuals of the *Warlord* and *Victor* comics that his Taid had bought him to go along with his true stories of war.

The small room was cold. The door was usually kept closed and the room seldom used. The narrow window looked out of the back of the cottage towards the sand dunes and the forest. The view was the best in the cottage and Dan thought he should use the room more. The sun was fading in the sky but still gave light. Dan was pleased that Annette would see his home for the first time in daylight. It had been full of his grandparents' love. He wanted her to like his home. His Taid who had an eye for a pretty girl would have approved of Annette, a good Welsh beauty and with brains too. He felt his Taid close by.

He saw Annette's car drive along the lane and pull up next to his Mondeo. He didn't want to rush out and seem too eager but then he didn't want to leave her on the doorstep. He threw a split log on top of the coals in the fire grate and he went to open the door. She had opened the low gate and was walking up the path. She was wearing a red coat and had her grey and pink walking rucksack with her in one hand and a bottle of red wine in the other. Her face lit up when Dan stepped out.

"Croeso a ty ma," said Dan having practised his welcome in Welsh for Annette's benefit.

"Da Iawn, Dan, Diolch a ti."

She followed him into the sitting room and looked around.

"It's a bit cold so I've set the fire."

"This place is amazing Dan." She was excited and nervous.

"Is it? Its small."

"But it's perfectly formed." Annette smiled at him.

"It's a proper Bwythyn Bach, I'll translate, its a proper traditional Welsh cottage, there are not many left that haven't been spoilt. There is a heritage one that has been renovated on Anglesey at Porth Swtan. You are so lucky to live here Dan."

"Er... yes I suppose I am."

Annette was still standing in the sitting room holding her rucksack. She was dressed in her teaching gear of black trousers and a grey jersey sweater with a red woollen military coat over the top. Her rucksack looked full and he offered to take it from her.

"I've brought some clothes to change into. Hope you don't mind?"

"Of course make yourself at home. Would you like to change now or have a cup of tea or a glass of wine?"

"A panad first, then wine." She hesitated before her next sentence. "Dan, I am free now. I've sorted it with Daffydd that we are over. Can I stay the night with you here tonight?"

"Of course you can Annette. That would be great."

Again, her face lit up and she crossed the short distance to Dan, put her arms around him, and pulled him close. He put his arms around her and with the arms of his jumper pulled up to his elbows his bare forearms rubbed against the wool of the red coat. They kissed deeply, their first time having cut free of excess baggage. She was not much shorter than he was so Dan didn't have to lower his head too much to reach her lips. They held on to each other close and she arched her back to mould into his body. The log settled in the fire behind them and sparks hurried up the chimney.

They broke apart. "We have all night, lets have a cup of tea first."

He showed her into the kitchen and filled the kettle from the sink before placing it on the top of the range to boil. Annette stroked her fingers over the oak table. Her eyes lit up again when she saw the Welsh Dresser. It delighted her to see the traditional furniture piece so obviously in its original place rather than sold as a rich man's trinket in a posh antique shop. To Dan it was simply the home he had grown up knowing. As he took in her pleasure at his simple surroundings he figured you never appreciate what is normal to you.

The kettle whistled on the stove and Dan swilled boiling water round in the light blue porcelain teapot to warm it before emptying, putting two teabags in and refilling it. He put a knitted tea cosy over the top, while he sought out two mugs and put milk in a small jug.

"My Nain taught me how to warm the pot like that when making tea. Would you prefer a cup and saucer?"

"No a mug is fine thanks Cariad."

They sat on the sofa, knees angled together but not touching. The tea was strong when he did pour it and the dash of milk that she put in turned the liquid an orange brown. She took a tentative sip then a longer gulp.

"Thanks, I was parched."

"You ok?"

"Yes, it has been a bit stressful but I'm here now. I didn't get much sleep on Wednesday. Somebody dropped me off really late and I couldn't settle." Annette pulled a holy angel face at Dan.

"Sorry about that."

"Hmm," she sighed at the recollection. "Anyway I survived Thursday at work and then needed to speak to Daffydd. We spoke about the end of the relationship but not about him moving out. He blamed it on me working nights but I told him we had problems for a long time before that. He didn't ask if there was anybody else and I didn't say. He's checked the weather on the web and reckons there will be good surf on the Lleyn for the next couple of days so he's gone down there today. He asked me if I wanted to go with him for the last time but I said no." She rolled her eyes at the thought.

Dan stayed quiet.

"He said he was going with friends so he can probably take one of his little dudettes. So I'm free tonight to be with you."

"If you want me, that is?"

"Yes I do."

"Well come on then. Where are we sleeping?"

Picking up her bag from the sitting room Dan showed her into his bedroom and followed inside. She put her rucksack on the bed and took off her red coat then reached into her bag and somewhat to his surprise pulled out a toothbrush.

"Do you mind if I brush my teeth?"

"No of course not."

He pointed her back out to the bathroom. The toilet flushed, the tap ran into the sink and after a couple of minutes to compose herself she came back into the bedroom. He had taken his big jumper off. Now he was waiting, standing at ease, in his jeans and a shirt next to the bed. He had put the bedside lamp on and drawn the curtains, the evening was approaching and it was still light but the act of closing the curtains heightened their sense of privacy.

She came over to him and this time she took control. She kissed him and then stood a little back and started unbuttoning his shirt. When the last button was undone, she pushed both hands inside the two halves that split apart allowing her entry to his torso. She scratched her fingernails across the hair of his chest and squeezed his tight pectoral muscles with a curved palm. She pushed the shirt over his shoulders and for the first time she saw his naked chest, shoulders and his flattish belly. Not bad at all she thought to herself and admired his strength and manliness.

She moved in again to kiss him and reached her arms behind him. She rubbed her hands up and down the strong latissimus dorsal muscles of his back before scratching her nails down the centre of his spine. The previous night in the car Annette had lain back and thought of Wales as he pleasured her. Now it was Dan's turn to groan with the sensations she gave him. He was becoming impatient and he reached down to the bottom hem of her jersey top and pulled it up and over her head. She wriggled her arms through the sleeves and threw the top behind her. Annette stood there in her bra, the angled cups pushing her breasts upwards and outward as it was designed to do.

Dan stepped back to admire her fully and saw that under her breast was a picture, a tattoo painted down the right side of her body. It was a long swirling Celtic design of a dragon in black line with hints of red and green. The tail started under her breast and went down her rib cage before the head and mouth of the dragon came across her tummy down below the line of her trousers and back up underneath her navel. He watched transfixed as his fingers traced the tail down her side before moving across to the dragon's head to the steel torque bar piercing in her belly button. Her body was slim and her flat stomach allowed her to carry the design. It had been unexpected and Dan liked it, found the unveiling of the secretive body art extremely erotic.

He undid the waist button of her trousers and they fell to the floor. She was wearing navy blue low cut brief panties and the full effect of the dragon's neck and head came into view. He retraced his fingers up and round the dragon's body to her bra covered breast.

"I had my belly button pierced so it looks like the dragon has a jewel in its mouth. Do you like it?"

"God yes, it's a beautiful design."

"Its Y Ddraig Coch, the Red Dragon of Wales from the Mabignonion; the book of Welsh Folk stories and fairy tales. My father used to read them to me when I was a little girl."

"Any others?"

"I was a surfer girl remember?" She turned

round and lifted her hair up with her hand. At the base of her neck there was a round symbol with a black half and a white half that slotted together to make a circle. "This was my first tattoo. The Yin and the Yang, it represents balance in life. I had it done when I was seventeen away on a karate competition."

Dan sensed that there had been a relationship but he didn't press for more information. His eyes went down.

At the bottom of her spine above her buttocks and along the top of the elastic of her panties was another Celtic design. This time, the tattoo was a complicated line of black swirls with a red heart in the centre.

"The heart is in memory of my father and because I liked the design. I'm not sure my father would have approved of the tattoo in his honour but it is important to me."

Dan rubbed his hand over the bottom of her back, feeling no lines or traces on the skin that the tattoo design was there. Annette had faced away from him and was looking towards the bed leaning over slightly. He rubbed his fingers one last time over the heart in the middle of the design and deftly used his hands to pull down her knickers; they fell down her legs and she shuffled her knees until they reached the floor. He caressed her now naked bottom, the muscles of her gluteus maximus were firm and rounded and his hands cupped the small cushion of excess fat at the top of her legs.

"I want to see you naked," he told her using his fingers to undo her bra strap. The brassiere fell open and, still facing the bed, she shrugged it off her. She was now naked, except for the black socks. Her back was towards him and he had a glimpse of her nipples as she lifted up the duvet and scrambled underneath. She bent her legs and pulled off the socks, threw them out from under the covers then pulled it up bunching with two hands to cover up to her face daring him to react.

"No Clothes!" she said.

"I want to see you naked," he repeated. She lowered the duvet back down to her chest, revealing the low swell of her breasts but not her nipples.

"More," he said standing over her. She relented, uncovering her breasts. From above they were perfectly round; her nipples were pale and small the same colour as the rest of her skin. As he watched over her they became pink and were now hard and smooth like the peas he had felt in the car. They stood out, like triangulation pillars at the top of a gentle slope.

"They are very small!" she said as she pushed her breasts up for effect.

"They are not that small. It's just that you are a tall girl and they look smaller. They look good to me."

She pulled the duvet down further, showing the whole tattoo and the top of the triangle of her pubic hair.

"Naked" insisted Dan and she flipped back the whole duvet to one side showing the whole of her body. She closed her eyes and held her hands by her sides.

His eyes ranged over her naked body and he drank her in. Her pretty face, her square shoulders, the slender body with her small breasts, her tattooed tummy, her slim waist to where her body swelled at her hips in a diamond. Then to her genitals and down to the long muscled legs.

"Absolutely stunning," he said and traced his index finger slowly down from her temple. He passed the eyebrow, down the side of her cheek, her neck, over her collarbone and across the firmness of her breast, tipping off the nipple. Then underneath the breast and along the tail and body of the dragon, he skirted round to the side of her hips and down the outside of her leg to her feet. She was long and tall and he had to shuffle his feet across to reach all the way down. She had her eyes closed to intensify the slow deliberate trek of his finger.

He returned back on the inside of her ankle, her knee and her inner thighs. He touched ever so briefly against the lips but made no move yet to investigate further. He scratched his way through her pubic hair and diagonally up to her neglected right breast that he had ignored due to difficult access in the car. As he brought his finger up on the far side of her neck, he opened his hand and caressed her cheek. As she opened her eyes he leant down to kiss her.

She moved over to the far edge of the bed and turned on her side to give him space. Her whole body language was inviting him to join her and she reached her hand up to make the pillow more comfortable. As she did so, her fingers found his old rubber hot water bottle tucked away under the pillow. Not exactly sure what it was, she pulled it out. Holding it between her thumb and forefinger. When she realised she threw it at him.

"Well you won't be needing that again tonight now will you?"

She again invited him in. Holding back the duvet.

"I want to see you naked too Dan."

He quickly let his jeans fall and he slipped on to the bed and pulled the cover over each of them. They held each other, naked together for the first time. She overcame the distraction of his wounded leg and lifted the duvet to look before kissing him once more.

She was ready for him to enter her and he stopped in consideration.

"Should I get a condom?"

"No, I'm on the pill, please just be inside me. I need you inside me."

He raised himself on top of her and lowered his hips down pushing her legs out of the way with his thighs. As his penis nuzzled against her lips she opened up to him and he entered her. Her body letting him feel his way deep inside her before she wrapped her legs around him and they moved together in a dance as old as time. Their hips rolled together finding a rhythm that satisfied both their need for affection, for intimacy and ultimately a shared climax.

They lay together afterwards; she rested her head on his shoulder, her dark hair falling on to his chest as she stroked him gently. He reciprocated by gently rubbing her neck and her upper back. They didn't speak but enjoyed the moment of satisfaction before he raised himself and dressed and left her to recover in the bed as he got up to make the Spaghetti Bolognese and put the garlic bread in the range oven.

26.

After their meal, they sat in the sitting room and talked about their future. Dan poked life back into the fire and when the logs were blazing away, he sat back on the small sofa next to Annette. She sat with her long legs tucked underneath her. Following their exploration of each other's bodies, she had dressed for dinner in jeans and a surfer's branded hooded top.

He had offered her a shower but she had been hungry for food and said that she liked the smell of his body on her own, not wanting to wash it from her just yet.

They sat together in the room with no television and just the fire for distraction. He offered the radio and she said yes finding a Friday night music concert on Radio 2, which played away gently without too much chatter. They agreed that the music was very different to when they were working in the pubs and bars and that tucked up in front of the fire was a better place to be. Dan tried to set the mood with just a side lamp in the corner adding to the low flames coming from the grate..

Annette leaned over to kiss him and then curled up against his shoulder. Dan moved his feet up against the armrest and they lay together afloat on the sofa with limbs intertwined. Occasionally disentangling to take a sip of wine they talked about nothing and they talked about the world. After their shared intimacy, the barriers were down. The fire crackled as a log settled.

"Dan, will you please tell me some more about your treatment after the bomb?" Annette had more questions for Dan and he answered honestly. She asked again about his scars and the rehabilitation he had received and the therapy and counselling which he had been offered but missed out on. He told her a little of his life leading up to joining up and the chronology of his Active Service,

She listened with interest. British Politician's insistence on interference in foreign affairs had led to a full life for Dan and his comrades and he had been flung around at their whim.

"Do you believe in service for queen and country?"

"I'm not sure. I was proud to serve and wear the uniform. If I hadn't joined up then I was going down the path of doing more crime. That stopped when I joined the Royal Marines. It was a better life."

"Then it all stopped when you were blown up?"

"I felt like just another injured serviceman thrown on the scrap heap and I was bitter that after all I had seen and done." She sensed that the pain was still not fully healed.

"When Gwilym was threatened outside the seafood factory I felt that it had dislodged the sense of inertia and melancholy that had hung over me. I was a good Sergeant because I was calm in a crisis. Nothing I have encountered since my discharge had lived up to that sense of danger and excitement that the confrontation with Stephen Williams triggered in me. Perhaps there is nothing in civilian life that will ever compare to the threat of being blown up and shot at?"

"You sound like you wanted to seek out the danger?"

"Maybe, even when I worked in the tough City nightclub before I signed up for the Royal Marines I found myself looking for trouble and seeking it out. I wanted the confrontation to prove to myself that I was alive. I enjoyed the boxing where it was one on one and then I found rugby and played as part of a team. Serving in the Marines gave me that constant confrontation by pushing me to the limits in training and then being unleashed on the enemy in a hostile environment. I've dealt with Chinese Triads in Hong Kong, Saddam Hussein's Republican Guard in Iraq, Bands of Armed Militia in Bosnia, Guerrillas in Sierra Leone and ultimately the Taliban in Afghanistan and they blew me up. And now back to drunks in nightclubs again?

Annette listened with a sense of trepidation. Her friend Diane's brother had signed up for a short service career in the Army and had been to Iraq. He had come out and rushed off to drive a delivery van. Diane had still been living at home when he had come back from Camp Bastion and he had woken with nightmares.

Dan had spent many more years in danger than Diane's brother and Annette wondered how he had coped with the sights he must have seen. He talked about it as though it was an adventure in uniform but naked in his bed she had seen his visible scars.

Now she worried about the hidden psychological wounds that she had glimpsed in her previous conversation about the Afghan bomb. She was deeply attracted to this quiet strong man and they had made love just an hour or so before with a passion that her body still ached to repeat. She wanted more of that passion and she wanted to know more of the man inside. It would have been easy for her to have plodded on with Daffydd. He was gone from her heart now and she wanted that space to be filled with Dan. It would not be easy but he had shown her he was a good man and she already could see a bright path that they lay ahead.

"You said you've killed, do you want to talk about it now?"

"Not really, it's locked away. If I said they deserved it then it sounds callous. I feel more guilty for the lives I couldn't save than for the ones I killed."

To move from the difficult subject of his wounds Annette made a show of admiring the carved love spoons above the fire and she disengaged from their embrace and took them down before sitting back down on the sofa.

"As a good little Welsh girl, I learnt the meanings in school. Can you see the hidden symbols in the intricate patterns? The heart and the knots stand for a long relationship and happiness. This one is carved with a heart for love and a cross for Christian marriage. This second one shows a diamond for good fortune and below that is a carving of two balls in a cage. This means there were two children in the marriage."

Dan didn't answer and Annette carried on. "On the other hand, of course they might not be a personal item and just have been bought in a craft shop."

"No it makes sense. I always thought my mum was an only child but Gwilym's wife Annie told me that there was a son who was killed. He was called Daniel too. I only found that out recently. My mother had been quick to leave here. I never understood the reasons they had always been kept vague. I wasn't even sure of how old my mother had been when she left here. Nor the relation in time to me being born. Annie told me that she was pregnant when she left."

Annette, her analytical mind whirring with curiosity couldn't understand his lack of interest in his mother's reasons for leaving the family home.

"Didn't you want to find out more about why your Mam left?"

"Not really, I suppose it's a bloke thing. Life as a kid wasn't great. We moved a lot, depending who

Mum was with at the time. Or escaping from."

"Bechod, bless, how sad!"

"I suppose it was. My holidays here were my safe haven. Mum tried, but she was a party girl and was always leaving me with neighbours. Perhaps I didn't want her to have stayed here because it wouldn't have been so special for me."

"What about your father?"

"I never knew him. He obviously existed but some of my mother's boyfriends were horrible men so I must have presumed he would have been like that too and didn't want to find out more about him."

"So you don't know who he was? Or where he came from? If she was pregnant then both your parents were Welsh."

"No, he wasn't ever part of my life"

"Don't you want to find out?"

"I have never thought it mattered. He didn't ever support my mother so he didn't deserve to be part of my life."

"Did she know who he was?"

"Was she that bad do you mean? I think she knew but didn't want him to be involved in her life after she had me."

"No deathbed revelations?" Annette held his hand with sympathy as she asked him.

"She is not dead, she is still alive. She actually met somebody decent and moved down to London."

"But you speak of her in the past tense as though she is dead."

"When she met this new guy, Trevor, I was just 18. I was starting to be a bit of a hard nut and to jump into trouble. I thought all her fellas were the same. She had been clean for ages and was holding down a job in the city centre. She was clever when she wanted to be. The estate we lived on was rough and it was a difficult place to raise yourself up from. She still liked to party but then only at weekends and I didn't mind that too much. She seemed to be in control."

Annette nodded him on.

"One night I came home from working in the club and some new guy was there, I thought he was shagging her in the lounge. I saw that there was crumpled tin foil on the tabletop in the kitchen. I thought he had brought heavy drugs into our flat and mum had taken heroin again. He was getting to his noisy climax on top of Mum and I saw red. I was starting to realise that the drugs and these men who abused my mother were always going to be there. I had been working so had a couple of drinks when I had finished. There had been lots of fights that night so my blood was still up. I was still on an adrenaline high and wanted to kill him. I can remember the rage in me."

He stopped talking and Annette stayed quiet to let Dan collect his thoughts. She was still holding his hand.

"So I dragged him off her and started punching him. He wasn't one of the hard men I was expecting. After a couple of punches he was on the floor, as though he had never been in a fight before. Mum stood up and started protecting him then, screaming back at me and I stopped."

"And?"

"It was Trevor, who was an accountant from London that Mum had met in her city centre work. He had taken her out to an Italian restaurant and they had brought some Garlic bread home in the tin foil, so it wasn't drugs. She had asked him up for a coffee and started kissing and they were being amorous when I walked in and clattered him."

He took a breath.

"It turned out that Mum had been seeing a bit of him and this was the fourth or fifth date. Why she brought him back to the flat without telling me he was a decent bloke I don't know. Mum wouldn't think straight some times."

"And what happened then?"

"Actually it did some good, at least for her. Trevor wanted to play the knight in shining armour and rescue her. He was doing some consultancy work and it was finishing up and he was going back down to London. He had his own house there and he asked Mum to go down with him for a new start. After punching him, I was never going to be part of that new equation and she left me in the flat. I lived there on my own for a few months before I joined the Marines and the flat went back to the council for somebody else to be re-housed in it."

"Did you not see her at all?"

"No she had a new life and got married. They pretended I did not exist so I was not even invited to the wedding. I was in Canada anyway on a training exercise so I couldn't go. She did send a note to

Taid here that she was married and for him not to worry about her. Taid showed it to me and I got the impression that Trevor had told her to write it. It did have an address and I wrote to her to say that if she hadn't heard that Taid had died and that he had specifically left the house to me in his will. I had a letter back saying thanks for letting her know and good luck in the future. Probably Trevor insisting she wrote."

"So you might have half brothers or sisters?"

"I possibly could do? Mum wasn't that old when she left 35 or 36. She could have had more children. But they don't know me?"

"After that did you ever meet anybody who you would have started a family with?"

"The Royal Marines were my family for a while but I was never totally against a family life. I did meet a girl in Hong Kong. We were getting along fine, then we ran into some trouble because of one of her friends and I was shipped out. It was the start of the first Iraq war and I was lent out to the Americans as a spare Boat Driver. We lost touch. I moved around so much that she might have sent me letters but I lost her address. It was all a mess. The Americans thought there was going to be a big D-Day type invasion of Kuwait. I wasn't posted where I should have been and I never heard from her again. We were close. She was the only girl I have probably ever loved. Or let myself love. It's a fact of life in the services that you love them and leave them. I had found my home in the Marines and I didn't want to tie her down. There was no point in looking for her. Besides, it was more difficult to keep in touch then without the Internet and all that stuff. As I got older, I had mates who tore themselves apart each time they had to leave their wife and kids. I went to funerals and carried their coffins while their widows wept. Why would I inflict that on my own wife?"

"So you were being selfless in not wanting to hurt her, where you?"

"No Annette, I was being selfish that I didn't want to get hurt myself. The Americans call them 'Dear John letters'. When a sweetheart writes to her soldier on the front line to tell them that she has found somebody else and doesn't want to be with him when he comes home. I have had friends who have had those and they used to call me lucky for not being attached. So I fell into believing them."

"What do you want now Dan? What do you want from me? Just a good time?" It was a sad story and she was crying openly now.

"Annette I do not plan on going anywhere for a

while. I would like to explore the chance of a proper relationship. I don't know if I will be good at it. But for the first time in my life I want to try."

"I want to try to?" She rubbed her tears away with the back of her hand and smiled. "Come on then lets go back to bed and try some more."

"Yes Miss!"

27.

"Annette, perhaps you should be going to Brendan's opening as a guest tonight rather than working with me," Dan said, as they finished their healthy meal sitting at the cottage's well-scrubbed oak table. The sun's rays streamed through the kitchen window filtered by the fresh leaves on the trees in the garden.

"I like working with you, Dan. I'm having fun. Its an adventure."

"I know you are but I'm thinking of your career. There will be some college brass going tonight and perhaps it would be better for you to be pressing the flesh and being nice to people rather than working as a bouncer."

"I am nice to people. Its you who bash them up."

"It wasn't people. It was Steve Drwg, the moron, trying to show off in front of his mates and that little tart in the short skirt."

"Well you showed him who was boss there."

"Maybe. He's not right in the head there. He's bulked up since I first met him, juiced up on the steds and he's taking too much white powder. It's a dodgy combination."

"Robbie says he's 'chwink'. Not right in the head. You can handle him though can't you Dan?"

"He's a big man in his own underpants. I've had a word with Frank about having him put on Pubwatch. Anyway forget that idiot. I wanted to speak to you before we start work tonight. I think you are a really good, Erm, what are we called now?" Dan grinned at here as she gave him a look.

"Oh yes Door Supervisor. You are the best female I've worked with and I'm really pleased that you are enjoying yourself but I want you to think about taking it easy and concentrating on your proper career and I just thought that tonight you might prefer to come as a guest rather than a bouncer."

"Dan we are leaving in an hour and I will be going with you to work a full shift. I will ignore that I am the only female door supervisor that you have ever worked with. I am actually looking forward to seeing the hotel all done up and the leather chairs and these tables that you say you have been putting up all week. Dan thanks for caring but I have been to loads of these receptions and stood there drinking warm white wine, eating stale vol-au-vents and listening to old men spout on about their businesses or their political careers while they try to look down my top or pat my bottom. Tonight I am going to be there as somebody different. Now do you think it will be ready in time."

"When I left this afternoon Brendan was standing over the workmen as they put their tools away. The disco will smell of paint but that's better than stale beer and vomit like when I first went in. The hotel foyer and bar looks totally different and that's where the reception is so it will be alright."

"Great now wash those dishes quickly then come into the bedroom."

"Stuff the dishes,"

"Come on then, I want you again. Quick and hard."

"Last night was good."

"Yes it was," her t-shirt was over her head before she reached the door. Dan chased after her.

Annette didn't work the doors on a school night and while Dan had been out at work her friend Diane had come round to view her new home. Diane had commented favourably on her fresh complexion, trim tummy and the huge grin on her face. Diane had been impressed with the cottage's location if perhaps not with the lack of modern conveniences. Annette had told Diane that she had no sense of romance and then brought her friend up to speed with her great sex life.

After much laughter Diane had been kicked out at midnight and Annette had been lying in wait for Dan when he came in. He had blood on his shirt from an altercation with idiots he said had been forcefully thrown out. He had also had another argument with Steve Drwg. Steve Drwg had backed away shouting threats and Dan was annoyed at the little shit and sat down on the sofa mulling it over.

Annette had been lying in bed waiting for him to come home and came out to greet him, wearing his dressing gown and was sitting next to him hearing about the events of the night. To calm him down she had sat with legs splayed across his lap and playfully opened the chord of the gown and distracted him from the idiots he had dealt with. He put his hands around and felt under the gown round to her buttocks. He had held on to the firm globes of flesh that had risen from resting on his thighs as she bent down to kiss him. He had grasped her hard to him and holding her tight he stood up. She wrapped her legs tightly around him giving out a squeal. It was a good job that it was a small cottage and that Dan was so strong. He navigated through the bedroom door and dropped Annette on the bed where she lay back showing off her tattoos and fit body in all its glory. He was in a hurry and took only a couple of seconds to be as naked as she was. He fell on top of her and took her roughly. She liked the manly smell of sweat and aftershave coming from his body and she raked his back with her nails as he drove hard into her in a quick burst of grunting passion. She liked it slow and tender but hard and quick was good for her too as her man claimed his woman with a strong thrust inside her.

That next evening after a few sweaty minutes Annette got up while Dan lay back on the dishevelled sheets of the bed. He closed his eyes in warm appreciation of the swift conclusion of their sexual union. Annette was ferocious in her passion for him and he responded in kind. He opened his eyes to see her long slim naked body stepping out of the room. He couldn't get enough of that body. It sent his heart racing.

Annette came back into the room with a towel wrapped around her body.

"Look at this old thing it doesn't cover my bits. I'm taking you shopping on Sunday, Dan. We really need some new towels and I'm going to try to buy you a new shower attachment to fit onto the bath taps."

"I thought we were going into the mountains again."

"Dan we really have to do more than work, have sex and be in the outdoors all weekend. I'm running out of clothes here and we need some new bed linen and towels. Then I thought we could go for a drink in the village pub, you haven't taken me there yet."

"I like you out of your clothes best."

Dan was still lying across the sheets and Annette stepped up to the bed. She ran her hand up the outside of his leg and across his belly. He raised his hand to meet hers as it travelled upwards and they clasped together, her long fingers fitting into his palm. His fingers still rough and calloused from years of dealing with salt water, ropes and boats, closed over hers. He squeezed to show his affection.

"I know you do and just for you I am going to wear my best black lingerie tonight. So when you see me you can look at me and know what I have on underneath."

He moved his hand and gave the towel a swift tug and it fell to the ground.

"Dan, will you stop that."

He pulled himself up off the bed, stood in front of her and pulled her towards him. She held him tightly with her arms up around his strong shoulders and neck. Their naked bodies as close as could be. She reached her chin up on to his shoulder and her lips touched his neck her breath murmuring in vibration against her skin. Over her shoulder he watched their bodies reflected in the oval mirror on the dressing table, his broad and strong and hers long, toned and narrow. He watched his thumb trace down her spine from the yin and yang circle to the heart in the middle of the Celtic swirls. He went past the tattoo and cupped the right cheek of her bottom.

"Dan, are you looking at me in the mirror?"

"Uhuh!"

She pushed him away and punched his shoulder.

"Enough messing. We need to iron these new shirts. Come on its time to get dressed and lets go to work."

28.

Side-by-side they marched across the car park wearing the black shirts with the hotel's new logo. They went up the steps of the hotel, through the big wooden doors and into the smell of paint, cleaning fluid and fresh leather. The foyer was scattered with the new leather sofas, tub chairs and coffee tables. Herded into clumps ready and waiting for the guests to arrive and hold business meetings or take afternoon tea.

Brendan's vision had become a reality and the smiling young girl behind the reception desk was wearing the same shirt as Annette and Dan, but without the tie saying 'Security'. There was a buzz of noise coming from the bar and Dan popped his nose in. The evening sun was shining over the harbour and out to the sea and the view from the windows was impressive. The last of the workmen, their working gear spattered in paint and plaster, were having a pint at the end of the bar. A small group of smartly dressed patrons were congregating closer to the door. Brendan was dressed to dazzle in a Kelly Green blazer and looked every bit the affluent hotelier. He was speaking to the smarter group by the door and disentangled himself.

"Hi Dan, Grand to see you, Great timing, the invited guests are just starting to arrive and its probably time these fellas at the end of the bar made a move."

"Sure no problem."

Dan went up to the five workmen, spoke to them politely. They finished their drinks and left immediately, thanking Brendan on their way out.

When he returned to Brendan and Annette he said, "Lets hope the rest of the night goes as smoothly."

"I'm sure it will all go fine, especially with this lovely lady looking after us." Annette accepted the compliment with a smile.

The bulk of Robbie came through the door and joined them. Robbie looked a mess but had a big smile on his face. Dan buried the Royal Marine sergeant's urge in him to snap, 'Smarten yourself up'. This was civilian time now and he took Robbie to one side and whispered to him to go and take some time to straighten his tie and wipe the remains of his dinner off his chin.

Robbie replied, "Yes boss" and went to find the toilets and a mirror.

When he returned he was marginally better, with his belly stretching the creases out of the new shirt, the biggest size available. Robbie was a night-club doorman to his size thirteen boots. Nightclubs were in the dark and the customers were usually too drunk to notice if a bouncer's shirt had been ironed.

Dan positioned Robbie and Annette on the Front door of the Hotel with instructions to open the door and be friendly. He sorted them out with their radios and Robbie was especially impressed with the earpiece that conducted sound through the bones of the ear so that the voices could be heard clearer.

"Much better than Frank's old crappy ones," he said and repeated the sentiment to Frank when he turned up a few minutes later, Robbie showing his employer how good the new radios were.

Frank's barrel chest was covered in a sharp

navy suit and a bright yellow tie. His round head was freshly shaved and he smelled sweetly of after-shave. He told off Robbie for not polishing his boots and then went to glad hand and network with the business and trade people from the town, most of whom he knew well.

Dan flitted in and out of the reception making his presence felt and being polite when he was asked a question. Brendan introduced him to peo-ple as his 'head of security', which was a grander title than he felt he deserved. Brendan was a char-ismatic man and he was playing the confident host, happy in his new venture. His positive personality gave his guests a warm vibe about this stranger putting himself at the heart of their town.

The longer the night went on the less Dan thought this pleasant party needed a heavy-duty bouncer like himself. While he smiled and nodded his head in polite conversation to the cream of the town's society, he would have to switch to a much darker personality if there was trouble later in the club.

Despite his tough upbringing he was an articu-late man and had never had any trouble conversing with the officer class. In the Royal Marines he had a rank and a status and was treated with respect. He noticed that here some of the men were making comments to their women about needing to be protected from him. One man made a comment about how scary it was to be in the presence of a bouncer. Dan kept quiet, smiled, nodded and left as soon as was polite. He went back out to the door to speak to Annette and Robbie, glad to be back in normal company.

"Sut mae Alwyn," Annette greeted a tall thin man coming up the steps. He was in his forties with a fashionable leather jacket and a gold earring.

"Dan, this is Alwyn Roberts. My head of department."

Alwyn held on to the handshake a moment longer than Dan was expecting and spoke to Annette in Welsh before turning to English for Dan's benefit.

"So you are the new man who has put a smile on Miss Davis' face? I must say I am impressed. I wouldn't mind my own handsome man. I bet he is the strong silent type, hey Annette bach."

Robbie, who was standing close, let out a splutter of mirth.

"Hush now Alwyn, you will embarrass Dan, now let go of his hand."

"I hear you live in an idyllic traditional

Bwythyn bach. I think I know it, my Nain and Taid lived in the village and I used to play on the beach."

"Yes it is lovely place to live. My Taid was known as Will Traeth so they probably knew each other."

"They probably did, it was very close knit community back then. I'm sure Annette's car parked outside your house has caused a few curtains to twitch in the village."

"Yes, I was told today that there are rumours running all around the village about us," said Dan with a warm-hearted glance at Annette.

"Well, she is a lovely girl and I approve, so when you want to invite me round for a barbecue and a bottle of wine then I will be there."

They were standing to one side at the top of the stairs next to the newly re-laid paving slabs of the terrace that ran along the front of the hotel. Brendan had said would it become an outside eating and drinking area in the summer. Tables had been ordered but would be delivered in a couple of weeks. A large strategically placed plant pot blocked off the entry while the cement was left to dry.

Alwyn took a break while other invited guests

walked up the stairs and the door was opened for them. Dan had done a brief dynamic risk assessment as they approached. He had taken the split second decision that the silver-haired couple in their fifties were not a heavy duty threat. Alwyn noticed the up and down look that Dan had given the couple.

Dan felt he should explain, "When you work the door you deal with so many idiots that you are constantly on your guard. At a reception like this you know there won't be trouble. But in a couple of hours there could be some drugged up lad with a chip on his shoulder that wants to attack you with a bottle. It makes you more aggressive and means you need a split personality, be polite and open the doors for the nice people and then scary as hell for the eejits."

Alwyn replied, "I can see you being scary if you wanted to be. I hadn't thought of it like that. We teach customer service at the college but I suppose dealing with drunks means that customer service goes out of the window."

"Not necessarily, Alwyn. Our job is to be there to ensure that the venue is safe for customers and staff who want to enjoy themselves and do their job safely. Certain behaviour, which is unaccept-able, say, in a family restaurant, will be allowed in a nightclub. But add alcohol and you create arseholes. Add drugs and you create unstable arseholes, who endanger the normal decent customers. That's who we sometimes have to deal with."

"You put it well Dan. Did Annette teach you that?"

"She's taught me a lot Alwyn. She's a good teacher and I am lucky that I did her course."

"Tell me, is Annette safe doing this job?"

Annette was listening and piped up, "Alwyn we have discussed this. I am capable and it is good that rather than just teaching the course I can do the job."

"Annette, I know you are capable cariad and you are right that as a lecturer you should be able to speak from experience. But I am interested in what Dan thinks."

"Alwyn, I agree with you. I have seen Annette deal with confrontations and she hasn't taken a backward step. I respect her for that, but because of the situations we deal with this job is never totally safe. I am doing this job for some extra money so I don't dip into my savings. Robbie here needs to pay for some extra treats for his kids. But this is a twilight world and we deal with a lot of idiots, sometimes that leads to friction. Annette has a good career and I wouldn't want this part time job to damage her future prospects. I would say to her that perhaps she should work with me over the summer and then concentrate on a promotion."

Annette commented, "I am here you know!"

"Again well said Dan, I think that the end of the summer will be a good timescale. Annette is seen as a rising star and I wouldn't want her career damaged if she was in trouble with the police. I think the management of the college will give her a few months before she gives up."

"I am starting to care about this girl and I don't want to see any harm come to her either. I hope to know her a long time."

"Bravo Dan, Di' Iawn. There you go Annette. Can you find another one like him for me please?"

"What happened to your friend from Manchester?"

"Ah... but he's not here again and he doesn't have a Bwythyn by the beach."

Alwyn looked on to the car park as a big Mercedes saloon pulled up and two males and two females stepped out.

"Now here is a man I wouldn't mind getting to grips with, Phil who runs my gym. Oh let me go in and get a drink otherwise he will think I know the lowly bouncers." Alwyn disappeared inside.

From their looks and similar stature the two men were obviously father and son. The son's female partner, a stunning long legged blonde was wearing a tight black dress showing not much less than the bath towel that Annette had complained about. Although Dan noted that coming out of the bath before Annette had not been wearing four-inch high heels.

The father was with a glamorous woman with auburn hair. She was not much older than his son, showing thicker legs and a deeper cleavage. Large pieces of fabric had been strategically cut away and his hand around her tanned bare midriff proclaimed ownership of a prized possession and showed to the world that she wasn't his daughter.

Frank Delaney seeing the car pull up through the window had come out to join Dan. As the two men walked up the steps, Frank pulled his stomach in and thrust out his hand to the older man.

"Haia, Brian, Sut ydych chi?"

"Iawn diolch a ti Frank. All good thanks. You know Philip don't you?"

Philip, the son, was well tanned, fit and strong. He was wearing designer jeans and a grey suit jacket tailored to take in his wide shoulders and broad back. Dan recognised from his stealthy economical movements that he was trained in martial arts. Under the jacket he wore a black cashmere crew neck sweater that hugged the muscles of his torso. The round collar was barely containing the well-defined neck muscles that showed throbbing veins and the tops of hidden tribal tattoos that reached up his neck. A thick gold chain, which would have dangled to Annette's chest, was stretched tight, edging the sweater. Dan automatically assessed the younger man as an opponent. He reckoned that if needed he could take him down but it would be a vicious fight.

Frank introduced them.

"Brian, this is Dan Richards, a new man for me and he is head doorman here."

"Dan this is Brian Williams and his son Phil. Phil runs the health club and used to be a national karate champion. Brian runs...er... a number of local businesses."

Dan sensed that Frank was tweaking the tiger's tale.

Brian dressed in a dark tailor made pinstripe suit with a purple silk tie on a pink shirt with a starched white collar. He reminded Dan of the big time gangster he had worked for as a teenager back in the city. Brian was perhaps in his late fifties or early sixties, not as bull-like as his son but not yet past his prime. Dan shook both men's hands when offered and noted that neither man tried to squeeze their authority into their handshakes. Like himself, they had nothing to prove and Dan relaxed, he wouldn't have to fight them just yet. He was standing slightly taller than both men but he knew that this was probably because his boots had a chunkier heel.

Phil had looked over his shoulder at Annette, but it was Brian who said hello to her.

"Is that Annette Davies, Sut mae?" Brian kissed her cheek and she replied in a flurry of Welsh that Dan couldn't keep up with.

She held out her hand and Phil took it.

"Haia Phil,"

"Haia Annette. You have a new job? Last I heard you were teaching in the college."

"I still am, this is part of doing the job rather than teaching."

"Are you still doing karate?"

"No. I've learnt a few new tricks since then."

"Me too. I'm into mixed martial arts now and I do some cage fighting. I'm a teacher myself now."

"I've heard that."

The fragrant blonde on Phil's arm was tugging to pull him inside to the party.

"Wait a minute, Julie. You came back home then after Uni. How is your Mum?"

"Mum's fine, getting on with life. I thought you were going to escape but you came back too."

"You know this place and the family, it never lets you go does it."

The blonde tugged again, she was slightly nervous. Phil twisted his torso past Dan nodding his head in acknowledgement and said "see you later," to both Dan and Annette

Dan looked over at Robbie who raised his eyebrows and blew out his cheeks. The air pushed out of his lips as he let the relief of the encounter with the town's reported hardest man escape.

Frank had stepped inside the reception area with the quartet and Dan followed them inside.

"Brian can we have a quick word?" The men stood to one side of the hotel foyer. "You need to know that Stephen is becoming a problem around town."

"Yes, I've heard that he is becoming to big for his boots. I think Cliff has been putting ideas into his head. I will have him spoken to and told to cool down. His Dad, John can't control him and he won't go out on the trawler."

"He's starting to attract attention, being too cocky. I thought you should know."

"Thanks Frank, I appreciate it. Glad to see you are doing well and running this place. I hope you can keep it open now."

"I heard Pat got sent down last year. Was sorry to hear that," said Frank.

"No you weren't Frank. No malu-cachu between us old friends now is there."

"No I wasn't sorry. Should have been put away years ago."

"But he had his uses, Frank."

"Everything is above board these days Brian. All my staff are licensed and pay tax."

"Good on you Frank. Well done. You should see my tax bill. Keeps the bastards in champagne and caviar what I pay them."

Brian looked over at Dan who was standing to one side of Frank in the same way that his son was one side of him. That meant that the two younger men were standing next to each other. Brian took in the similarities in their height, shoulders and the blue eyes that matched his own. The two glamour-puss women were looking at their phones.

"Where are you from?" Brian asked Dan.

"I was raised in Liverpool."

"Oh. I thought I recognised you but if you aren't local probably not."

"My mum was from round here but went away before I was born."

"Nice place to live isn't it. But not many jobs, if you need one come and see me."

"Frank's looking after me just fine, but thanks I

will bear it in mind."

"We had better go in. I will deal with Steve Drwg," Brian shook his head "what idiot calls himself the 'Bad'.

"Cliff would have done," said Frank.

"That's true. Families hey son. Come on Phil lets go in."

He nodded his acceptance of the issue to Frank and Dan, then went into the crowd of people with a smile and a hand outstretched, like a Yankee politician in the run up to an election. Phil walked to one side and slightly behind, part protégé and part minder. The two glamorous females trailed behind.

The night rolled on and two hours later Dan was ready to open the discotheque doors when Brendan gave the go ahead. There were already a hundred people who had made the effort to come early and they were standing waiting outside. One of Dan's lads had gone out there to form the semblance of a queue, which snaked across the car park towards the brick gateposts. Small groups were joining the back as he watched.

He checked his watch. Brendan was going to bring through the remaining guests from the party in about ten minutes so they would see the club first. Then the general public could come in. Entry was free for this first night.

Dan had swapped a younger doorman with Robbie on the hotel bar to allow the big man to run the disco's front door alongside another big lad, Kevin, who he had worked with and trusted to be sensible. Annette was going to be inside with Huw, who was the soldier who he had trained with for his Door Supervisor's course and the others would be spread through the club. He was just about to do a radio check to the different locations when a police car drove through the car park gates.

It drove up to the front of the queue and Dan bent down to be polite. The police sergeant in the driving seat was Emyr, Gwilym's son in law.

"Haia Dan, How's it going? This is Inspector James," Emyr introduced the police officer in the passenger seat.

"Hi. Emyr, we are just about to open. Do you want to come in and see inside?"

The Inspector answered. "Dim Diolch. Not today thanks. How many are you expecting tonight?"

"Not sure, we have a capacity of five hundred so we have geared up to expect that."

"And what time are you closing?"

"The License gives us until two."

"Ok, I closed this place down before and will do it again. So make sure they all behave."

Police Sergeant Emyr and ex-Royal Marine Colour Sergeant Dan exchanged a look that said a lot about how to deal with superior officers.

"The inspector will be finishing at midnight and I'm on a late so I will see you later Dan. Pob lwc boi."

The white car with 'Heddlu' in black letters on the bonnet, with fluorescent blue and yellow flashes on the side and blue lights on the roof rack drove off.

Dan went to the door and double-checked that all was ready before calling through on the radio to Brendan that they were ready for him. Brendan had liked the idea of having a radio himself and his voice came back through Dan's earpiece saying, "Roger that, Okey-Dokey, coming over now, on the way...er over." Much to the amusement of Robbie and Kevin.

29.

The music was already blasting around the club when Brendan came over with a crocodile of about sixty people, leftovers from the launch party. Phil Williams nodded to Dan as a courtesy to acknowledge that he was the boss as they were ushered in. Dan noticed that Annette had lowered her head as Phil had walked past. He had put her next to Robbie and given her the clicker to count people in and out. On Dan's instructions Kevin was lining up the good-natured queue of early arrivals. Dan waited five minutes, giving the chance for the VIPs to buy drinks and then he let in the public hoi polloi.

The entry policy was a smart casual dress code, over twenty-one in age and customers must be able to stand vertically upright without falling over.

Brendan and Dan stood to one side and watched Robbie and Kevin do their job. If they looked young they would be ID checked and a small number of people were turned away. Others joined the back of the queue as fast as the boys could move the front through.

"Is everything ok so far?" asked Brendan

"Yes if its going to be this busy we will need crowd barriers to form the queue and stronger lights on the side of the hotel down to the car park. There are too many shadows by the bushes and round the edges."

"Ok, Lets start making a list and see what can be done before tomorrow night and then before next week," Brendan said surveying his new domain. "This is great. I always wanted my own nightclub. There are some great looking women here too."

"Yes, I'm used to it on the doors but I suppose you are not used to the short skirts and high heels. It's an older crowd than normally round town. You should see what the eighteen year olds wear?

"What, they show more flesh than this?"

"Yes Brendan, if you want to run a nightclub then prepare to be shocked."

"My ex wife could never understand why I wanted to own a hotel but I had great craic growing up. Some of my mates from back home are coming next month. We will have a blast."

"Ok, we will have ironed out any problems by then. Were you pleased with the reception party?"

"Yes very pleased, everybody seemed to like the place. The rotary club wants to hold their meetings here but the chairman was quite drunk by the time he left. A councillor introduced me to Brian Williams who wants to take over my supply chain, reckons he can save me money. I told him I'd speak to him but I know a shakedown when I see it. I'm not just some peat bog paddy straight off the cattle boat."

Dan had already spotted that there was a steel core beneath Brendan's affable exterior.

"At least you are not English. They welcome the Irish here but they rebel against the English," said Dan.

"True, like all good Celts should. Bash the Sassenachs. Where are you from Dan?"

"Good question, some times I think I'm learning to be Welsh but at other times I feel very English."

"I see you have got yourself a good Celtic colleen."

"Annette, yes, she's great. We are trying to keep it quiet."

"I can tell by the way she looks at you. Good-looking girl, bet she's got a temper. Watch those flying plates."

Dan laughed, "There speaks a man from experience."

Brendan rubbed the side of his head in mock pain, "and the lumps out of me to prove it. Red-headed Irish, Dan. You know the type of woman, pull the pin and wait for the bang. I miss her though."

"Well take your pick." They watched as a gaggle of girls in high spirits went through the doors.

Dan stepped over to turn two lads away from the queue for being unable to stand up properly and they huffed and puffed in frustration as he told them to come back tomorrow. There was always an excuse to turn away an unwanted customer.

By midnight they had easily reached their capacity of five hundred people and they started turning people away. Some stayed in the hope that the policy of 'one out, one in' would not take too long but it was a new club and those inside were staying there. There were minor incidents; the couple of lads that Dan had knocked back for being drunk had tried to climb over the high wooden fence to the smoking area at the rear fire exit of the club. Dan had anticipated that and there was a call from the doorman positioned there for back up. Robbie had gone round and chased them off across the hotel's lawn. The music could be heard from the hotel rooms when the back door was left open and Dan had his man stand opening the door and shutting it again, which worked to cut the noise down and also to show the security presence.

Dan went inside to check on positions. Annette was in the reception with the clicker and she winked at him as he went past.

Inside he placed his back against a pillar with the best view of the dancefloor, bar and towards the main door. Given free rein to run the club he was enjoying himself. There were tweaks to be made before the Saturday night but for an opening without a dry run rehearsal the venue was running smoothly. Brendan's bar manager was not as good as he had made out to be and was running round flustered. Brendan had thanked Dan earlier for in-troducing him to Carol who had gone in for an interview. It sounded promising and Dan hoped that Carol would be able to find some happiness away from the pressures of the tied village pub.

Brendan was standing with the DJ in his box and Dan saw that he was enjoying himself dancing away like he would have done twenty-five years before in the Irish town he had grown up in. Dan hoped that he would find whatever it was he was looking for in taking on this place.

The DJ who had been resurrected from previous incarnations of the club was playing disco tunes that Dan recognised from the eighties and nineties and the customers were dancing and drinking. The track playing was the Waterboys, '*I saw the whole of the Moon*'. Then the music turned to Black Box's "*Ride on Time*". When that finished the DJ shouted into his microphone.

"Boys and Girls lets give a great big Croeso Cynnes Cymraeg, A Warm Welsh Welcome to the man who has reopened the Bay Disco. All the way from Ireland, Mr Brendan O'Casey."

Brendan was given the microphone. "Cead Mile Failte." He shouted into it. "A hundred thousand welcomes. ARE WE HAVING FUN?"

The place went wild and the DJ put on "*Tell me Ma, when I come home*", which led to a lot of bad

Irish jigging.

Dan's eyes tracked around to study any threats. Phil Williams was inside at a booth overlooking the dance floor watching his two female companions dance. His blonde girlfriend, Julie, was too beautiful to be chatted up by all but the most drunken males. If they did summon enough courage then she pointed over at Phil and they backed away. The same went with Brian's girlfriend. Dan had heard from Frank that she was a Latvian dancer Brian had picked up along the way. She moved with sensual grace, her English was quite good and it looked like Phil's girlfriend had befriended her. Frank had told him that Phil's mother was divorced and paid off a long time ago and his father liked showing off the current girl on his arm. The procession of leggy blondes and brunettes was a certain sign of Brian's wealth and virility as much as the open top Porsche Carrera that Frank said he drove around town in the summer.

Brian's girl was obviously out of bounds. Dan saw that Phil was protective and also admiring, as were most red-blooded males in the place. From her looks, age, flirting and the occasional caressing touch between them Dan wondered if there was a twist to the relationship. Dan, sober and standing apart from the merriment of the venue's customers, detected that there seemed to be an undercurrent of tension between Phil and the two gorgeous looking women.

Picked out by their muscles, tattoos and tight T-shirts three of Phil's cage fighting friends had joined him through the queue and were sitting in the booth. Phil had ordered a bottle of champagne and the group were being flashy with their enjoyment of the bubbles. Dan heard a shouted conversation that the place looked better than it had ever done and that the music was good. The music was too loud for anything else to be discussed. Phil seemed to know a lot of the people in the club probably from the gym, a few girls went over and from his vantage point Dan watched their body language, a hand on Phil's muscled shoulder and he reciprocated by a pat or a squeeze on their tight bottoms carefully out of sight of the dancing girlfriend.

Dan guessed at the meaning of the touches. Most gym instructors he had known took advantage of the available admiring glances of bored housewives. The music had moved on to the electronic beats of a classic dance track and Dan saw Phil watching the two girlfriends dancing away. Dan figured Phil for a big beast in this small town. Perhaps if they lived in a city he would have more opportunity to go out and show the blonde off. It was interesting that he had come back when everybody had said what good prospects he had given up. Phil had known Annette and pretty well by the looks of their body language. Phil shared her liking of karate and of tattoos and Dan wondered if he had a Yin and Yang circle too. Well everybody has a past. She was with him now, that's what mattered.

Dan watched Phil reach into his pocket to pull out his phone. He looked at the screen and Dan saw him swear under his breath as he read the message and then text back.

Phil looked up straight at Dan and raised his hand in a half greeting. They were weighing each other up although Dan's intuition sensed neither animosity nor threat.

His earpiece spoke into Dan's ear, "Dan to the front door, Dan to the Front door." It came over crisp and clear.

He pressed the mike button clipped to his tie. "On way. On way."

When Dan went outside Steve Drwg was in front of Big Robbie and the other doorman Kev. He could see Steve remonstrating with them. Steve in trousers and a shirt had three mates with him and he wasn't going to back down in front of them. Dan could see that he was offering to fight the two bouncers.

Annette had stood in position to keep the door closed and she opened it to let Dan out.

This idiot calling himself Steve 'the bad' was in front of Robbie who had moved him backwards away from the door. Dan tapped Robbie's elbow and he stepped in front to take over the confrontation. Dan had dealt with him on a door the week before and he was like a spoilt brat, ranting and raving for being told that he couldn't come in the club.

The pupils of Steve's eyes were black from cocaine and his neck was red with the veins sticking out. His muscles were pumped inside a tight T-shirt but they were steroid pumped rather than naturally built and it was not the same. Steve was almost incoherent mixing up his English and Welsh words, not in control of his emotions.

"Don't you know who I am!" ranted Steve. It was a statement of fact not a question.

Steve's eyes were starting to bulge and there was white foam gathering at his mouth. He was balling his fists and working himself up.

"Calm down Steve."

"Let me in. LET ME IN. I am going to come in." Steve was almost crying in frustration at being refused entry.

Dan had turned to one side to improve his vision so that he could see any further threats. Steve's three mates were watching awestruck as their leader lost the plot.

Dan could see the door and Annette held it open as Phil Williams came out.

Annette holding the door said to Phil "isn't that your cousin? Do you want to speak to him?"

Phil replied "Not really. But I suppose I better had."

The door was opened for him. Dan cursed. He put his feet into a defensive stance. This could go bad and quick. Steve would be easy, Phil would be harder if he joined Steve. Dan wasn't sure which way it was going to fall.

Steve looked behind Dan and his cousin Phil came into his view.

Steve was wailing, "They won't let me in. Tell them to let me in."

Phil walked past Dan and in front of Steve. Dan took a step back to switch the emphasis away from himself as the cause of Steve's anger. Phil was talking Steve down and Steve seemed to be listening. Steve was poking his finger over Phil's' shoulder at Dan.

Phil told him to "Cae dy Geg," which Dan knew was shut your mouth.

Steve tried to push past Phil to get at Dan but the elder cousin pushed the younger one away. It was with the strength of benching a loaded bar bell and Steve staggered backwards. Phil moved forwards and pushed Steve again then slapped him across the face. With distance between Steve and the bouncers Phil growled at the watching friends to take him away. They dragged Steve by the arms and disappeared through the gates.

Phil turned back to the bouncers and apologised for Steve's behaviour. "I'm sorry lads."

Dan said, "It wasn't your fault. Thanks for helping out."

Phil replied, "He texted me that he wanted to come in. I figured he would try to cause trouble. He has to learn the facts of life and he has to grow up." He took a breath, "Families, you know how it is."

Dan didn't, his family were all dead or estranged from him.

30.

The music slowed down and at two am it stopped altogether. There was a satisfied buzz from the customers as they left the club. It had been a good night and they said they would come again.

Brendan was standing on the door next to Dan and the satisfied and somewhat drunken customers thanked them both on the way out. To protect from the chill Dan closed up his black jacket with the embroidered hotel logo that matched their shirts, it had been a present from Brendan to welcome him to the job. The new zip was stiff and he had to give it a sharp tug to pull it upwards.

Brendan's Irishness had helped the night flow

and a guy in a striped shirt shouted "top of the morning to you" at him as he weaved past on his way home.

"Which self respecting Irishman says that for fecks sake," said Brendan to Dan.

There had been a few niggles but on the whole the night had been a success. One of the lager pumps had broken and needed to be fixed before tomorrow and they ran out of glasses so they needed an extra glass collector. On the trouble side, apart from Steve Drwg who had disappeared into the night, a male had been thrown out for taking drugs in the toilets and two fights split up. Not bad for a first night. Brendan was pleased, the bar manager was not as good as he had said he was but Dan had been proficiency itself.

Annette was standing a few paces away and Dan left Brendan to speak to her.

"You ok?"

"Yes great Dan, I've had fun. It's a going to be a great place isn't it?"

"Yes a good atmosphere and not too many idiots. Brendan's offered us a drink afterwards for the boys. Are you ok to stay for one?"

"Yes I'm fine. It's a good team isn't it? They all look up to you, you know?"

"They've done well. You've done well. Annette. It is going to be a good summer."

"Thanks Dan, we won't stay too long, I want to get my handsome man into bed. Do you remember what I'm wearing underneath?"

"Oh yes, I remember. Black and lacy. Sounds good. Then we can have a leisurely lie-in tomorrow and then I think we deserve a big fry up. I've bought the sausages, eggs and bacon."

"You have food and sex on the brain. Dan cariad," her green eyes flashed at him.

Dan would always wish that he had taken up her challenge and kissed her there and then in front of everybody.

"So do you Annette, now go and help the lads get this lot home. Sooner they go, sooner you can get me into bed."

Annette looked over her shoulder and blew him a kiss as she skipped over to Robbie. That image, frame frozen in time would burn its way into Dan's soul.

The door team were joining the customers on the car park. There was plenty of noise and hilarity. Brendan was worried there would be complaints from guests in the morning. Dan was not sure what to do about that. Some of the customers were hanging around, others were going through the gates. He watched a young and recently met couple disappear around the side of the hotel towards the privacy of the undergrowth.

Annette was to one side of the car park nearest the bushes. With the other door staff scattered across the tarmac she was moving people along and asking them to be quiet as they went home. Phil Williams came out of the club with the two females and his three tattooed cage fighting friends. He looked over at Dan and gave a thumb up sign.

Dan walked over to Annette with a sense of relief. The night had gone well. Brendan was happy, the team had gelled well together and that idiot Steve the bad hadn't come back. Annette was happy and despite the time he was wide-awake. She gave him a big smile.

He switched back to his operational awareness. He really did need to sort out the lighting in the car park. There were too many shadows and Annette, his Annette, was standing close to the edge of the darkness. There was movement behind her in the bushes.

It wasn't a courting couple. It was Steve Drwg, who was now coming striding towards Dan. His muscles were fully pumped and he came on with menace.

"COME ON YOU BASTARD. I'LL SHOW YA," he shouted at Dan.

Steve was holding his right hand down by his side. In the sodium gloom Dan couldn't see what he was holding, if anything.

He was not going to take any chances. Steve was going to be slow and a couple of blocks should knock the knife out of his hand. Then Dan would flatten him.

In that split second Dan, the trained man, had already seen the outcome in his mind.

Annette was to his front and was turning to see Steve advancing on Dan.

If she had stayed out of the way then Dan would have dealt with the incident himself and put Steve down.

Whether she thought she could deal with Steve, whether she was being protective of her lover or wanted to prove herself with this raging bull would not be known.

She didn't see the knife held in the boy's hand and she stepped into Steve's path taking up a karate stance but blocking Dan's defence.

In a refereed karate bout then she might have stopped the knife and knocked it out of his hand as Dan had planned.

This time Steve's hand was already moving and the fishing knife, the same one that Dan wished to heaven he had thrown into the dock months before, struck Annette at the top of her stomach and plunged into her flesh.

The blade went upwards, entering just below her sternum. Still intent on striking Dan he pulled it out.

A taxi drove into the car park through the brick gateposts. The headlamps hit on to the scene. Steve still had the knife in his hand and in the flash of light there was a black liquid spouting from the tip of the blade.

Annette's body was crumpling to the ground when Dan went past her. His swinging right fist connected with Steve's jaw. Dan's punch knocked Steve sideways. The knife was flung out of his grip and it arced high into the air and fell into the bushes.

As Steve was falling the toe of Dan's boot hit him in the groin. Dan put his full force into the kick. He needed to clear Annette's assailant out of the way.

Steve's body contorted forwards and Dan's left fist hit his cheek and put him down on the floor insensible.

If Dan had known that Annette was already dead he would have carried on Steve's destruction with boots, fists, teeth and head. Instead, his training took over and he pulled himself back from the abyss.

Annette lay on the floor. Life had already left her sightless eyes. Dan ripped open her shirt revealing the wound piercing her white skin just below the black satin bra. He did his best to block the wound and ripping his jacket from his arms held it over the wound in a battlefield action. Punctured by the knife the heart had stopped pumping the blood and the wound was dry.

Annette Davis, 29, full time lecturer and part time door supervisor was dead within seconds, possibly before she fell to the ground. Certainly before the ambulance arrived with blue lights to the hotel car park to join the police car and the small groups of shocked partygoers.

The police, already on their way for a routine check, turned up within seconds. Emyr reached Dan first and with Robbie they tried to help. Steve Drwg was unconscious and was left to lie there.

The ambulance came and dealt with Annette first but they could only confirm that there was no heartbeat. Dan already knew this. He had seen death before.

He was still on his knees leaning over Annette's body when the paramedics released him from the responsibility of his efforts of resuscitation. Only then did the realisation hit like a steam train.

For the first time he looked around. The flashing lights illuminated the scene. His eyes scanned around the horrified bystanders until his gaze locked on Phil Williams, who lowered his head in shame. Dan now had a score to settle with the Williams family. He knew he would destroy them.

Author's Note.

Firstly I hope you have enjoyed reading this novel.

After talking to my trial readers I thought I would expand on my own experiences and their relevance to the plot of Splinter.

I am from the city of Liverpool but have always been drawn to North West Wales and moved to live here full time in 2006. My wife is Irish and partly the reason was to be give easier access to the ferry at Holyhead bit it really is a fantastic place to live. Like all rural areas there are problems and as former Director of the Anglesey Tourism Association I should say that I have highlighted and accentuated these for dramatic purposes.

I have led a varied and full life and have pulled some of this work of fiction from my experiences and the rest from my imagination. There are a couple of recognisable locations because I didn't feel the need to reinvent the location for Mount Snowdon and Chester is the closest main shopping town. North Wales towns do have shops but for the purposes of my story a trip on the train to Chester was more of an expedition. The town and village are a composite of North Wales towns and villages that I know well.

My Grandmother lived on Anglesey and we visited her regularly. As the eldest of four children I couldn't wait to escape the family and met up with friends from Liverpool who had a caravan close by and then made local friends playing in the village rugby team visiting local pubs and dodgy hotel discos along the way.

In 1991 I met Rob and Andy Kemp playing rugby. They had moved from Sussex to buy a whelk boat and refusing to acknowledge the difference between London and the rest of Southern England everbody called them cockneys. I helped out on their boat 'Big Foot' at holidays and weekends They worked hard but struggled with bad weather and bad payments.To me it was an adventure but it was a hard life and I appreciated that I had a proper job to go to on Monday morning. At the time the price of whelks was approximately £150 per tonne. The Kemps gave up the fight and sold Big Foot to be a mooring barge in the Menai Straits and the boys to work on land. Less than two years later Whelks were discovered as a delicacy and the price shot up to £650.

I have lived in North Wales for the last six years and after fifteen years of being a travelling Sales rep/director I made the mistake in 2007 of buying a hotel business advertised as being in an 'idyllic location'. Running a fifteen bedroom hotel with a 60 cover restaurant and a public bar in a remote Welsh coastal village is a hard slog. Some people loved our efforts and some begrudged us any success. In the end I couldn't make any money and escaped.

Since then perhaps it would have been sensible to have gone where the more lucrative work was. But I had served my time building a successful business and had my fill of motorway traffic jams and airports. I love this part of North Wales and I am fortunate that my wife loves it too. Its a lovely place to live but there are few jobs outside the public sector and I am not a government employee type of person.

So I went on to do a few different types of jobs. The nighttime economy kept calling me and I went back to being a bouncer, which I last did in the

JR Sheridan

early nineties. As I describe in the novel it is a brave new world of licenses and criminal records checks and I have worn a blue badge on a fluorescent strip of elastic around my arm outside various pubs and nightclubs around North Wales for a couple of years.

I've wanted to write for years and after the hotel I set out to write a book about that hotel business and the lessons I learnt in my 4 long and (record-breakingly) wet summers that I ran the place. Following a lot of effort and universal rejection from literary agents I put that book to one side and changed tack and I started to develop the idea for a novel. Dan Richards as a character has been knocking at the back of my mind for probably more than twenty years and for the first time I have been able to develop him into a 'real-life' character in a fully completed novel.

From my Grandfather's stories of his adventures in the Royal Navy I had planned to join up myself all through my childhood. I was in the Cadets and was due to join when I left school. Before I was due to attend my final interviews I took a few months to travel and from my father's recommendation I went to Hong Kong. I went for two or three months with my rugby boots and I stayed for two years. On my return to Blighty my self discipline to fit into the regimented life of the services was blown away.

Since then along the way I have met serving and retired members of the armed forces and at times wish I had joined up as I had planned at 18. It is said that old soldiers never talked about what they saw and locked it away. The modern culture is to be open and talk about your feelings. New technologies make it easier to communicate with home but how can you tell a mother, wife or girlfriend what you have seen. This is fast becoming a topical issue that I believe is a time bomb that will blow up in the face of the politicians who send their soldiers, sailors and airmen and women to war. It has happened throughout the centuries but in the twenty first century there is less tolerance by families and the general public to be accepting of the fate of combat veterans.

In the book, Dan Richard's way of dealing with his experiences by going head down to get over his wounds and work on Gwilym fishing boat is a creation of my own but I am told is not unrealistic. I have been told that the "splinter" dislodged by violence leading to an improvement is also credible. I thought Dan might enjoy his liaisons with Carol and Annette as a sign of his brighter future and had written the scenes to show his journey before I thought whether I should or not. Take them as an integral part of his rehabilitation.

On the door you meet a range of characters

ranging from those you want to protect to the likes of Steve the bad. When I worked as a bouncer twenty years ago drugs were rife and there was the rave culture of ecstasy and acid. Then cocaine was a yuppie drug and now it is among the most common. Another difference is the easy access to steroids. Steroids, or steds, or juice have a distorting effect. Add cocaine and alcohol and you see the pupils go black and a young lad thinks he can take on the world. Paranoia and impotence are all factors that lead to frustration and often that frustration turns into violence.

I am also a qualified Close Protection Officer and in the clubs we occasionally have reality TV stars who are paid to do a personal appearance, where they are mobbed by the fans. Mainly the celebrity is well behaved and we have had more trouble with the wannabees who are hanging on to their coat tails. This celebration of easily won fame is part of modern youth culture. Admittedly I have had to google some of my 'charges' to see who they are but the punters already know.

"Steve Drwg" type of characters do exist and it disturbs me that round the towns where I work I see a comparison in the way that the drug dealers are often treated as minor celebrities in their own right and as personalities that the young and stupid aspire to be. Hence the tattoos, the steds, the cocaine and that question when you stop them coming in, "Don't you know who I am?"

Quite often on the door we see a young one, male and female do something particularly daft. When I had started the book one of my older colleagues and myself had a conversation that a lot of customers we deal with still have to learn about the 'facts of life'.

Daft in a country town could lead to embarrassment, tears, threats or violence. In a city daft could lead to much worse. In my experience there is an awareness in a city of a million people of the potential for meeting that one nutcase with nothing to lose. My character for Steve Drwg wouldn't survive in a city. There would always be somebody who was bigger, tougher or less prepared to put up with his arrogance. That is a sad fact of life and I try to show the differences between levels of society with the Christmas Eve incident in the pub.

In Splinter the hero, Dan, is an ex Sergeant who has been around the block and the villain is a young small time gangster, a big man in a small town. Black and white, good and bad. Some women might say that Dan's failure to commit to a relationship is selfish and bad in its own way. Reality is never as cut and dried as in a novel.

The week that I finished the first draft of Splinter and was choosing an editor and investigating methods of publication I was working in a night-club on the Thursday night. It was one of those full moon nights when you expect trouble. Too many blokes, not enough women willing to dance with them always causes tension. I had been on the door but had gone inside and was with a colleague watching the dancefloor. I had seen a group of five males going in. Three older with a couple of younger lads. One of the youngsters, tall with cropped blonde hair, had been looking for trouble and had been told to calm down. I saw a fight on the dancefloor and stepped in to separate it.

I felt a bang and the youngster had punched me in the face. I split up the fight and we threw the lad who punched me out of the fire exit. All the time his father and uncle were telling me that he had been started on and it wasn't his fault and he was just "Two days back from Afghan". Instead of having him arrested we sent him on the way and I told the father to explain to his son in the morning what an idiot he was. The father, an ex squaddie himself, knew he had a long term problem to deal with.

Having just finished writing my book, which deals with an ex-serviceman's road to rehabilitation, I put the punch and my first black eye for a good few years down to poetic justice. Most weekends myself or my colleagues have to deal squaddies who feel aggrieved that their role is not appreciated by the public they serve. "What have you ever done for your country?" is a common question and often leads to threats or tears. This is surely a time bomb waiting to explode.

I have thoroughly enjoyed writing this novel and I hope that my enjoyment shows. It is not an academic work in any way but I hope I have done justice to Dan's problems and his road to rehabilitation. He will have to deal with the aftermath of Steve Drwg's use of the knife and his own association to the Williams family. As I write this I am halfway through Book 2 in the Facts of Life Series and hope to publish before the end of the year. I have also already written a Novella about Dan's early career in the Royal Marines and yet another scrape he finds himself in.

If you would like to contact me to ask questions or make suggestions please look on www.jrsheridan.co.uk for news, blogs and details of upcoming books.

JRS

ABOUT THE AUTHOR

JR Sheridan lives in North West Wales,

He has lived a number of different lives
and has travelled extensively,

From a bouncer and crisp salesman in
Hong Kong, to award winning
businessman selling materials for false
legs in Liverpool, then Hotelier and
Restaurateur on Anglesey and back to
Door Supervisor again.

Along the way he has picked up many
ideas for future books.

For more details on the author and
information on upcoming new books
please check out

www.jrsheridan.com

20785670R00234

Made in the USA
Charleston, SC
24 July 2013